THE MADAGASCAR PIGEON

John Thom

There's more to come about the exploits of Jaguar Beault. Watch for future thrillers currently flowing down the suspense pipeline from **Bat & Ball Press**. Especially...
Termination Determinators
The Nuclear Armageddon Endgame
Evil in Silicon Valley

Contact the author at: **jaguarbeault@gmail.com**

Bat & Ball Press
San Fransisco

ISBN-13: 9780961124212
ISBN-10: 0961124210
Library of Congress Control Number: 2014900283
Bat & Ball Press, San Francisco, CA

Dedicated to my superior grandkids, Anthony, Mai Ly, and Alana, with best wishes that they enjoy long lives filled with happiness and health...and get stinking rich from the phenomenal sales of this book and the collateral incomes from its movie franchise, television shows, video games, annual bubble-gum trading cards, and a clothing line that will be so fantastic that it will make runway models actually smile.

1

The city wore its famous fog like an old coat tailored to fit a 42-long hanging over the shoulders of a 34-cadet. Thick and lots of it. Fog silently echoed down every hill and along every street and alleyway. The cold and damp painted my window, obscuring the view from my second-floor office to the street below. I cursed the fog. I cursed the blocked view. I felt trapped. I felt alone. I felt separated from the pulse of my town, from the character every person here is defined by to make them different from every other person. Whatever the poop that means. I felt separated from the edge, yes, the edge, where I spend most of my time. I am in investigations, a shamus, a gumshoe, a private dick. No jokes, please.

I go by the name Jaguar Beault. It's not my real name and the reason I use it is not a story I like to tell. So I don't. I take on cases where I can make a buck. I'm easy that way. I'm not proud. I turn down cases if my radar tells me there is something too fishy, too screwy with the client. I turn down these cases even when business is slow. Business is usually slow. But a screwy client is just as likely to stiff me with a bad check as to sue me if I don't make him – or her – happy. I'd lose that lawsuit every time because my job is not to make people happy. Hire me to solve a problem. That's my job. I charge a hundred and twenty-five dollars an hour plus the expenses I run up – legitimate expenses. My car is no longer under warranty. It surprises me when it passes the state's comical smog test. I'm licensed to carry a weapon. It's been fired. It's a gun.

If you haven't figured where I work, I'll tell you. It's San Francisco. I locked up a place in the city back before it would have cost me too dearly and where today rent control means I can afford it. I also live in the city. My commute to work is from my bedroom to my desk. I work and live in the same space. There is a drawback doing it this way. I can't leave my work at work. It's always there over on the desk. Or on the floor. The hallway outside my door serves another half dozen offices where I'm friends with some and not friends with others. I like the yin and yang of that.

Sometimes a knock on my door will be the start of a profitable relationship with a client who has money and is willing to pass some of it along to me. Sometimes I get a knot in my gut when I hear knocking. I never know.

This time I called to the door, "It's not locked." The knocking came again. "When I said it's not locked," I hollered, "I meant that you should come in." Gad. She was easily five-ten or five-eleven, four or five inches under my height. She was thin in a way that you didn't need to tell her to eat more. In deference to the damp from the fog, she wore a pants suit and a long coat. They still complimented her figure. Her face, under a stylish hat, could have come from the pages of a glamour magazine.

"Sorry for not calling first," she opened, "but since you come highly recommended, I wanted to get over here right away." Recommended? Me? I spent a moment trying to think who would have recommended me. As I said, business has been slow. "I'm not good with figures," she said, (I made no comment about hers, though I could have come up with a few) "and I need professional help." Blackmail, I thought, embezzlement, maybe insider trading.

"Let's talk about it," I told her.

"Okay. My regular accountant retired and he's been doing my taxes for a while. Now I need a new tax man."

"Tax man."

"Yes."

"I don't do taxes."

"Sure you do."

"No I don't. Hell, I should know if I do taxes or not."

"Yes you do. You're Jason Bevalaqua, the tax man."

"No. I am Jaguar Beault, the private detective. Jason Bevalaqua, the tax man, (and the floor's resident horse's ass I could have added but did not) has an office at the end of the hall." She was still laughing when I heard Bevalaqua's door open and then close. As I went back to the crossword puzzle I was struggling with, I said to myself that dame is more than a few furlongs short of a full marathon.

She came through the door without knocking this time. Same dame. I sat up. "I'm using the extra knock I did yesterday, Mr. Beault." She giggled and pronounced it "beault" and I did not correct her. "I hope that is all right by you."

It wasn't. "I coulda been naked in here, lady, this is my home," I scolded her. That didn't seem to mean anything to her. She just strove on.

"It turns out I do need your services."

I came close to telling her I provided more than one kind of service to my women clients, but I resisted the urge. Probably a good thing because I think she was reading my face and would have disliked my kind of humor. Instead, I countered, "Just what is it you need, Miss? Miss? Uh, miss?" A bit of a dim bulb, she is. "I was trying to learn your name when I was repeating miss." Here I did that quotation thing in the air with my fingers.

She told me her name. "It is Phyllis Gunn."

"Gunn, huh? Sounds dangerous."

"At times."

"Now?"

"I don't know yet."

Phyllis Gunn told me she had a story. A troubling story. A story that cried out for help. My help. She needed Jaguar Beault. She was nothing if not overly dramatic. Before she began her story, she asked, "Mind if I smoke?"

I frowned and let a count or two pass, then answered, "It's okay by me, but only if it means you are on fire." She smirked. It didn't matter. I don't like smoking. I gave it up years ago. Tell the truth, I hardly started. High school. Sitting around with the guys. Actually at a table near the guys. One of them came over and offered me a cigarette. "No, thank you, I don't smoke." "You do now." He was on the wrestling team. I wasn't. "Smoke this," he commanded. Instead of inhaling – what did I know – I exhaled and spit the cigarette straight onto his shirt. I explained it wasn't on purpose. Nevertheless, he kicked the stuffing out of me.

Miss Gunn put her cigarette back into her purse. "Do you have something to drink?" she asked.

"I have coffee. It's fresh. I've just made it."

"Coffee? Don't you have something stronger than that?"

"It's nine forty-five in the morning, Miss Gunn, a little early to be knocking back liquor, don't you think?"

"It's five forty-five in the afternoon somewhere, Mr. Beault, so what's the big deal?"

I didn't answer that remark. I could have told her I was not a character from a 1930s or 1940s black and white film always just two steps away from a bar with ice and glasses and booze and soda water. I had been down that drinking road briefly, and what few memories that were not blotted out by my expertise at it are not happy ones. Worse than that smoking thing. At least I didn't get the snot kicked out of me when I drank. Not that I remember, that is.

"I hope you are more cooperative in our professional relationship, Mr. Beault, because so far you are not showing any concern for my needs."

"We don't have a professional relationship yet, Miss Gunn, and my lack of cooperation so far, as you say, is just my being a Good Samaritan and keeping you from the poisonous effects of the tars and nicotine in tobacco and the mind-numbing consequence of alcohol consumption."

"You some kind of meathead, Mr. Beault?" She thought she had me there.

"Yes, Miss Gunn, I am, and aren't we all." Ha! I had her there.

"But..." she started. I held up my hand and stopped her.

"Why don't you simply tell me why you need my help? Wouldn't that be a good idea? Then we can get past this childish yapping."

She blushed. "Okay." She told me she had just arrived in San Francisco aboard a tramp steamer. A tramp steamer? I didn't know there were any of those around in this modern age. Shows how much I know. When she neglected to indicate where from, I asked. She equivocated, saying, "Oh, East Asia or so." Or so? East Asia or so? Cripes, East

Asia is huge. That much I do know. It could mean a million different places. I pressed the question. I thought it might be pertinent. I'm a detective. I like to dig into things.

"It doesn't matter, Mr. Beault," she said, "I'm here now and that's what is important." I decided to let it slide for the moment. She continued. She said other passengers on board the *Queen of Diamonds* made her frightened by their intense interest in her. *Queen of Diamonds*? She told me that was the name of the steamer. Made sense. I made a note of that. I asked about the people with this intense interest in her. "Passengers on the *Queen of...*" Egad. That much I had figured out.

"Miss Gunn," I interrupted, "can't you stay on point here? I deduced they were passengers. What I meant was for you to tell me more about them."

I had her attention again. She said there were three in particular. There was the Pole who seemed always to be just within eyesight whenever she was out of her cabin. On deck. At meals. From time to time he tried to engage her in conversation. She was polite in return, only there was something about him, his manner. Creepy, she decided.

There was the Pole's henchman, a disgusting man who said not a word while he sent threatening messages through his close-set eyes. "He is a short, ugly, impassive man with the skin of a lizard. He made me tremble," she said.

And last there was Ms. Wu, an enigmatic woman who was now friendly and smiling and then distant and cunning.

"Cunning?" Yes, Miss Gunn said, saying Ms. Wu tried several ways to discover Miss Gunn's travel purpose and destination. Wary of the Wu woman, Miss Gunn feigned indecision and admitted only to an unplanned itinerary. I told her the Wu woman was undoubtedly not from Poland and the Pole's other minion was perhaps from an indeterminate background.

"Have you been to Poland, Miss Gunn?"

"Poland? Why ever do you ask such a strange question as that?"

"Not so strange, Miss Gunn, when one of these seemingly conspiratorial passengers is of Polish origin. You may have had truck with him at a previous time."

"What the hell are you talking about?" she snapped, her back arching.

"The Pole," I said.

She laughed and sagged back into her chair. "Oh, I see. He is called "The Pole" because he is extremely tall and very slender. He makes quite a sight, I'll tell you. His appearance would be amusing if he were not so treacherous."

Okay, he's not Polish. I made another note to that effect.

On arrival in San Francisco, Miss Gunn went on, she saw that the three passengers followed her from the steamer. In her taxi she could see the three of them in a taxi of their own motoring on the roadway behind her. At the hotel, she registered quickly and was just entering the elevator when she saw the same three coming in the front entrance.

"Perhaps it was a coincidence," I told her.

"Coincidence? Are you serious? Coincidence? How could it be a coincidence?" she exclaimed rather strongly.

At this point I changed my mind about coincidence. Couldn't a been, I concluded, under the circumstances she had been describing. Definitely not a coincidence. Something was up. I had gone off track. Wasn't the first time. Keep going, I urged her.

"When I was in East Asia I acquired a...a thing, a souvenir," she said hesitatingly. "I saw it and I liked it. I was going to carry it with me when I developed a bad feeling, so I asked the merchant to ship it to me."

"You had a bad feeling? What was that from?"

"I don't know. I can't explain it. It was just a...a feeling."

"Did it have anything to do with the souvenir you bought? Is it valuable?"

"No, not at all. No. It would have nothing to do with that. It is such a simple little thing. Just a trip's souvenir."

"What is it, this simple little thing, this souvenir?"

"Nothing really, a trashy little statue. Plastic probably."

"Not so trashy that you arranged to have it sent separately. To where?" I asked her.

"To San Francisco."

"You live here?"

"No, yes, I do now."

"In the hotel." It was not a question.

"Temporarily."

"Where then was the statue to be delivered?"

Miss Gunn reached into her purse and brought out a cigarette. When I did the "uh-uh" thing, she pouted and pleaded. "No" settled the issue. I was thinking about that smoking experience in high school and the pounding I got. When I said to her that she owed me an answer, she raised her eyes up to mine and said, "To you."

"To me. That seems odd."

"I had no one else to trust, Mr. Beault, no friends, no family here in San Francisco. I thought choosing a man in your line of work would be a safe harbor for my, uh, souvenir."

"You picked my name out of a hat?"

"Not exactly. You'll recall that I told you that you came highly recommended."

"As a tax man."

"Ah, yes, well, that, I mean, was, uh, not entirely true."

"But entirely false."

She gasped. She reached for a tissue in her purse and dabbed at her eyes and at her nose. "You're being cruel to me, Mr. Beault, and there is no call for that. I've come here quite innocently to use your professional services, and I feel as though you are playing with my emotions."

What a load of crap that was, pulling a Scarlet O'Hara on me. *Oh, my stars, what will I do now?* she could have said. When I began to respond, she raised her head and in a new frontal attack demanded I give her her property and she would reward me with payment for services rendered. I stared at her.

"Where is it?" she accused me.

"Where is what?"

"My package."

"Well, you see, Miss Gunn, I receive lots of packages destined for distraught females who return to San Francisco on tramp steamers from foreign ports, East Asia included" – I'm dripping with sarcasm as I say this – "so I would need to know precisely what it is that you arranged to send me so that I could turn over the correct one to you. You can see, can't you, that that would be the professional thing for me to do?" She was trying to frame an answer when I said, "What is so important about this souvenir statue you are expecting to receive through my office?"

"I'd rather not say."

I may not be the sharpest needle in the pin cushion. I know that because I have been told in so many words. Be that as it may, it was occurring to me that there was something rotten in the state of California and right here in my humble homestead. This dame was a couple of marbles short on the Chinese checkerboard of life. I had had enough. I stood up. "I do not have your package, Miss Gunn," I said in my controlled rage, one I'd practiced before. "It has not arrived here. I have no way of knowing if or when it will. If it does I will contact you and you can come and claim it. It'll cost you one hundred dollars. I want fifty now – in cash – and fifty more when I put the package in your hands. And don't think I won't be happy to be out of this arrangement. Write down where you will be and how I can reach you. In the meantime, don't call me or stop by my office. I don't want to hear any more of your tall tales or have to keep telling you your package has not arrived. I am an honest man. I said I would call when it arrives and I will. Good day." When it looked like she was going to make an objection – to what I didn't care – I held up my hand. "Good day," I repeated. She left, leaving two twenties and a ten on my desk.

2

I live, and work for that matter, in the Outer Richmond district of San Francisco. Not far from the ocean. The Pacific Ocean. It's the biggest natural feature on Earth. If you haven't seen it, you do not know what you are missing. Come to my city and see it. I'm not even doing business with the visitor bureau when I advise this. I recommend it free of charge. I decided to take my own advice. I went to my car – good, it started – and drove up to Geary then west out to the water, swinging south past the famous Cliff House onto Great Highway with the Pacific on my right then past the western edge of Golden Gate Park where you see the two big windmills. I kept my speed coordinated with the traffic lights at thirty-five miles an hour past the San Francisco Zoo turnoff before slipping onto Skyline. I exited onto Highway 1, California's historic north-south coastal roadway. Highway signage said the next nine exits would put me somewhere in Pacifica, that funky beach town that time seems to have preserved like a bumblebee in amber in the 1950s. I was hungry. I know a spot that does me just fine.

When you are in the private eye business you learn to take what comes when a need or an urge pushes on you. Your time isn't always at your command. Those are the days you are skulking around trying to keep an eye close to a wandering husband, or wife. Or chasing a bail jumper. Or when you are waiting for potential witnesses to show up to ask them a few questions or to slap a subpoena on them. Or when you are bouncing from one county office to the next hoping to find just the one clerk who knows (1) what she is doing and (2) will do it for you.

I guess this is my way to defend a personal taste I have cultivated over the years. Yes, fast food. Purveyed from square-fronted buildings acknowledging no responsible architect and surrounded by drive-thru lanes like moats guarding a castle and seen from afar like a collapsed rainbow for all the colors in their marketing image, colors you wouldn't choose if your life depended on it. Of course, some would argue that your life does depend on it when you choose some of the culinary fare at food-served-fast places.

Here's an exception. Down in Pacifica's Linda Mar neighborhood perched on the ocean shore like flotsam washed up on the sand with nary anything else around it is a restaurant with a Mexican theme. Pretty essential. Have you, like me, ever tried to calculate how many days will elapse before you have a Mexican food deficit requiring a quick fix? Not many, right? What makes this location remarkable is that it has a close-up ocean view. You can smell the view along with the Mexican aromas. And it looks more like a cabin than a brick and mortar and neon box. It's a Taco Bell. I had a taco salad and a diet soda. I do this about twice a month. And I don't apologize.

Back in the Outer Richmond I trudged up the flight of steps to my office-slash-home. I tossed my keys on my desk, glanced at my phone – no messages – tossed my 3 Musketeers onto my dining table (I do eat at home occasionally) and went to the bathroom. The candy bar is the irreducible postscript to a Mexican meal for me. I don't have Mexican food without topping it off with a bite of chocolate. You may do the flan thing, but not me. There's a tiny all-purpose store around the corner from my place run by a Chinese family whose patriarch looks like he is a veteran of the Boxer Rebellion. These folks seem to live forever. Very nice people. I wonder if they eat Mexican followed by chocolate. Oh, I tell you this because it's where I bought the candy bar.

Just as I was about to tear the wrapper off the 3 Musketeers there was a heavy thumping on my door. "Jesus effing Christ," I cursed, "that door's made of wood not steel. Take it easy." Didn't work. The thumping repeated. I scurried over to the door and pulled it open. "Hey, take it..." I stopped as a short, slender, salt-and-pepper-headed fifty-ish looking man dressed in seafaring clothes, leaned into me now that he wasn't being held erect by the door.

What he mumbled I could not make out. There was no question he was in some sort of distress. He stumbled into my room around me. He was clutching a package inside his coat. I helped him to a chair where he looked up at me and coughed "Beault?" He pronounced it my way. "This is for you." He pulled the package from his coat and shoved it into my hands. "I'm done for it," he said, "it's yours now. Good fucking luck." With that he rose and turned for the door. He didn't get there. He fell forward onto his face. It was then I noticed the blood on the chair where he was sitting.

It was just my luck – fucking luck, I suppose, like the dead guy had wished on me – that the two San Francisco homicide detectives who showed up later after the original appearance by the beat cops were Lieutenant Joseph Blough and Sergeant Richard Headley. The three of us had a history. Homicide was on scene because the beat cops determined that several bullet holes had reasonably contributed to the death of the dead man lying in a pool of blood on the floor in my room. Police know stuff like that. As for me, I figured I was going to have some explaining to do.

"Lieutenant Blough," I hailed him.

"It's Blough, asswipe, and you know it." Oh, correct, I told him by way of apology. I mess with him because he messes with me. Fortunately, I get away with it most of the time. If I didn't get away with it, I'd pay good because the lieutenant leaves the impression that he doesn't have to take crap from anybody...officially or unofficially. Except for some years on his face, he looks like a young athlete.

"You kill 'em?" Blough sniffed at me. I answered in the negative.

"You know 'em?" I answered in the negative.

"Why's he here?" I answered that I did not know.

"He just shows up and drops down dead? Croaks in front of you?" I answered in the affirmative.

"Whater ya holding out on me, Beault, there's gotta be something?" I told him nothing, meaning I wasn't holding out anything from him. That was a lie. I didn't say anything about the package I had hidden.

"Me and Headley think you're lyin." Headley had not said a word the whole time, so I don't know how Blough knew that his partner thought I was lying. Maybe they use ESP. "That right, Headley? Think he's lyin?" Headley nodded. Well, there you are, Headley did think I was lying.

"I'm not lying," I said, "it happened just the way I told you. I would know more if the guy hadn't bought the farm so fast."

"It doesn't make sense," Blough said, rubbing his chin.

"You got that right."

"And no ID on him?" This directed at the officers who had been standing in my doorway.

"We couldn't find nothing on the body, lieutenant. No nothing." I was reminded that they don't teach grammar at the Police Academy.

"We expect you to be downtown no later than noon tomorrow, Beault, to make a formal statement. You got that?"

"What's to state, Blough? Guy plows against my door. I open it. He stumbles in and lands in my chair. I don't know who he is. I'm asking him what's the matter. He's not answering. He gets up and falls down dead. Write that down now and I'll sign it." I thought that would cover it. "Wait," I said. "Bevalaqua down the hall has lots of enemies. Maybe this guy came to lodge a complaint against him. Down at the end of the hall that way," I waved. Didn't want to miss a chance to put another burr under that horse's ass's saddle. Bevalaqua's saddle.

Blough scowled. "Downtown. No later than noon tomorrow."

The coroner had arrived and had done whatever he does to stiffs. Then the dead guy was wrapped up and carted off. Crime scene guys had taken pictures. I don't know what they'd do with those. Just a dead guy sprawled on my floor. Maybe they are into scrap-booking.

3

If you don't count the stupid trip downtown where I was ordered to make a twenty-five-word statement to the cops, I had two pressing matters at hand. No, three. First things first. I ate my candy bar. Second was an examination of the package the dead guy delivered with his last breath. Then third was a visit to my neighbor.

I picked up the package and guessed the weight at something well over ten pounds. The covering material was a soft cloth secured by duct tape. The all-purpose gift wrapping. I was impressed. When I cut through the wrappings I was met with the oddest thing. It was a statue. No, a statuette, maybe fifteen inches high. It was a bird of some sort. Damnedest thing. Odd, like I said, yet also unexpectedly reminiscent. A statuette of a bird rang a bell somewhere in my head. I examined the bird to no avail. It was what it was. A bird statue and an ugly one at that. To be fair, I'm no art expert. What came to mind was Miss Phyllis Gunn and her bewildering story about a package coming to me from East Asia. Bewildering now after a dead guy had entered the equation dropping it in my lap.

Well, if that's the way it was going to be then I had better get to work. I am a detective, which meant I had a leg up on you amateurs who might find yourselves in this puzzle. Look at the facts is where I started. Miss Gunn appears. Check. Package arrives. Check. Dead guy on my floor. Check. Cops arrive. Check. Candy bar. Check. Open package. Check. That left only one more task, again not counting that pointless drive across town tomorrow to police headquarters.

This one had the potential to be the toughest of them all. Down the hall to where Miss Gunn had detoured recently. To Bevalaqua's.

He's a real horse's ass. Ask anybody. He does people's taxes. I bet his repeat business is about five percent. He must have been a breech baby... through the smallest birth canal in the history of womankind. Crushed what little brain he had. That's if you really believe he was born of a woman. Did I mention he's a horse's ass? It merits repeating, I'm telling you. Ask anyone.

His office is about fifty or sixty feet down the hallway at the end like I already told you. It's a painful walk for the very reason that he is down there. I have rare interface with the guy, and it's usually listening to him bitch about something he thinks I've done or haven't done. I don't know why he has it in for me. I'm not the one who turned him into a horse's ass. Somebody else has to take the credit – or blame – for that.

His door was open. He doesn't live in his office like I do in mine. He probably lives in a cave. No, it'd be a stable since he's a horse's ass. His office interior is a desk and file cabinets and chairs for himself and his unlucky clients. I doubt that he has any friends.

"Beault," he shouted when he saw me at his door.

"Bevalaqua," I shouted back.

That's usually the extent of our interfacing if he's not complaining about something.

"Saw the cops," he said, "you under arrest?"

"No."

"Did you kill that guy?"

"What guy?"

"The dead guy on your floor."

"Oh, that guy."

"Yeah, did you kill him?" I said no.

"The cops think you did."

"How do you know that?"

"I can tell."

See? A real horse's ass. "I didn't kill him and they didn't arrest me."

"They will. It's just a matter of time. You don't look innocent."

"Screw you."

"What do you want, Beault?"

"I did you a favor the other day."

"I doubt that."

"I did. I sent Phyllis Gunn to you. She needed help with her taxes."

"No you didn't."

"Yes I did. She came to my office by mistake and I sent her down the hall to you."

"You're full of shit."

"Well, I won't deny that, but this time it's fact. What was it, Tuesday or Wednesday?"

"I don't know no Phyllis Gum."

"Gunn, not Gum. Hold on now. She is a tall dame, a real cutie, dressed in a pants outfit. Sure, you saw her."

"I saw *her*, but Phyllis Gunn isn't the name she dropped on me."

"That's interesting."

"To you, maybe, but not to me."

"So, did you do her taxes?"

"That's none of your business, Beault, but I'll tell you anyway. No, I didn't. She wasn't here about taxes."

"That's strange. Why would a beautiful woman come here looking for you?"

"Eat shit and die, Beault, I know lots of beautiful women." (Those would be the ones he helped cheat the IRS, most of them probably still doing time.)

"Yeah, lots of beautiful women, sure, no doubt about that, Bevalaqua. Can't argue with that. What did she want then?"

"It was shocking what she wanted. She wanted to know about you."

"Me?"

"Yeah, could she trust you."

"Trust me for what?"

"I don't know, just trust you. She kept asking me about you, so I finally told her you were too dumb to be trusted, a failure, a dropping of sparrow crap on somebody's shoulder, a guy who would borrow from Peter to pay Paul and then tell Peter that Paul stole all your money when Paul was actually a prince among men. When I looked up from my computer she was gone. Musta decided there wasn't anything more to learn about you."

15

"I am sure that she decided she could no longer remain in your exalted presence."

"I've got real work to do, Beault, not take money from old ladies to have you sneak around their rutting husbands. Why don't you take a hike?"

"I'm going. By the way, what name did she give you?"

"I'll tell you."

"Thanks."

"For five hundred dollars."

4

What I had was around fifteen pounds of an aviary-themed composition important enough to put a few bullets in a guy. I wonder if the cops will ever ID him. Not my problem, except I would be interested. He knew my name. I should know his.

But back to the bird. I had another avenue I could explore. I am acquainted with a professor of cultural anthropology at a college here in San Francisco. I could ask her. Emily. She might even cooperate, but that hope could as easily be dashed. Emily and I are...were...well, it ended in a bit of a mess. It's got nothing to do with why I use my new name. Let's just call it a misunderstanding and let it go at that. Besides, if you keep at me for what happened, I may get testy. Remember, I'm a private eye and I am licensed to carry.

I *am* a private eye and I have the gadgets to prove it. One of my favorites is a pen with a digital audio recording capability. I can be talking to someone, maybe a perp, and I hit a switch and everything he says gets recorded. Son of a bitch could be cooking his own goose without knowing how or why. It maybe violates a few of his Constitutional protections, sure, but that's too bad, and it might be different if he hadn't chosen to go into the crime business is what I say. Another one of these toys is a tie clasp with a miniature camera connected. Right there in front of the perp and he doesn't know it. What a doofus. God, I love these gadgets.

Emily was on my mind. I hauled out the bird and shot pictures of it from all angles with my very conventional and fancy digital camera. I use this one in my work sometimes.

I didn't call the college. Emily would have said no when I asked to see her. She would have said hell no if she was having a bad day. If it

17

were a really bad day, she would have said no you effing a-hole bastard and the donkey you rode in on. I know that doesn't make sense, but it happens to be a direct quote from her when we were on a date this one time. Oh, the memories.

I re-wrapped the bird and put it in a cloth sack. I drove to my gym and carried it to my locker in the men's dressing room. I put the lock on and spun the dial. It's a combination lock. The bird was nested in a safe place. Now off to see Emily. The gym. It's been a while since I was there to work out. Something else to put on my to-do list.

I got lucky with a parking spot near the campus and headed for Emily's building. I'm not a stalker, I just happen to know where her office is. Inside, I saw her door was closed. Just then I heard people walking my way. A few students holding books and backpacks, Emily among them. She stopped abruptly nearly causing a couple of students to collide into her. She put her hand to her mouth. I am sure she was stifling a scream. I know how to read her face. I put my hands up to show I was not a threat. You know, I come in peace.

"Are you all right?" her students asked her. She was staring at me. The students in turn looked over at me. The guy who comes in peace.

"Yes, I am all right," she told them, "I'll see you tomorrow."

She brushed past me to her door, unlocked it and went in leaving it open. I took that for an invitation to follow her in. She went to her desk and put her school trappings down. Books, folders, mobile device, her purse, too. She looked at her phone for messages. None. She turned on a desk lamp. She looked at her watch. I remained motionless and silent. She looked up at me. Just looking. Then she came around her desk toward me. Oh, good, I thought, a welcoming hug for old time's sake, no hard feelings, let the past be in the past, we've matured, grudges, if that was what they were, are unhealthy, let's be friends at least. When she reached me she hauled off and hit me squarely in my solar plexus. Has this ever happened to you? Man, that hurts. Knocks all the wind out of you. Worse is that you think you have a collapsed sternum. I thought mine was. So much for let the past be in the past.

Emily is just under average height, has short brown hair and deep green eyes. She's fit as a fiddle, real good on the tennis court – where she probably gets her strong right arm – and has a shape like an hourglass. She's a college professor and as such she doesn't pay regular attention to the current fashions for ladies. She doesn't need to dress for her job. She has tenure. When she does pay any attention to her appearance, she is a very pretty girl. It helps a lot, though, if she doesn't speak. She accompanied that punch to my belly with a common question she asks me, "Why are you bothering me, you shithead?" Apparently, one of us still carried that grudge.

It won't be very instructive for me to go into any details about how I growled with pain and slowly got my breathing back to near normal and how long it took for me to have a voice. Suffice to say it was help-ful that Emily had two hours between classes. I was on my hands and knees when she went back to her desk, sat down and began sorting through her class materials. She knew from experience how long it would be until I had my wits back to explain why I was there. She's a bright woman with a good memory of previous shots to my solar plexus. Evidently, we were not done with that bit of rancor. And, boy oh boy, did I hurt.

"I've told you before, Emily, I don't like it when you hit me like this," I said when I had regained my composure. "It hurts. It hurts like the devil and you know it."

"What do you want?"

"I want you to stop doing that to me," I answered her.

"What do you want *here*?" she barked at me. She said it in a way that could have been followed up with "you dumb turd," another of her favorites with me.

"Oh." Through the torture of short breaths I told her about Miss Gunn, the dead guy, the cops, the package and Bevalaqua. "Is he still a horse's ass?" she asked when I finished with the part about the tax man. I didn't need to answer. She knew. And I was trying to conserve my words. Each one hurt when I spoke.

"So what does this all have to do with me?" she said.

"Ah, well, that's the cool part," I said when my breathing was sorta normal. "I want you to look at some pictures and tell me if you know what it is."

"What what is?"

"Why the thing that came in the package, of course."

"Show it to me," she said sternly, again in that tone that could have been followed up with "you smelly fart." Emily, you see, has, at times, a crudely developed way with words. I've heard them.

I brought out my camera and handed it to her. She attached it to her computer with a wire and an exasperated sigh. She pushed a few keys and waited while the drive pulled the images onto her screen. While she waited, she stared at me and not quite so lovingly as in a few of the old days.

The first image appeared. It was the bird. Thank God for that. At least I hadn't screwed up the photography. One by one she flipped through all the pictures, all the angles of the bird. A couple of times she glanced up at me when a new and different angle appeared. After the last picture, the computer screen went blank. "That's it?" she said.

"Yes."

"I'm surprised you didn't take a picture of yourself with your pants down."

I snickered. "I don't do that anymore. Come on, you know it was just that one time, and it was a practical joke."

"Not a funny one."

"Yes, I know that now," I said, massaging my solar plexus and another memory. "Can you identify this thing?" I asked as much to change the subject as to get to the bottom of the mystery.

"Basil, what you have here is..."

"Jaguar."

"What?"

"I'm not Basil anymore. I'm Jaguar Beault." I thought she was going to choke, she laughed so hard. "Come on," I said, pleading. She didn't come on, she plainly saw this as funny. I waited.

"Okay, Bas...uh, Jaguar (she laughed some more), you have something here. Something rather special. I didn't think I'd ever see one." My ears perked up at this and my other senses perked up as well. My solar plexus throbbed.

"What is it, this bird?"

She related the story. Centuries earlier, possibly in the Renaissance era, a tribe of natives on an island off the east coast of Africa decided that a cache of jewels and gems and other precious stones they had procured from an itinerant missionary held divine powers because the valuables fell into their hands at the same time a troublesome drought was interrupted by a rainy spell that helped reconstitute the fields for their crops. Grains and fruits and vegetables reappeared and the tribespeople had a resurgence of foods. The missionary, uh, well, he disappeared. The confluence of missionary, jewels and rain had to mean something, so the valuables were elevated in their esteem. Not all the tribespeople were as theologically oriented as others. The ones less religious selfishly reasoned they could get damn rich selling the trinkets to some greed mongers from Europe or somewhere. Some rich French, for example. There were plenty of them tripping around Madagascar experimenting with colonialism. Conflicting objectives within the tribe.

When the tribesmen who wanted to sell the valuables were identified, the tribesmen and tribeswomen who revered the gems and their purported powers settled the issue by an old custom. They did it "out of court" so to speak. Fearing that others in the tribe might come to the same unhealthy ambitions as the now-departed and godless ones, the remaining elders of the tribe took matters into their own hands and decided to conceal the jewels. Three statuettes were crafted in the form of a totem important to the tribe. The statuettes were molded – so the legend contends – with hollowed-out interiors and a secret entry gizmo. There the jewels could be hidden. Not the best scheme, but a scheme nonetheless. Everyone in the tribe was aware of where the booty might be. Unbeknownst, however, to everyone in the tribe save a few trustworthy and honorable elders was the fact that a fourth secretly crafted statue was destined to hold the gems. Three were red herrings. The irony of a red herring was completely lost on the tribe. A fish is not a bird. The statues, of course, were birds or, more precisely, a bird. The holy totem of the tribe.

"What you have here, Bas...er, Jaguar," Emily proclaimed, stifling yet another sarcastic laugh, "is one of the four. It is the Madagascar Pigeon."

Now it was my turn to laugh.

"What's so funny, don't you believe me?" she demanded.

"It's not that. I believe your story. But Madagascar Pigeon? Their holy bird is a pigeon? Is that the extent of their imagination? The only thing a pigeon does is beg food and shit everywhere."

"Well," she said, "it's not my place to question somebody's religious ways. That would be a full-time career." I was considering that, still laughing, when she said, "Where is it? Did you give it to the Gunn woman?"

"Oh, no, I haven't seen her since that day she came to my office. The second time."

"Well, where is it?"

"I've hidden it."

"Where?"

"There is mischief afoot and a dead guy. It might be better if I don't tell you. Keep you out of the equation – and out of danger – if you get my drift."

"That's very protective of you, noble, even, though I don't remember you had such a virtue. What happens if you show up like the dead guy, you know, with bullets in your belly?"

I hadn't thought of that. On the flip side, if I was lying in a pool of my own blood peering at the Pearly Gates, where the Madagascar Pigeon was going to reappear wouldn't mean jack shit to me. Madagascar Pigeon? Somebody in Africa must have been a comic.

"Where is it?" she asked again. "You could have the one with all the jewels. The odds are four to one. Not bad, huh?"

"Actually, I think the odds are three to one since there's only four statues. Three are empty and one isn't, if you believe the legend."

"You know, Basil," she said to me, "you really are a nerd. What difference does it make what the odds are? We've got the chance to solve an ages-old puzzle right in our hands and you are doing arithmetic. Four to one, three to one. I should have hit you in the mouth. Keep it from flapping. Maybe next time. Where the hell is it?" If she could knock me senseless with a blow to my tummy, just think of the damage she'd do to my face, my nose, my teeth.

"You been working out?" I asked her.

She answered, "Where – is – it?"

I told her. My gym locker. I may be a nerd. I am not a dumb nerd.

My instincts about Emily and how she would be the person to enlighten me about the statue proved correct. I had the answer and more. The African background, the presence of potential riches, the name of the thing, Madagascar Pigeon. It was time to leave. I thanked Emily and moved to the door.

"Wait," she said. Here she came. The hug, owed me now that we were in a confederacy. Two peas in a bejeweled pod. When she came near, she reared back with that right arm of hers. Oh, lord, I mumbled as I covered my mouth, my nose, my teeth, and she got me right in the solar plexus.

As I crossed the campus in the direction of my car, students stared at my hunched-over figure, my faltering stride, my groans. Twice school security officers inquired about my obvious stress. "I'm okay, really. Something I ate, I guess. Thanks for asking." God, that hurt. Still had all my teeth though.

5

When you have been involved with a woman and things don't work out between the two of you with a storybook ending and then she punches you – twice on the same day – in your solar plexus, you aren't too surprised when she doesn't call to ask after you – even if she thinks she's on the verge of some academic accolade for discovering a hidden treasure spoken of in sketchy terms in her pedantic textbooks. Besides, what was all this *we* shit? "*We've* got the chance..." and "right here in *our* hands..." My emphasis. Her presumptiveness. It's my statue. Well, Miss Gunn's if you can believe her cockamamie story. She doesn't even give out her real name. Bevalaqua, that horse's ass, said she did not use the Gunn name with him. How do I know she bought this souvenir in East Asia and sent it to me? More practically, how will she know it arrived if I don't tell her? I'm the only one who knows where it is. Ooops, and Emily, too, now. Why'd I tell her? Oh, that's right, she would have kicked the snot out of me. But nobody else knows.

Right about here, my door swung open – why don't I lock it – and in walked The Pole, his whaddyacallit minion, and Ms. Wu. It was easy to identify the trio from Miss Gunn's description. "So, Mr. Beault, the private detective," he assessed me. I began to respond when he offered, "Buddha, you look awful, what did you run into?"

"Yeah, well," I said, clutching my abdomen, "you ought to see the other guys."

"Doing your private dick thing, eh? Bringing wayward husbands back to their marriage beds, peering into other people's windows, skip-tracing drunks to their local saloons, following..."

"I get it, what do you want?"

"Okay, Beault, let's cut to the cheese here. (Cheese?) We know you've got it. It's not yours to keep, and it certainly isn't yours to give to Miss Gunn. That's the name she's using right now, correct?"

My solar plexus still hurt and everything near it. I looked from The Pole, way up high, to his minion and then to Ms. Wu. They seemed very expectant. Confident, even.

"You have me at a disadvantage, mister. First, who the hell are you people, and second, whatever is this it you are referring to? And, third, who is this Miss Gum?"

"Gunn, dammit!" he exploded.

"Where?" I shouted, "who's got a gun?" Pretty good joke that. The Pole did not get it.

"I hope a gun won't become necessary, Beault. We are men of experience and good sense. We can bargain fairly."

"Bargain? Bargain for what?"

"If you wish to play it this way, we will have it your way. This Miss Gunn character has something that belongs to me. She slipped away from us with it. Your name was known to us. She is now in San Francisco. You are in San Francisco (Tell me something I don't know) and I am reasonably certain she has come to you with a fabricated story about an item she has sent to you. To repeat, it is not hers, it is mine." He stopped. I said nothing.

When a moment passed, I said, "Oh, are you finished?" The Pole nodded. I'd say ominously. "Most interesting story, mister, only I don't see how I fit into it. I'll admit that a Miss Gunn appeared here recently, but it was mistaken identity. She was in fact seeking a tax preparer who also maintains an office in this building. When I discovered her error at arriving at my door, I redirected her to her desired location. That is the beginning and the end of my involvement in your fantasy."

"I do not believe you, Beault."

"I am sorry to hear that, but there is nothing I can do about it. Where you place your faith is beyond me. Now as the day is drawing near its end..."

"Did Kluszewski give it to you when he came here?"

"Klu-who?"

"The man who died in your office."

"Oh, that poor man. His name was what? I didn't get that from him. At death's door, he was unable to speak. I shall pass his name along to the police. They will appreciate that information. His murder is most troublesome. You know, do you, that he was murdered? Shot several times. Fatally. With bullets. Know anything about that, do you?"

"Did he give it to you, Beault? I do not wish to keep asking. I want to know and I want it."

"Whatever is this it you keep talking about? The only thing this Mr. Klu-ski gave me (and here their eyes widened) was the job of cleaning up the blood he left on my chair and my floor."

"Let's shoot him," Ms. Wu said in cultured English. She had pulled a gun and it was pointed at me. We all shifted our attention to her. Me especially. "Then he will tell us where it is," she added.

She didn't say, "Let's discuss our options; let's look at the pros and cons; let's think on this a moment; let's test the waters of debate; let's exchange views on this; let's canvass opinions; lets take up alternatives." It was just, "Let's shoot him."

"If you shoot him, my dear, he will not be able to tell us anything." I pointed at The Pole and nodded assertively in agreement with his correct analysis of the situation.

"Yes, of course, I know that," Ms. Wu said. "We will shoot him in his knees. That is almost universally convincing." I didn't care for this woman.

"We are not Barbarians, dear, we have other means to convince Mr. Beault to do the right thing."

To me, he said, "I am aware it would be fruitless to search your office, Beault. You seem a clever man, and I suspect you have hidden my property in a remote and safe place. I am a patient man, although I do have precious little of it left as it relates to you. I – we – will return tomorrow afternoon at five o'clock. At that time I will expect you to give me my property. I am sure you agree that I do not have to add "or else." The three of them left. I clicked my pen, turning off the recorder. Hell of a gadget.

The Pole got that "or else" thought right. It is never a friendly phrase. I remember one time...the door swung open again and just as I

27

was wondering if The Pole had a change of heart, in walked Miss Gunn. No, she dashed in and shut the door. She even locked it. She was wearing a new outfit. Black leotards, an azure knee-length skirt, a crimson vest and a cozy-looking jacket to ward off the still-foggy city chills. And a hat of some shape. I re-clicked my pen.

"I was hiding outside. I saw those awful people here. I couldn't let them see me. I am so afraid, Mr. Beault. They frighten me. What did they want? Did they talk about me? Ask about me? I don't know who they are. It is so frightening." Then quiet. I guessed at that point she had run out of words.

"Why, Miss Gunn," I greeted her, "so nice to see you again. Are you enjoying your visit to the city? It's too bad we are in such a foggy period, though it does add mystery to San Francisco, don't you think?"

"I...um...yes...no...I don't know..."

"Cut the act, sister," I said savagely. "You have played me for a sucker. I ain't no sucker, you got that." I was rising from my chair. "You come waltzing in here with a load of lies and a tearful face and you want me to pant like a lapdog. A guy's dead and I've been threatened with a gun. Nobody's told me anything I can count on. You tell me your souvenir is coming to me. Those bozos who just left tell me it belongs to them. What the hell is this it, I ask. Nobody tells me. And all I have to show for it is a lousy fifty bucks."

Miss Gunn collapsed into a chair. "I apologize. You are right, Mr. Beault, I have not been entirely truthful with you."

"Have you told me anything that is true?"

"Certainly, yes. Did the package arrive? I have the other fifty dollars."

"Let's go back to the truth instead of changing the subject. For example, your name isn't Phyllis Gunn, is it?"

"You are a clever man, Mr. Beault."

"Gee, I just learned that a few minutes ago from your friends."

"They are not my friends," she blurted. "They are thieves and liars and murderers, yes, murderers no doubt. They want what's mine, and they'll stop at nothing to get it."

"Your souvenir, you mean."

"Oh, uh...yes...have you seen it?"

"Let's get back to your name. We should be better acquainted if we are to do business together."

"I am Mrs. Dexter Covington."

"You are married, yet you do not wear a wedding ring."

"My name is Alice, Alice Goodbody."

"Nice try."

"What can it matter what my name is? My life is in danger. I must have it...my souvenir...so I can escape from these ruffians."

"All right, no names for the time being. Here's an idea. Why not tell me your story – from the beginning. Maybe then I can help in some way. I *am* a private detective, after all. You tell me your story and I'll take notes – with my pen here – jotting down anything that resembles the truth. Go ahead."

She went ahead right to my face. What a stewpot of untruths that was. I know there are times when I operate at the lower end of the dimmer switch, but come on, did she really think I was going to buy the detritus she was selling? And the whining. Like a five-year old.

"Now that you have heard my story, Mr. Beault, will you please give me my possession? I really must get away from the others. Oh, and here is the fifty dollars I still owe you."

"Keep it. I haven't earned it. I said I would take the money when I put the package into your hands. I can't do that. The package hasn't arrived."

"Dear me," she said, "I was certain you had it. So certain that I brought this along" – here she pulled a gun from her purse – "in case you were so stupid that you would try to dupe me. As you can see, Mr. Beault, I am not easily duped. I will use this if I have to."

"Wouldn't that send me as well as the whereabouts of your souvenir to the grave? Not the ideal plan for you to follow."

"I'll use it."

"Yes, maybe. This is the second time today a woman has held a gun on me with the aim of shooting me. If I couldn't give her what she wanted because I do not have your blasted toy, then I cannot give it to you for the same reason."

"Let's not quibble, Beault (what, no Mr.?) I know that Captain Kluszewski came here. I heard that he died here. He gave you the package. It was his job. So where is it?"

"Not here because he had no package to give me. Maybe he lost it between the time you shot him and when he got here."

"I didn't shoot him."

"Who did?"

"It...I don't know. Why should I know? It could have been anybody. One of those ruffians. Yes, one of them."

"Miss Gunn, Mrs. Covington, Miss Goodbody, whoever you are, this is taking us nowhere. Let's join forces. I have no interest in your souvenir (a little white lie) except for the fifty clams I'll get. You seem anxious to find it. If you hire me to find it – you do have money, right? – I'll do my best to locate it. I'm a professional at that sort of thing. A hundred and twenty-five dollars an hour."

She stood up, put her gun back into her purse and turned toward the door. "I'll call you," she said as she went out. I gathered I did not at this moment have a new client. I clicked off my pen recorder.

6

The phone rang.

"Beault."

"Hi, Bas."

"Oh, hi, Gren." It was my brother. It was good to hear his voice. Grenville is the minister of a church over in the Castro District called the Congregation of Brotherly Love in the Name of Jesus Christ.

"How are you doing?" he asked. He's a good guy. We have different lives and different interests, but we love each other.

"I'm doing okay," I said not so convincingly. We talk to each other a lot and see one another several times a month.

"That sounds to me as if you are *not* doing okay," he responded. Despite our differences we know each other like open books.

"I won't bore you with the details. How are you doing?" I asked him. Our parents are long gone. They had good lives but sad ends. They drenched us in love and friendship. Could not have asked for more.

"I want to bore *you* with some details," he told me.

"Uh-oh, want me to come over?"

"If you would, please."

"Half hour okay?"

"Yup."

His church is a gutted and converted large billiards hall abandoned years ago on a street a half block off Castro Street south of Market. He's a big, articulate guy who got all the good looks, size genes and intelligence in the family. I'm two years older, and I used to tease him out of habit until one day I looked up at him and gulped. He grew about five inches and put on forty pounds over one night, I always believed.

31

I was never jealous of him, just proud. He has a big following of what I would call parishioners but he calls congregants and brethren. They worship him. No, they worship God. They think Grenville is "the berries" as the old saying goes. The congregation is about eighty percent male. The females in the congregation resent the hell out of him. He thinks it's cute. Years ago when he told me he was gay and how he had embraced the revelation and how he wanted to make a difference in his community and I saw how happy he was, I almost wished I was gay. I'm not. But *c'est la vie.*

Grenville said there had been a theft.

"You don't lock the place?"

"It's a church, Basil, I leave the doors open. God doesn't shut us out, why should I?"

"Because this is San Francisco, not heaven. There is an element that doesn't obey the rules, even God's."

"I hear the crimemeister talking."

"Yeah, maybe, but who's the one got ripped off?" I asked him.

He raised up his hands. "I accept the blame."

"Let's go over the missing items in more detail. I have an ache in my stomach – oh, I'll tell you about that, too – that tells me we may be onto something affecting both of us."

He showed me the statuary. Told me how members of the congregation donated statues to the church in an unexplained generosity that started when the building renovation was complete and the church looked empty. There were statues of Christ, the apostles, the archangels – mostly men, incidentally – and one of Harvey Milk. These were intermixed with more conventional Christian iconography. His word, not mine. I asked him to tell me what was missing. He described them. Uh-huh, I murmured. How many, I pressed. He told me. Uh-huh, again. When did this occur I told him to tell me. He told me. Uh-huh.

"Let's sit down. I need to tell you what's been going on over on my side." I went through the whole thing, leaving out nothing. He's my brother, for Pete's sake. I owed Grenville the whole truth.

"You've been playing in a dirty sandbox, bro, ever think of hiring a bodyguard?" he asked me.

"Hiring one? I am one. Well, I could be one if I wanted to be. I just don't want to. That is some tough duty."

"You're the detective. What do you make of this?"

"Greed and more greed," I said, "which is the easy answer because greed is almost always a leading motivation for crime."

"That's true in my business, too."

Missing from Grenville's church were four statues of doves, the bird of peace. That twanged my antenna. I'm a detective, remember? I told you I am at the start of this tale. I have people with guns and belligerent attitudes poking around in my knickers looking for statues of birds and then you have statues of birds purloined from your brother's church. I'm not good at arithmetic (that's not just false modesty), but I can add one and one and come up with a connection.

"What's the connection?" he asked me.

"I don't know, but there's got to be one. Unless we hear that the crooks in this town have given up on carjacking luxury cars to go into swiping mute birds, this has to mean certain people assume that I sneaked the Madagascar Pigeon to you for safe keeping."

"That makes sense. It's no secret we're brothers. Even though," he said, "we don't look alike because I am so much handsomer than you, folks will still know who we are."

"What, you're doing stand-up now?"

"Always planning ahead to my Sunday sermons. I'm thinking of doing the Ugly Prodigal next week. You'd be the star."

"While you are making ha-ha, don't forget that if my theory holds up you could be in a lot of danger. When the pencil necks who stole your statues find they are useless to them, you may get a return visit. You ever buy a gun?"

"Yeah, sure, my church is an armory. I've got a whole magazine downstairs with enough guns and ammo to overthrow Canada. Only I don't want to. Too cold up there."

"Whew. You oughta be writing for Jay Leno."

"Who?"

"Yeah."

"Come on, who's Jay Leno?"

I changed the subject. "Do you have guys in the congregation who could keep an eye on you and your church? Maybe a neighborhood watch sort of thing. I could hold a class on how to marshal their..."

"Basil, they're gay, they're not helpless. I've got members who are veterans. Vietnam, Desert Storm, Afghanistan. Others are cops. A couple of ex-pro linebackers."

"Oh, yeah, who?"

"I'll put the word out. Anybody wants to mess with the church, we'll be able to deal with it. The church is important to them."

"You're important to them."

"I'm only God's handmaiden."

"Don't turn into a martyr."

"That's last on my list."

"Famous last words. Literally last words."

At the door as I was about to leave, Grenville tapped my arm. "She said her name is Mrs. Dexter Covington? Phyllis Gunn? Where does she come up with names like that? Alice Goodbody?" We had a good laugh over that.

In my car on my way home I wasn't laughing. There wasn't anything funny about the goons I was dealing with who were turning their attention on Grenville. I know he could easily take care of himself in a fair fight, but he can't dodge bullets. I was worried for him.

7

Let's see, I had a dead guy they had to scrape off my floor, a trio of ruffians – one of whom was voting to shoot me – who said I had to turn an it over to them by five o'clock tonight, a tall dame with a pocketful of names with a gun of her own she also pointed at me, an ex-whatever who could punch me in the solar plexus like George Foreman, a brother unfairly linked into my troubles, a floormate who was a horse's ass who proved it with every encounter, and no clients active enough to be throwing a lot of money at me. All I needed now was...and sure enough there was Detective Lieutenant Blough and his silent sidekick waiting at my door when I came up the stairs from my sweet roll and coffee shop down on Balboa.

"Beault," he said.

"That's *my* name," I said.

"Where ya been?"

"Why?"

"Cuz I wanna know."

"Live with disappointment, lieutenant."

"You bein a smartass, Beault?"

"Sometimes, but not now."

"Been out shootin strangers again?"

"Again?"

"Yeah."

"Are you accusing me of shooting someone?"

"Maybe."

"Do I need a lawyer?"

"A P.I. needin a lawyer, who'd a thunk?"

35

"What do you want, Blough?"

"Let's talk."

We talked. He told me they had opened a homicide investigation on the dead guy in my room. I congratulated him on their perceptiveness. A dead body with three or four bullet holes.

"So you decided it wasn't a suicide, eh?" I challenged. He reminded me that he and his mute partner – that would be Sgt. Headley – were armed. I got the message. And I also had to go over my explanation of the poor guy's death even though I had dutifully gone downtown and signed my sworn statement to the exact same effect. Being the good citizen I am, I said it all over again. Blough said he doesn't understand why Kluszewski chose to die on my floor if I didn't know him.

"That makes two of us," I agreed. Probably three of us, but Headley hadn't offered an opinion.

"You're lying to me, Beault, I just know that, and when I come across the truth I am going to wrap you in San Quentin irons." I guess he wanted to go easy on me. San Quentin is just a few miles north of the Golden Gate Bridge and home to "Q," California's rather notorious prison for hardasses, and close enough, he seemed to be suggesting, for my friends to come see me during visiting hours.

Later, when Blough and Headley were gone, and I had finished some chores, I looked at my watch. Mickey Mouse said it was past four o'clock. That meant The Pole, his weird minion and the armed Ms. Wu would be by in less than an hour for the it they demanded or, alternatively, else. I didn't like else. When there was a tap on my door I jumped. What, they're early, or did I miss the daylight savings time change again this year? I collected myself and said, "It's open." In walked the strangest individual I had ever laid my eyes on.

"Mr. Beault?" she asked. I was struck dumb. She was just over five feet tall unless she was wearing heels that I could not see under her draping. Then she would have been even smaller. Not smaller, shorter. Smaller would not fit her. She may have been five feet around as well as five feet tall, which would explain the tent-like covering she sported. It was a forest green with alternating white and yellow vertical pinstripes. Vertical, I imagine, to diminish the girth appearance. Did not work. The collar around her substantial neck came up to just under her Adam's apple. Huge dark glasses covered her eyes and more of her face than conventional frames. Her hair was pitch black and matted down around an oddly shaped head and worn short. Her ears stuck out like open doors. Her hands at the end of arms you would expect to see on an adolescent were in gloves. Or so I assumed. One hand was. The other was lost in an oversized handbag flowing from her shoulder. Navy blue. Printed on one side was "Pier 39." I didn't figure her for a tourist. I am, after all, a detective. I detect and discern. She was something else.

Finally, I could answer. "Yeah, I'm Beault."

"Oh, good," she said in a high, squeaky voice. "I have come to the right place."

"How can I help you, ma'am?"

"Ma'am?" she squealed. "You goddam son of a bitchin bastard. My name is Lorenz, Marcel Lorenz. I'm no ma'am." Adam's apple, of course. I saw it. I should have recognized him for that. Gals don't have Adam's apples. Do they? Then I looked to see if he was wearing a tank of helium gas to make his voice so high and squeaky. I thought it was a staple of his diet. Draped the way he was I could not see any attachments.

"Sorry," I managed, "I'm having a bad week." Then I added, "Sir."

"Well then, Mr. Beault, I am going to make your week better." Oh, I smiled, a new client with money.

"Great, how can I help you help me?" I said teasing the situation.

"You can hand over the Madagascar Pigeon to me so that I will not have to kill you."

And for the third time (fourth if you count the not-so-veiled threat by Lt. Blough of his being armed along with Sgt. Headley) I was staring down the barrel of a gun. Evidently, his gun had been in the handbag along with his other hand. It was a formidable gun. Being the cool character I am, especially in the face of danger, I quietly assessed my options, glancing to see if I had an avenue to subdue this overgrown pumpkin. All I could see to do was click my pen.

"Don't try anything stupid, Mr. Beault, this gun is loaded."

Was I that obvious, I thought, as my options narrowed? I could not think of anything to say, so I said, "I'm sorry, you want me to do what?"

"Hand over the Madagascar Pigeon." As I had when I first heard that name, I began to laugh. More like a giggle. Madagascar Pigeon. What on Earth! It was also a tense giggle, brought about in large part by the continuing presence of the gun. I was at the receiving end of that gun.

"Do I amuse you, Mr. Beault? Are you perhaps laughing at my appearance? I know I sometimes elicit an uncommon reaction from people."

"No, no, Mr. Lorenz, not that at all. I was reacting to what you said. Madagascar Pigeon. What a comical name. Whatever is it?"

"Do not play the jester's role here, Mr. Beault, I know you have it and I want it. Give it to me now."

Though the gun was still pointing at me, I had collected my wits a little bit. A bit of wits, that's your intrepid P.I. "You are mistaken, Mr. Lorenz, if you think I have a bird belonging to you. I do not."

"My patience in this matter is very thin. You have the Madagascar Pigeon, having received it from Captain Kluszewski when he was here the other day." Patience was running in short supply with all these jerkheads.

"The dead guy, you mean? Indeed, yes, he was here. But he gave me nothing, well, except for a scare. It is not the usual visitor here who drops dead on my floor."

"Captain Kluszewski was charged with the statue, Mr. Beault, and charged further to deliver it to you in this very office. From Miss Gunn, whom I believe you have already met and transacted business."

"Oh, yes, Miss Gunn. Or do you mean Mrs. Covington or Miss Goodbody?"

"She is winsome, is she not? And, yes, I mean her in any guise."

"Well, Mr. Lorenz, everything you tell me may be true. However, your Captain Kluszewski arrived here without your bird. I can only guess that he was separated from it before he reached me. Maybe he had been distracted because he was full of bullet holes."

A pall of uncertainty fell across his face. That was reassuring to me. I gambled. "If it is any consolation, Mr. Lorenz, I will have to tell the

same tale to three other people who have expressed an obsessive interest in this risible bird. They in fact are due here within minutes."

"Three?" he croaked. Fear replaced the uncertainty. Ah-ha, a clue.

"I wonder if you might know them. One goes by the unusual moni-
ker of The Pole. He has a slovenly associate and an enigmatic female
friend I know only as Ms. Wu."

Lorenz clutched at his collar and quickly scanned the room. "Here?
Now?" he gasped.

"Yes, here and now...in, oh, about ten minutes. Care to stay and meet
them?" I needled him. "You seem to have similar collecting goals."

"Shut up," he shouted. "Sit down," he told me. "Over here," he
pointed at my swivel chair. He came up behind me.

8

My head hurt so bad I wanted to cry. I blinked. I *was* crying. The tears made a fog of what I was looking through. The hurt made everything else incomprehensible. My brain was on pause. I would have shaken my head to restart it, but something hinted to me that that was a really bad idea. I reached up to my head. Something sticky all over it. I don't use a hair tonic.

I heard someone say, "He's moving," like that was a scientific breakthrough. Moving? I touched my head again. Not a hair tonic. Blood. Then "Can he talk?" What kind of stupid question is that? Of course he can talk, I thought. Been talking all my life. Since I was about four and a half. "Ask him what happened" – "You ask him what happened" – "What happened?" Presuming I was the one who was supposed to be telling what happened and underscored by the fact that it was my head covered in blood, I began to tell them what happened.

After a long jumbled explanation, I heard somebody say, "What's with him? He can't talk." But I have been talking, telling you everything that... I passed out. So I was informed later. Later my head still hurt, my eyes were fogged, I was probably crying again, and I was propped up on my sofa. How'd I get here? Dumb question. Even if I learned how I'd got there I would not have given a crap. Ms. Wu leaned in and wiped my eyes with a tissue and then with another she wiped my nose. Ms. Wu? Oh no, are they here? Then I heard someone say, "That is so Oriental, my dear, the sweet soft touch of Asian benevolence." The Pole! Ms. Wu backed away after having suggested The Pole screw himself, although she said it less lady-like. "Are you with us now, Mr. Beault?" The Pole asked me. I coughed out an answer even I could not decipher.

This stupefaction went on for several more minutes before I could ask, "What happened to me?"

"It looks as though someone split your head open," The Pole told me. "Do you know who?" Not do you want an aspirin or can we call a doctor or do you want an ice pack. Just do you know who. What a buttface.

My brain was still on pause. I didn't know who...yes, I did. I whispered "Lorenz." The Pole grasped my arm. "Hey, that hurts," I mumbled.

"What did you say?"

"I said that hurts."

"Did you say Lorenz?" he asked. I nodded. I should not have done that because it made my really sore head throb some more. Pay attention, Beault, I cautioned myself.

"He was here?" I didn't nod, I blinked. Even that hurt. "Did he take the...no, he would have killed you." Oh, happy thought, I thought. "So where is it?" he raised his voice. "I said I would be here at five o'clock to get it and it is now past nine."

My head ached like hell, but I did have the capacity to sound mad. "I am sorry, Pole, if the fact that I have been mugged to near death has put you off your schedule." Then I repeated what I had told him yesterday. "I do not have your item. Captain Kluszewski did not have it when he expired here the other day. I have learned since then that it is a strangely name bird."

"The Madagascar Pigeon," Ms. Wu said as if on cue. She also said it with unconcealed awe.

"Where did it get a name like that?" I said. "Every time I hear it I want to laugh."

"You are not laughing now, Mr. Beault," The Pole observed, "because you have seen it and now you are coming to the realization that it is invaluable."

"A pigeon? Invaluable? Hell, step outside and grab one," I whispered. "There's hundreds out there all the time pooping on the sidewalk. Dime-a-freakin dozen. Invaluable, ha, I say. By the way, I am not laughing now only to prevent my head from exploding. I want to avoid that."

Round and round we went. Where is it? I don't know. You have it. No I don't. Where did you put it? Nowhere. You're a jerk. You're an ass.

No I'm not. Yes you are. Na-na-na. I was exhausted. I needed to crash. I also needed to find Marcel Lorenz. I wanted to pound that lily-livered coward. I had come to the conclusion it was he who caved in my head. I was pistol-whipped. What a horrid term: pistol-whipped. Crap, did that hurt. First, I would crash. Crashing is good when your head is caved in and it's covered in blood. Your own blood. I didn't care if The Pole and his two sidekicks gave a rip. I had to crash.

I did. I crashed. Which means I went to bed. I slept until about noon the next day. I felt a little better but I was far from healed. My head still hurt. Incidentally, here is some advice: don't ever get pistol-whipped. It's rank. More than that, it stinks. Or is that the same thing? I think I'm digressing. Am I digressing? Never mind. I showered, trying to clean the blood from my hair and elsewhere. I ate some sardines on soda crackers and then heated a can of pea soup. I spent about fifteen minutes dialing for something interesting on the radio. No luck. Checked once again to make sure my door was locked. Okay, okay, I am digressing, but you would, too, if you were as troubled as I was. I had troubling things on my stoved-in mind. I had the Madagascar Pigeon. I was told it was invaluable. Is that better than valuable? Doesn't make any sense to say it that way. In-valuable. Weird. I had been threatened by shady characters that they'd kill me if I didn't relinquish the statue. I could do that. I could give the damn thing to one of them. Then the others would carry out their threats. That sounded like a lose-lose situation to me. Troubling, see? I did not have a good answer, so I chose one from the not-so-good answers. I telephoned Emily.

She didn't pick up until around the tenth ring. "Yes!" Not hello or this is Emily or something friendly. Just "Yes!"

"Oh, hi, it's me," I started.

"Who is me?" she crowed. She knew. She had heard my voice many times before.

"Me, Jaguar,"

"Oh, you, Basil."

"Look," I said, "sorry to be a bother, but I think you will want to know the way things have developed over this Madagascar bird thing."

"Why am I going to care?"

"Things have gotten very strange...and tense. Actually very dangerous."

"Dangerous for me?" she asked.

"Well, no, for me."

"I'll ask you again, why am I going to care?"

Criminy, I thought. "Emily, I know you have it in for me. Let's forget about me. Surely you are interested in the M.P."

"The M.P.?"

"The Madagascar Pigeon."

"You still have it?"

"Sure, that's what I'm trying to tell you. There have been developments."

"Oh, spare me."

"No, really, strange developments. I've been threatened with a gun. In fact, three times."

"Aren't you being a bit dramatic?"

"No, three guns, three different times. One of them used one on me."

"You were shot?" Just a question, no real emotional attachment to the inquiry.

"He hit me with it."

"He hit you with a gun. Isn't that sort of counter-intuitive?" This woman hates me if you haven't figured that out.

"Listen, Emily, we need to talk. I could use your input. Besides, you'll want to know what else is going on with this statue mystery." She relented and I suggested we meet for a quick bite. You know, in a public place where she would be less inclined to slug me in my solar plexus in front of strangers. I named a place. What I heard on her end of the line was a harrumph. Instead, she named Harris' Restaurant on Van Ness. That's a costly place, I said to myself. Drat! Well, dinner was my idea, so I said okay and how about six o'clock.

"Six! Shit, what are you a hundred years old? You gotta go to early-bird specials to save a buck? Nine o'clock and not a minute before. Or after. Make a reservation. I'll meet you there." She hung up. What's wrong with six? I get hungry early.

9

When the phone rang a few minutes later I did one of those fist pump things. Emily! Calling to back off some. Come to her senses. Shouldn't be dumping all over me the way she had been. I let it ring a few times. Like she does. "Yes!" I exclaimed, like she did.

"Mr. Beault?" Not Emily.

"It is pronounced beault."

"Is it?"

"For as long as I can remember." Then nothing. "You called me. Can I help you?"

"No, but I can help you," the voice said. Wait a second, I thought. I'd just heard that same thing recently. Somebody – Lorenz! – saying that same kind of thing as an alternative to my shooting death. Hearing it now did not improve its implications.

"Just how can you do that?" I played along.

"I represent someone who has an abiding interest in ancient artifacts," he said.

"Really, but I'm hardly ancient." I love doing that. Lightens moods. And my mood certainly could use some lightening.

"Droll, Mr. Beault, very droll. Allow me to explain."

"All right, splain it to me." I almost added "Lucy" but didn't.

When a moment of silence passed, the voice said, "It will be to your advantage, Mr. Beault, to hear me out without interruptions. I hope I do not have to say that again." I could almost hear the phrase "or else."

Whew! "Please proceed," I agreed.

"I represent someone who has an interest in something you have in your possession for the time being. This individual is prepared to make you a fair but generous offer for it. He has the resources to meet this offer. You should have no misgivings about that. What he proposes is that I meet you within the next twenty-four hours when I would give you – in cash, mind you – five thousand dollars. You in turn would give me the Madagascar Pigeon you currently hold."

Five grand, I thought. That's a hell of a lot more than the fifty bucks the Gunn woman still owed me for the bird. A guy with less scruples than I had could be tempted. I sat there musing about my scruples, such as they are. Then I heard the voice again. "Are you still there, Mr. Beault?"

"Oh, are you finished? I didn't want to interrupt you. You told me not to do that."

"Yes, I am finished except to establish a time and a place to complete our transaction."

"Well, sir," I said, "I may be the last one chosen for softball at the company picnic, but I am not so naïve to think a call like this does not come without a portion of suspicions."

"Suspicions?"

"Suspicions, yes. I do not know you. I do not know the person you represent. I have no way – and I am a rather resourceful private detective (I boasted) – of knowing if you are telling a whole truth or if you are grasping at the straws of unsupported rumors. You could be working for the FBI or the CIA or the NSA."

"You prove perceptive, Mr. Beault, I like that. However, I can't imagine why the FBI or the CIA would have any interest in the Madagascar Pigeon. Then again it is often hard not to put plenty past the NSA. I may have a solution to ease your suspicions. I feel as though I am authorized to modify the offer. A new proposal. I, on behalf of the person I represent, will send to you by messenger one thousand dollars – again, in cash – as a token of our sincerity. This thousand dollars, let us call it a you-can-trust-me fee, will be in addition to the five thousand dollars for the item itself."

Well, well. The bargaining begins. The subtle negotiating. The give-and-take of the deal to come. The...

"Mr. Beault?"

"Oh, sorry, I was just...you know, I don't know what to call you, your name."

"It's irrelevant, but you can call me Blankenship, Hugo Blankenship."

Hugo Blankenship? What, his mom and pop hated him? Hugo? How does a guy with a name like that ever get beyond third grade without a barrelful of complexes set upon him by kids with real names, names like Basil and Grenville? Okay, my own dad had a sense of humor.

"Mr. Beault?"

"Oops, sorry again. I've been thinking, you know, about your offer, about the person who you say you represent, about an item you believe me to have. Why, I'd like to understand, do you believe I have this thing?"

"Oh, come now, Mr. Beault, that does you no justice. It is patently clear that Captain Kluszewski had the Madagascar Pigeon and that he was well paid to deliver it to you. That he had to give his life to hand it to you is his bad luck." Bad luck? I wonder what the good captain would call it.

"What you say is correct, Mr. Blankenship, all but the part about hand it to me. As I have told Miss Gunn, The Pole, that Lorenz character, even the cops..."

Blankenship burst into my explanation. "The Pole? Lorenz? You know these people? You have seen them? They know about the Madagascar Pigeon? They have offered you money for it? This is most disturbing."

"This is disturbing? Try a pistol-whipping," I said.

Then Blankenship again. "The police are involved also?"

"Sure, it's a homicide investigation. Your Captain Kluszewski didn't die of the heartbreak of psoriasis. He had four bullet holes in him. That's usually four more than the handbook calls for."

"Oh my," Blankenship despaired, "this changes everything. The Pole, Lorenz, perhaps others. I will...my employer will want to accelerate this transaction immediately. In fact, to show our good faith he will...he authorizes me to double our offer if you can give us the item straightaway."

"He sounds to me to be a generous individual. Make it double even your new offer and I would have to decline."

"But why?"

"Because I do not have the Madagascar Pigeon. (I keep telling this white lie.) As I tried to explain earlier, the captain did not have this thing when he came to my office. Its whereabouts are known only to the one who got to him before he arrived at my office."

"I don't believe you," Blankenship yelled into the phone.

"Join the crowd," I told him with a smile on my lips.

"I want that statue. I demand it, and I will do whatever it takes to get it."

"Hugo, Hugo, Hugo," I soothed before I noticed he had hung up.

10

Things were heating up. Here I was sitting on a hot property. It started out at a hundred bucks from Miss Gunn, then it was five grand from Hugo, then another thou – that good faith fee – then double up when it came clear there were other players in the game.

Then there came a tap-tap, tapping at my door. I think I had locked it. Tapping. Tapping? Not that cretinous Marcel Lorenz again. Where's my fucking gun? I got it. "Who's there?" I asked at the door.

A woman's voice, "It's me."

Hell, that could still be Lorenz with that squeaky voice of his. Could be a trick. "Tell me who you are," I called out.

"It's me, Phyllis Gunn, open the door." It *was* she. I let her in and re-locked the door. She was annoyed with my caution. She said, "What is the matter with you...oh, my God, what happened to your head?"

"It was a message from a recent visitor to my home and office who took exception to my description of pigeon statue events. Exception enough that he pistol-whipped me." Here I winced. She didn't.

"How dreadful for you. Was he a client?" Dreadful? A pistol-whipping? A first-rate one at that and all she can say is how dreadful. And he? Why not she?

"You could call it dreadful, galling even, Miss Gunn, but for the life of me I cannot find the words to wrap around this experience. And, no, he is not a client." I stared at her. "I wonder if you might know the gentleman. Goes by the name of...Lorenz." Definite reaction. Tried to suppress it. She couldn't. "I believe you and he have similar collecting interests, similar, not so surprisingly, to a growing bunch of bird aficionados."

"I don't know what you could be referring to, Mr. Beault. I know no one with the name Marcel Lorenz."

"Never heard of him, what?"

"Quite, never heard of him."

"How is it then, Miss Gunn or Mrs. Covington or Miss Goodbody or whoever the hell you plan to be today, that you know him as Marcel (this I emphasized) Lorenz? I did not tell you his first name when I brought him up as my attacker. This is a tried and true detective device we use to dismantle liars. Works every time. Worked here with you."

"Oh, Jaguar, (now it's Jaguar?) please don't treat me this way, so mean." Here she tried to cry. "You are my only hope for retrieving my souvenir. You do have it, don't you, so that I can take it with me?"

"Enough already," I said to her. "Who is this Marcel Lorenz?" She slumped into one of my chairs and put her purse on her lap. "While you are trying to come up with an answer as untruthful as everything else you have told me in our brief encounters, remember that I can reach my gun before you can reach yours." She put on a smile that said you win. She slipped her purse off her lap onto the floor.

"Marcel is a slime, a wretched man who is without any morals, integrity, honesty, or anything that might redeem him. He was just a few steps away from grabbing the Madagascar Pigeon. I am sure you know all about my souvenir by now, Mr. Beault, so I won't try to conceal my interest in it. As I say, he nearly beat me to it, but I was luckier than him. We were in Shanghai. I knew who had the pigeon, he knew who had the pigeon."

Here I broke in. "The Pole and his cohorts, they also knew who had the pigeon in Shanghai?"

She let out a sigh and agreed, "Yes, them too. They are a treacherous band. That Ms. Wu is a real piece of work. I believe she would strangle her own mother for ten yuan."

"Yuan?"

"Chinese money."

"Oh, ah, of course, I knew that." I had probably forgotten.

She continued. "I made it onto the boat and noticed The Pole and his crowd were also sailing."

"Lorenz on it, too?"

50

"I don't know. If he was I did not see him."

"Not see him? How could anybody not take notice of that subhuman? Musta not been on board, that's for sure. Oh, sorry about the interruption."

"In the meantime," she went on, "I had your name and address and had already arranged for the delivery of my souvenir to you. I did not want the pigeon in my cabin."

"Captain Kluszewski had it? Not the merchant you lied about when you said that's how it would be sent."

"Yes. I'm sorry about that. I trusted the captain more."

"How much did you trust him?"

"Twenty-five hundred dollars."

"Not the one hundred you were offering me to put my life on the line."

"No, yes, I mean I did not think anything like this would occur. It all looked so simple. The captain would bring the prize to you unnoticed because no one but me knew he had it."

"That has proved to be short-sighted. The four bullets in the guy tells a bright detective like me that someone else knew he had your prize as you call it. Unless you shot him."

"The poor man dying like that...what...me...I didn't shoot him," she yelled when my comment had sunk in. "I've told you that before."

"Spare me, Miss Gunn, you have no love lost over his untimely departure. Your only concern is the Madagascar Pigeon, which raises the question, what do you propose to do now? It is gone."

"But..."

"It is not here and the other interesting thing is that not only you are baffled, but also The Pole, his dreary friends, Marcel Lorenz, and now Hugo Blankenship must be equally baffled." At the mention of Blankenship, the Gunn woman's jaw dropped. "Just as I suspected," I said to her, "another charming member of the cast of characters looking for the thing. How is it you know him?"

"He is married to my sister. He was the one who first discovered where the statue might be hidden all these years. He has extensive business dealings in Asia and..."

"Doing what?"

"Business. Let's just call it import-export."

"Let's call it what it is, shall we? He's a smuggler."

"That's a crass term."

"It's a crass world we live in," I said.

"Let's not quibble. It's unimportant. He found where it was and had plans to recover it. I knew of his plans and beat him to the statue."

"That's not a positive signal of familial compatibility in my book. You played him for a sucker. I'll bet he was miffed at that."

"He has threatened to kill me," she said.

"Well, that certainly fits the mold of this deadly little soap opera we are all a part of, doesn't it?"

"All this should show you how urgent it is for me to get the statue and disappear. My life is at stake," Mr. Beault.

"You pulled my name out of a hat for a hundred dollars. You put my life at stake, too. I think the urgency is not for you to disappear, but for me to get you people to believe I don't have the bloody thing and you guys go look elsewhere. I want out of this."

"You told me the other day that I could hire you to look for my item."

"That was before I was threatened by guns more than once and pistol-whipped by a giant pumpkin. No deal. A little bit of income ain't worth the grief you all have brought me." She leaned down to her purse. I brought my gun out quickly. "Don't do something dumb." She shrugged. I told her I had a dinner appointment and she left. I don't think she was very happy.

11

At Harris' Restaurant, where you enjoy elegant dining, though my usually empty pocketbook has scant memory of that, I went to the bar and ordered a drink from Robert, a club soda over ice with a lemon slice. We chatted for a moment. He knows what I do for a living. A living? God help me. It was about nine-fifteen. I walked to the dining room where Emily was sitting. I carried my drink in front of me...in front of my solar plexus in the hopes she would see the disadvantages of slugging me through a glass. It worked. She didn't get up to hit me. She did glare at me, however, glancing down at her watch. "I told you not a minute before nine, you jackass, and not a minute after. You are hopeless."

"Good evening to you, too, Emily. You look lovely." She looked the same as always. I have found it advisable to make respectable reference to a woman's appearance. Most notably to Emily's appearance.

"Sit down, Basil (that again, ugh). So what's so effing important that you had to see me on short notice. Wait a minute. What's wrong with your head? You been giving yourself haircuts again? What a cheapskate. What can they cost you? Fifteen lousy dollars?"

"It's a lot worse than that. Let me tell you."

Telling her took us through drinks. I told her everything except the part about Grenville's church getting ripped off. Mentioning my brother to Emily is like lighting a roman candle. She would start gushing until she ran out of breath. She has a thing for my gay brother. She's not alone in that, I confess, but she...well, the way she carries on drives me batty.

The way she was ordering and eating I just knew she pegged me for the bill. What, no Dutch Treat? She makes a lot more money than I do. Hell, street performers make more money than I do. And she's got tenure. I get death threats and pistol-whippings. She did me one favor, though, she listened. I'm not so sure she sympathized with the fix I was in – looking down gun barrels, getting pistol-whipped – because when she finally spoke, she said, "Let's order dessert, something really wicked."

What did I ever see in this woman? Anyway, I got a hot fudge sundae and so did she. After every other bite from hers she would reach over and take a spoonful from mine. And not in that way when couples would share romantic glances. She just wanted more of the ice cream. Before you wonder about her, let me tell you that she was genetically engineered to not put on weight. When the bill came, she pushed it closer to me and said, "Don't pay that yet. I want an aperitif." An aperitif? Now she's turned into a snob. At my expense. I'm going to have to turn to bank robbery. Hey, I do have a gun. I could buy a mask. No, that won't do.

"The picture is clear, Basil (stop saying that! I'm Jaguar), you are up excrement river without an oar." Finally she was offering her reaction to the tale I had told her. Maybe, just maybe, she will have some useful guidance, I hoped. I hoped, too, that she would be into this topic of a potentially valuable artifact. She took a sip of her drink – this aperitif thing – and was about to go on when someone edged up to my chair, leaned in, and whispered, "Mr. Beault, I am aware you have the statue..."

"Hey, asshole, I was talking to him. Don't be a putz and interrupt without an invitation." Emily at her best table manners. Do you suppose she talks to her students that way? Ah, that's right, she has tenure. She can do anything she likes so long as it doesn't leave a trail of blood or a campus building on fire. Teachers unions, don't you just love 'em? Sorry, another digression.

"Excuse me, madam, it is Beault I am talking to, not you, so butt out." I could have warned him about Emily's propensity for delivering superior solar plexus blows, but I wanted to see where this was going.

"Butt out? Look here, you prick, I could kick your ass from here to the kitchen if I was so inclined. I haven't put somebody your size down in a week or two so..." She stopped because the intruder, still leaning in close to me had drawn his jacket back revealing a gun. Just great!

Another gun. This case – one for which I was earning zilch – was turning into a guns everywhere feature film. Do you sometimes wonder at times like this when you have faced the opening of the barrels of half a dozen pistols over the past few days about the Second Amendment? It gives anyone the right to pack heat. Even guys like Marcel Lorenz who apparently knows how to use both ends of a gun, which reminded me and I massaged my head, which still hurt in lots of places. Then I had a really scary thought. I looked at Emily. Is it possible she's packing? Oh, shoot, I'm digressing again. Sorry.

"Now if you will allow me to continue," he said glaring at Emily, "I will say once more that I know you have the statue, Beault, and I expect you will give it to me."

"Statue? What the hell are you talking about?"

"Don't mess with me. Kluszewski brought it to your office before he died."

"What's going on here? Has somebody started a website reporting on the comings and goings of Jaguar Beault? And who are you?"

"Clint Westwood." Emily laughed out loud and I coughed.

"You just made my day," I said. He slapped me across the back of my head. It must be an easy target. It hurt like hell again. "Ouch, don't do that, it hurts like hell," I jumped.

"I'll do more than that, Beault, if I don't have the Malinese Mallard by noon tomorrow."

"The what?"

"The Malinese Mallard, what Kluszewski gave to you." All the while he's leaning in to me trying not to talk too loud. It's an upscale restaurant, and I noticed he was trying not to disturb other patrons.

"What in the name of John James Audubon is a Malinese Mallard? Don't you mean Madagascar Pigeon? That's what everybody else is calling it."

"Everybody? Who? What are you talking about?"

"Oh, let's see, do you have an hour while I name them all? There's Phyllis Gunn, The Pole, Ms. Wu, Mrs. Dexter Covington, Hugo Blankenship, Marcel Lorenz, that twerp who hangs around The Pole, wait, he doesn't call himself that. He doesn't even speak. Then there's

Alice Goodbody." I saw Emily mouth "Goodbody?" "Have I forgotten anyone? Sure, Joe Blough."

"Who the hell is Joe Blough?"

"Oh, just the homicide detective lieutenant of the San Francisco Police Department investigating Kluszewski's murder. Do you know him?"

Westwood grabbed my shoulder. "Tell me you have not given it to any of these people."

"Hey, that hurts, too," I said pushing his hand off my shoulder. "I have not given the Malinese Mallard to any of them." I saw him relax. "I have not either given any of them the Madagascar Pigeon. Or the Oregon Duck. Or the Australian Emu. Or the Patagonia Parrot."

"Good," he reacted.

I continued, "Because I do not have any of them. I have not had any of them. I do not expect to have any of them."

"But..."

"No buts, Clint. You seem to be pretty well tuned into this drama, yet you have not heard that Kluszewski didn't have anything to give me when he chose my office to draw his last breath. With so many bullet holes in him, it is surprising that he was airtight enough to breathe at all." I thought that was funny and winked at Emily. She raised her eyebrows.

"But..."

"Ah, I said no buts. You are going to have to look elsewhere for this damnable thing. I ain't got it."

Westwood looked down at me and said, "I'll get to the bottom of this, Beault, and if you are down there you'll wish you'd never met me."

"Mr. Westwood, I already wish that."

"Humph," is all he had left. He turned and went for the exit.

Emily finished her aperitif and pushed the check even closer to me. "Thanks for dinner, it's been a lark."

"Huh? What are you saying? Don't you see the trouble I'm in?"

"Very much, yes, I see the trouble you are in. That man, for example, is prepared to kill you. You also testify that some or all the others who make a claim for the statue are prepared to kill you. You know what? If I were you, I'd be careful."

"That's it?" I whispered. "I empty my soul over this goddam thing and show you how much danger I am in and then you see this first hand with Clint Westwood tonight and all you can say is be careful?"

She thought for a moment. "Yeah, I guess so."

If there is one thing I learned about Emily Birch-Aspen, and I learned a whole lot in the short time we were an item, it is that she has no heart. Did I tell you about her name? Birch-Aspen? She was married a short time to this guy who did not come up to her expectations and standards. She dumped him but hyphenated her name, keeping his as part of it as a designation of triumph. She took his name and she was damned sure she was going to keep it. Something in the back of my mind tells me she is motivated by some scheme that gets her into her ex's bank accounts. She probably has his balls in a canning jar at home.

It's not a stretch to suspect that she's got an empty jar set aside for mine. Nevertheless, I went home way more than a hundred dollars lighter for that dinner with Emily. Dinner with Emily. Sounds like the title of an off-Broadway comedy-romance. It isn't. It's just one more way she likes to stick it to me. Did you notice she didn't say word one about the Malinese Mallard? Who's to say she isn't tuned into that? She's a cultural anthropologist. She knows ca-ca like that. This Malinese bird might be worth more than the Madagascar one. I won't put it past her to try to turn a profit on her new information. While all I get from her is "be careful." I'll sleep on it.

12

Well, sleeping didn't help. The truth is I can't make heads or tails of Emily. I don't know why I even pretend. So onward and upward. What's next? Move? So I won't have gun-packing antique collectors out for blood? My blood? Naw, I like San Francisco. It's got it all. This from a guy who can barely afford it. I'll take my chances. What a dumb shit. I hate to admit that last thought, but if the thumping on my door had happened just a tick earlier...never mind. The knocking. What's this then, another gunslinger just rode into town looking to notch Beault on his gun stock? "Who is it?"

"Open up, Beault, it's Blough." Perfect.

"You gotta gun, don't you, Beault?"

"Yeah."

"What's the make, what's the caliber, registered?"

"You have an itch, Blough, and I think you want me to scratch it." I looked at Headley to see if he liked my palaver. Who could tell? He just stared at me.

"I'm here on official business, so let's play this straight." I got my gun and handed it to him. He looked it over, took out the shells, and put it in his pocket.

"Don't you need a warrant to seize a lawfully registered gun from an American citizen who has no criminal record and with rights under the Second Amendment of the United States Constitution?" I looked at Headley. No change.

"No," Blough answered.

"You going to tell me what's on your mind?"

59

"You aren't going to like it. Where were you yesterday, say around noon?"

"Right here."

"Doin what?"

"Nursing a headache."

"A headache, huh, how...wow, what's with the hair and your head?"

"I had a run-in with the alternative use of a pistol."

"A pistol-whipping?" I nodded carefully. "A pistol-whipping, Sergeant Headley. Brings back memories of the old days, don't it?" Headley is actually smiling now. "When bein a cop had some real, what's it called, latitude." He looked at me. "Just kidding, Beault. Pistol-whippings are not an authorized use of force out in the field." He did not include "down at the station" as part of the unauthorized territory. "Who did that to you?"

"Some guy who stopped by and didn't like the answers I gave him to his questions."

"Oh, yeah? His name wouldna been Lorenz, would it? Marcel Lorenz?"

How the hell does word get around about me so easily? I just met this guy. "You know, I'm not sure I got his name," I answered. "He was busy pistol-whipping me."

"That must have pissed you off real good, right?"

"It annoyed me, yes."

"Annoy you enough to put a slug in him from this gun?" he said, patting his pocket.

"He's dead? Are you asking me if I shot this guy?"

"No, I'm asking you if you murdered this guy?"

"I haven't murdered anybody lately, Blough, so the answer is no."

"Maybe ballistics will tell us different. I'm thinking hard evidence will mean more than your denial."

"Have it your way, Blough."

"I always do. So, Beault, word on the street is you are into some major scam. Something about a bird. Is that what Kluszewski gave you before he died not five feet from you? A bird?"

"He didn't give me *a* bird, he gave me *the* bird by dying, like you said, not five feet from me. Can't say things have been very good for me since then. Hey, answer me this. You got an autopsy report on Kluszewski, right? And Lorenz, too."

"Kluszewski, yeah, Lorenz in a day or two. They may need a backhoe to get inside that fat dude."

"What got the captain? I'll bet it wasn't a .38."

"You're clear on that one. It was a .32. Lorenz? We'll see."

"Got a mystery on your hands, don't you?"

"I don't know, Beault, I'm not a private eye like you, I'm just a lowly policeman."

"You got any suspects? Besides me?"

"The investigation is continuing." That translates to none of your business, or in Blough's case, none of your fucking business.

"This has been great fun, lieutenant, sergeant. I expect you'll return my gun after your ballistics pros tell you I'm clean for Lorenz, too."

"He pistol-whipped you, huh?" Blough laughed. There was nothing funny in that. Cops must have a different sense of humor. A jaded sense.

They were gone. That's all that mattered at the moment. Except for the fact that I was now unarmed and there were at least, let's count, one, two, three, four, five, six, seven, seven people, no six, Lorenz is dead, six people willing to shoot me for the Madagascar Pigeon or the Malinese Mallard or just because they don't like my looks. Custer had better odds than this.

The phone rang. It sounded like trouble. Why? Because that's all I had been dished lately, and I hadn't heard what good news sounded like in a long time. I answered it anyway.

"Mr. Beault?"

"Yeah."

"Oh, good, my name is Archimedes Pym and…"

"No it's not."

"Yes it is."

"No it's not. Nobody calls up somebody and says, 'Hi, I'm Archimedes Pym'. That doesn't happen."

"I'm sorry you feel that way, but please take my assurance that is my name. Your name was given me by Ms. Birch-Aspen who..."

"Emily? Emily gave you my name?"

"Yes, she and I are colleagues in the Anthropology Department."

"Of course you are. That's super. Colleagues. Anthropology. Emily, eh? That's super."

"Are you quite all right, Mr. Beault? You are alarming me. Ms. Birch-Aspen said you had recently suffered a serious injury."

"I am quite fine, Mr. Pym. Doctor Pym, is it?"

"Well, Professor Pym, but no need to go there."

"Okay. Yes, I'm fine. You called?"

"Tell me about your injury. Emily, Ms. Birch-Aspen that is, did not give me any details."

"I was pistol-whipped."

"Not out in the field, I suppose. You were down at the station?"

I chuckled. I was starting to like this guy. "No, it wasn't the police. They are innocent. Of this anyway."

"Someone else then."

"Someone else then is right. Emily referred you to me?"

"She did." Professor Pym filled me in on his background and his teaching post and his professional relationship with Emily and his particular areas of study in old stuff. How one of his responsibilities was to ferret out treasures for the college's museum. When, of course, he added, the acquisition costs were acceptable to the budget and the museum's board, and no covenants with foreign countries were broken regarding the legality of importing antiquities to the U.S.

"So you're a treasure hunter, professor?"

"No. Well, I suppose in some ways that is what I do. But I'm no Indiana Jones, let me assure you."

"You own a gun?"

"A gun! No, I would never. I detest them." That was useful information. I could leave him off the list of those who might shoot me to get the prize I held and that I assumed he would gladly take for his museum.

"I agree, guns are detestable. Tell me then what Emily told you," I asked Pym.

"She tells me you are involved in the search for some unusual statuettes."

"Entangled is more like it. I'm in the middle of something that I don't understand completely. It has also put me in a real pickle. Emily filled me in on the Madagascar Pigeon. That's a real corker, isn't it?"

"When we deal with cultural behaviors beyond our own experience and history, it is likely we will not understand them completely," Pym said. "You are correct about that. We must still respect that which we cannot believe or explain. I like to offer as an example how a foreign visitor to our country would be expected to understand American football. Impossible to rationalize it to someone who did not grow up with the endless media bombardment of the sport or its encyclopedic rules or the almost religious fervor its followers exhibit." I didn't say anything. I felt I did not need to have my comments on the record.

"The Madagascar Pigeon," he went on, "is a prime example of a cultural difference." He paused.

"Is there more?" I asked.

"Much. It is why Emily said I should talk to you. She overheard at dinner a reference to the Malinese Mallard. She knows of my keen interest in that subject. Do you know what it is?"

"I haven't the foggiest idea. (That's San Francisco-speak.) The only mention of it so far is from Clint Westwood, and that was only briefly before he took flight when I named a passel of people snooping around the Madagascar thing. Just another part of the entanglement I was describing."

"Yes, Emily said there was a growing crowd looking for the item."

"Growing? Try mushrooming. Every few minutes, it seems, another felon shows up pointing a gun at me saying I get shot if I don't surrender some statue. I think I'm in the wrong line of work."

"I sympathize, Mr. Beault, but do you have any avenue of escape from this predicament?"

"I could hop a plane to Costa Rica. They don't make statues of birds down there, do they?"

Pym laughed. "No, I don't believe they do, at least not any that carry the burdens like the Madagascar Pigeon." After a hesitation, he added, "Or the Malinese Mallard."

"Do you intend to enlighten me about that one?"

"Yes. The Malinese Mallard originates in Mali. You know where Mali is, Mr. Beault?"

"In the South Seas, I believe."

"No, it's in northern Africa."

"Ah, yes, that Mali," I recovered.

"Yes, well, it is notable as the host country to that old and romanticized trading crossroads called Timbuktu."

"That I have heard of."

"Good. Legend has it that sometime in the distant past, the timing lost now to passing centuries, certain nomadic traders ventured on camels and on foot from caravansary to caravansary..."

"Uh..."

"...oases is perhaps a better descriptor for these stops, Mr. Beault. Anyway, arriving in Timbuktu they carried with them treasures that tempted other traders who stole a quantity of extremely valuable precious gems and jewels."

"Thieves."

"Thieves, yes. As is customary among thieves there was no honor lost. It is no surprise that greed permeated this den of thieves. This dishonor among the thieves led to arguing over the spoils and then to wrangling and eventually to fighting. Certain scoundrels grabbed what they could from other scoundrels and ran for it. The treasure scattered and probably dissolved into a short spree of hedonistic spending and living. However, the legend claims that a valuable residue survived the fate I just described and was – for safety sake – encased in a statue of a mallard duck."

"What is it with these birds?"

"A curiosity, I concur. Perhaps it was coincidence born from a reverence of an animal with the capacity of flight, which humans have envied since the days of Eden. Regardless, the legend says this statuette bore precious stones which today would equal a king's ransom."

"Have you seen it? Is there only one? How do you know of its description?"

"It may not exist."

"What!"

"It may not exist. As I say, legend has it. We know only of the story, oral traditions, until early in the 19th century when the legends around it were written into a few books, likely as not by adventurers who were seduced by the tales. There is no evidence that there is a Malinese Mallard. Unlike the evidence that there is a Madagascar Pigeon."

"What evidence is there that that one exists?" I was so caught up in the possibility that the mallard thing might be a fraud, a fake, I forgot that the evidence for the pigeon thing was in my own locker at my gym. It had been in my own hands.

Pym answered. "It was in your own hands and is now in your locker at your gym."

Emily! When did I have the brain fart that prompted me to tell her what I had and where I had it only then to completely forget? How many pistol-whippings did I...no, it wasn't during a pistol-whipping. It was one of those solar plexus episodes. I am in the wrong line of work. I was searching for something intelligent to say to Professor Pym when I heard myself say, "Now what?" Oh, the perfect rejoinder.

"If I were you, Mr. Beault, I would be careful."

Be careful? That's the same advice I got from Emily and it hasn't done me any good yet. Is that what they teach in academia? Okay, class, there is danger afoot so, you know, be careful. What a load of manure that is.

13

I was hearing from too many people with birds or dead bodies (mine) on their minds. That scared the number two out of me. What the heck was going on? I was frantic. I know private eyes are not supposed to get frantic. We're tough, hard-bitten, stare-danger-in-the-face sons of bitches who don't take no shit from nobody. Then again, Miss Gunn had a gun. The Pole had a gun. Ms. Wu (oh God!) had a gun. The Pole's minion had an insane look and no doubting had a gun. Hugo Blankenship likewise no doubt would have a gun. Clint Westwood had a gun. Blough and Headley both had guns. They probably had guns on their ankles. Even I had a gun...oh Christ! I don't have a gun. Blough took it. Ballistics has it. I do have a backup. But it's just a little popgun compared to the big dogs I have had to stare down recently.

While all these nutjobs who weren't cops were out emptying all the gun shops of ammo, I could see Blough sweet-talking some judge into signing a warrant for my arrest. Just as likely Emily and Archimedes Pym were conspiring to torture me to reveal the combination to the lock on my gym locker so they could get the Madagascar Pigeon and fence all the jewels and run off together to Costa Rica. Why did I put that idea in his head?

On top of all this my solar plexus still hurt, but only when I had to breathe, and my head still ached. I was pistol-whipped if I haven't mentioned that before. I am definitely in the wrong line of work. I may walk down the hall to Bevalaqua's and see what it takes to become a CPA. I could do people's taxes. Oh pee! Maybe Bevalaqua has a gun. Not exactly a pleasant reverie all these thoughts, and what had been gloom was now turning to despair. I had to shake this off. How about an hour in the gym? Oh, yeah, right, so any one of those gunslingers could follow me to the only thing that separated me from a trip to the mortician. No, what I'll do... The phone rang.

Priceless. Here I go again. Yet another nut job telling me he has a gun and he wants a bird he thinks I have. "Give me the Okinawa Ostrich, Mr. Private Eye, or I will shoot you in the solar plexus with this bazooka after I pistol-whip you into oblivion." Oh well.

"Hello."

"Blough."

"And..."

"You can come get your gun down at the station."

Down at the station, eh? The putative place for police pistol-whippings. "Why do I have to go all the way across town to get my gun which you took from me right here in my office?"

"Because if you don't come all the way across town you won't get it back, will you?"

"Um, sounds like I won't. By the way, I'm going to make the leap that your ballistics boys decided my gun hasn't killed anybody this month. Am I right?"

"Usually not, dickhead, but in this case yeah. Are you coming or not?"

"Who do I see?"

"I don't give a crap. Just identify yourself."

"While we're being so chummy, can you tell me what the autopsy on Lorenz showed?"

"Yeah, it wasn't your pretty little .38."

"That's a Police Special .38."

"Trying to impersonate an officer of the law, Beault? That's a crime, too."

"Funny again, Blough. What got Lorenz?"

"It was a .32"

"Same as the one that got Kluszewski?"

"You're getting kinda nosy, Beault, why should I tell you?"

Somebody knocked at my door. "Just a second," I yelled, "I'm on the phone."

"What's all that about?" Blough said at his end.

"Somebody's at my door. I told them to wait. So what gives on Lorenz? I just maybe might be able to help you solve a case or two."

"Well, well, it must be Christmas and the San Francisco Police Department just got a gift from Santa. Help solving a crime. From a private dick. Hey, Headley," Blough shouted, "we'll be able to retire now that the crime solving is in the hands of shamuses."

"Are you finished, Blough?"

"It was from the same .32." He hung up.

It was easy to make the connection. A .32 got Kluszewski and a .32 from the same gun got Lorenz. Somebody who has been sticking a gun in my face was a murderer. I was hoping that I'd seen all the bad guys who had a criminal interest in the pigeon thing. If not, it would mean a new player and that would not be good news. Yeah, but which one carried a .32? Could be either a man or a woman. A .45 or 9mm more likely went along with a man. Bit much for a woman. Lotta recoil. Then again...

Knock-knock. Oh, crud. I went to the door. "Sorry, I got lost in thought. Ah, Miss Gunn, come on in. Didn't mean to keep you waiting." Not when she might be carrying a .32. I tried to remember what her gun looked like when she pulled it on me that time. I couldn't.

"My name is Lavernia Lavender, Mr. Beault, and I need your help."

"You are..."

"I can see you are confused by my name. I am Phyllis's twin sister. We are identical twins."

"Identical twins."

"Yes, I am fully aware that you have met her and that she has relayed a saga of mysterious characters, a sea voyage, and a missing statue. Mostly what she has told you are the facts. The part that is not true is that the statue does not belong to her but to me." What could I say? Nothing. So that's what I said.

"Before Phyllis set sail from East Asia to San Francisco," this woman continued, "she tricked me and my associate into revealing where the Madagascar Pigeon was secreted. She stole it from me, Mr. Beault. I have since learned that Captain Kluszewski delivered the statue to you as she had arranged. I gather she paid him a tempting sum. On the surface it would have looked like easy money for the captain to simply drop the package at your doorstep. Which he has done. Consequently, now that you have heard this truthful explanation, you will see it means you can give the statue to me, the rightful owner."

I was about to commit a non sequitur. "Do you want some coffee? I can sure use a cup."

"No, thank you."

I poured myself that cup. "You said you had an associate in East Asia. Who was that?"

"That is irrelevant, Mr. Beault."

"Humor me."

"His name is Marcel Lorenz."

"Uh-huh. Does he claim half ownership in this thing you are looking for?"

"You have an inquisitive mind, Mr. Beault."

"I do. It comes from my many years in detective college. I finished first in my class." I didn't. There is no such thing as detective college.

"Mr. Lorenz will not have any objection to your giving me the Madagascar Pigeon," Miss Lavender said.

That thought crossed my mind and I agreed with her. "I suppose not."

"I have other matters to attend to in San Francisco," she said, "I'll be on my way if you will give me...oh, my gracious, I apologize. I did not mean to overlook the fact that Phyllis probably made a financial arrangement with you." She began rifling through her purse. "An arrangement to pay you for your trouble and service. What was it? How much was..."

"It was five hundred dollars."

She snapped her head up. "Oh, no, it was only..."

"Only what, Miss Gunn?"

"My name is Lavernia Lavender. Didn't I tell you that I am my... Phyllis's identical twin?"

"Now you mention that, yes, you did tell me that. How is she, by the way?"

"I hardly can say. I must confess that we are not close. The point is that we hate each other."

"That's sad. Broken family ties. Who would think? It is so hard to keep sisterly bonds alive when there are disputes. Any madness in your family?"

"That's insulting. What could make you ask such a thing?"

"Just more of my inquisitiveness. Here's something. I'll give you the short answer because I have a nagging feeling you are better informed about this whole matter than you are letting on. Okay? Yeah, okay. I don't have the thing, this statue. Captain Kluszewski did not drop it on my doorstep, as you suggest. What he did drop on my doorstep was his own dead body. Then..." I stopped. Eff it. I was not about to tell that story for the millionth time. So I said, "Say, what kind of gun do you carry?"

"I...it...I don't have a gun," she said as she clutched at her purse.

"That's smart. They can be so unsafe." I stood up and stepped over close to her. "Let me walk you to the door." She would not be able to draw the gun she said she did not have in her purse while I was this near her. "Thank you for stopping by. I hope you have more luck finding your pigeon thing. Why don't you ask Mr. Lorenz if he has had any luck."

"He...I can't..."

"Yes, that might be, well, inconvenient. Good-bye, Miss Gu...Ms. Lavender." Lavernia Lavender? Where does she come up with these names?

14

I drove across town and got my gun back from the police station. I felt a little better. When I got home I loaded it. I felt a lot better. While down at the station, I did not get pistol-whipped. It was a good day. Any day without a pistol-whipping is a good day.

Oh...listen to this. I'm going across town to...well, you know why... and traffic is slow. Duh, it's San Francisco. Slow due to the many cars, the many drivers of cars who don't know how to operate them, and the army of street digger-uppers stationed every four or five blocks throughout my city. Bright orange cones and maybe three city employees wearing colorful vests and displaying stop signs directing cars into a single-file flow through narrow gaps where I am convinced the crews were in the process of making potholes. If that sounds cynical, just ask yourself this question: How else could so many holes in the streets show up without the input of professionals? I waved at the guys with their signs, one pointing "stop" at us and two showing the "slow" side. Pick your poison highway conduct.

You've guessed, I guess, that my car is of mature years and shows evidence of reaching its design limit. For example, my dash-encased A.M.-F.M. radio has not worked in a long time. Always optimistic, I almost always fiddle with the knobs in hopes of some sounds.

Having negotiated that narrow gap where the potholes were appearing and the traffic was inching forward, I headed onward on the street with normal boundaries. I won't tell you which street for fear that I will put blame on just one over the many others that are under the same watchful eyes of the pothole crews. Why put the slam on only one street, right?

As if on cue, my world went ker-klump, ker-klump as my tires nosed into and out of a pothole. And then..."...we're back. Let's go to Wally in San Jose. Wally, you're on Talkin' Sports. What's on your sports mind?" My car radio is working. Huh! All that slapping of the dash above the radio I had done in days and years past was over-matched by the more decisive power of a San Francisco pothole.

"Am I on?" "Yes, Wally, you're on, that's what I said." "Oh, okay, hi, this is Wally." "Wally, call again when you are back on this planet." "Let's go to Ray up in Petaluma..." I turned the radio dial. "...And I've been right about this ever since she was elected president and formed her own Camelot of Incompetence. There are just not enough right-thinking voters in this country. Stay tuned. After these important messages, I will be back to repeat what I have told you about..."

I spun the dial. "...Traffic and weather with our own airborne Captain Maxine Manahan. Where are you Maxine?" "Above the 880, Kenny, where there's a backup southbound from the junction with the 580 all the way to 98th Street. Three overturned cars blocking the left lanes seem to be the problem. Keep your head down when you pass that point just in case...although the Highway Patrol believes the gunfire has stopped. North of there the Caldecott Tunnel is closed westbound with a jack-knifed semi. I don't want to make light of this, Kenny, but the backup will probably reach all the way to Sacramento. It's a mess."

"Busy day, eh, Maxine?"

"You betcha. There's more. Over on the peninsula, the 101 is a parking lot between Moffett Field and the 280 in the city. Can't see what happens past there because of the fog." "Which direction, Maxine?" "Funny, Kenny, good joke." "Not a joke, Maxine, just want to let our listeners know." "It's the 101, Kenny, so it's both directions, northbound and southbound." "What appears to be the problem, Maxine?" "Same thing as every day, Kenny, cars."

Kenny said something silly. Then, "Better news on the weather, I hope, Maxine." "Fog, Kenny, until about mid-day when it will turn to low clouds. Temperatures will be normal for this time of year. Bring along a sweater or coat." "Thanks for your report..."

Ker-klump, ker-klump. The radio ceased talking.

15

Coming back from a quick lunch around the corner, I was unlocking my office/home door when Bevalaqua shouted down the hall, "Hey, Beault, kill anybody today?" Always the clown, which translates to equine anal opening.

"Not yet," I said back to him, "hold on right there while I get my gun. I'll shoot you as a public service. Then the IRS can close out their investigations into your peculiar interpretations of the tax code."

"Ha-ha" is all he could muster. Horse's ass.

I went in the door, closed it and locked it. Better safe than pistol-whipped. The phone rang. Oh, goodie, which of my new playmates was calling to tell me how close to death I was because I wouldn't give them a bird. I did a roll call in my head, eliminating Marcel Lorenz since he was over-filling a cold-storage shelf down at the morgue. I didn't pick up the phone, but that didn't stop it from ringing. What the hell.

"Hello."

"Jaguar Beault" he blurted in a voice obviously camouflaged, "you have a bird statue you will give to me if you wish to see your dog again." I don't have a dog. I don't even like dogs. Dogs are flea circuses. They shit everywhere you don't want them to, and then they cherish the moment you have to bend over and pick up their droppings and cart it off. Yes, this opinion annoys more than half the population of the western world and above seventy-five percent of the residents of my city. But, hey, just watch those dogs and their owners and see what I mean.

"Who is this? Is this that snotty kid who's always playing phone tricks?"

"It's me...Emily."

"Oh, hi, you know that's not funny. There's some serious poo-poo going on around me."

"I know. You are in some deep shit. What have you done about it?"

"What I always do. I ask Grenville what he..."

"Grenville! Oh God, how is he doing? He's such a dear."

My bad for bringing up my brother's name to this woman. "Don't soil your panties, Emily. Stay focused. He's fine."

"You are so right about that, he is fine. Fine. Why couldn't you be more like him?" This crock again.

"Thank you for your kind thoughts."

"And him being...God, what I wouldn't give to be a man. You've seen Grenville, yes?"

"Yes, Emily, he's my brother. We see each other." I sighed.

"Did he ask about me? I know if he wasn't...he's such a dear. Did he ask about me?"

"Yes," I lied, "he asked how you were."

"What did you say, what did you tell him?"

"I said you still had the best right hand in the ring."

"You didn't!"

"No, I said you are busy at work molding immature minds into brilliant thinkers." That's what happens when you start with a little lie, you find yourself on a downhill slope with no brakes. "Did you call for some reason besides drooling over my unavailable sibling?"

"Ooh, don't say that. There's always a chance."

"Emily, they don't change. They take an oath." I wasn't deliberately trying to aggravate her.

"When you see him again, give him my love. All my love."

"Will do."

"Tell him..."

"Emily! Give it a rest." She's worse than a thirteen-year-old brat gushing over the latest pre-pubescent off-key YouTube sensation with a mother living her failed music career through her no-talent offspring. Did that sound mean-spirited? Good, I intended it that way. Comes from an impression I have of the current pop scene.

"You called," I said into the phone.

"Oh yeah. Professor Pym said you and he talked."

"Yes, he called me. I appreciate that."

"Was he helpful?"

"If you think it helped for him to pour more fuel on the fire of missing birds and nefarious bird hunters. All he did was widen the mystery. I admit though that he was trying to give me a better appreciation for the fix I'm in."

"His heart's in the right place, Basil (ugh), give him that."

"Okay."

"What'll you do next?"

"I'm going to Sausalito."

"You're going to Sausalito. That sounds like a metaphor."

"There's an antique store owner over there who I need to question. Well, not really an antique store, more a second hand store. Okay, it's a junk store. But it's got great stuff." I explained to Emily what happened at Grenville's church, about the stolen bird statues. How the coincidence was too much to slough off. "She knows this business like the back of her hand."

"She?"

"She, yeah, if anyone knows what's what with these things, she'll know."

"She?"

"You sound jealous. Are you jealous, Miss Emily?"

"I'm not jealous, Basil (My name is Jaguar!!), it's only that I didn't know you had any women acquaintances. Ones who didn't cost you a hundred dollars a night." Crap! Oh, and what she said there is not true.

16

The next day I got in my car and when it started I drove up to Geary and headed east toward Park Presidio, the roadway that would take me to the bridge. I adjusted my rearview mirror getting sticky stuff on my hand from the duct tape holding the glass in the mirror frame. How that ever broke I can't remember. I wanted the mirror to be functioning for me. If I were to be tailed I wanted to know it. That robbery at Grenville's church suggested those dirt bags clamoring for the pigeon thing would not stoop too low to find out where I had it. I kept denying it to their faces that I had the wretched statue, but I knew they did not believe me. So someone could be following. I kept my eye on the road behind me as I turned north anticipating again the thrill I get when the Golden Gate Bridge comes into view. One of the great vistas in the world if you want my unbiased opinion. Even on the bridge itself I kept looking back to see if there were any suspicious cars. I did not need to expose Miriam to any dangers from these scum. Miriam was innocent in the whole affair. Miriam owned the junk store I was headed to.

I passed the sign announcing Marin County and a short way later turned off U.S. 101 on Alexander Avenue leading into Sausalito, one of the Bay Area's most picturesque villages. So picturesque you can't get there most days because of the tourist throngs. So don't go there anymore. Listen to what Yogi says. "Nobody goes to that place anymore because it's so crowded."

What the heck! Did I say the robbery at Grenville's church? What a dope. I know better. I'm a trained private detective. That wasn't a robbery. A robbery is when the bad guys try to throw their weight around, or throw *your* weight around, threatening the victim like. No, this was a burglary at Grenville's. You burgle when you sneak around and break in to – well, I don't mean you meaning you, I mean you if you were a burglar – and break in to snatch things that don't belong to you (the burglar).

Sorry. I'll try to work on this digression problem I have.

Sausalito sits on Richardson Bay with a view to Angel Island and hills in the east and to the skyline of San Francisco to the south that you pay for if you live in town. If you live in town you are rich. There's about a hundred yacht clubs and about a million yachts. They are owned by rich people who wear deck shoes and Dockers pants and sweaters they wrap over their shoulders instead of pulling them over their heads. They talk "yacht" to one another in polite terms. The few I have happened to meet are really nice people.

I didn't see anyone I recognized as I turned off Bridgeway onto Caledonia to where Miriam's store is. Neither did I see any unwelcome pigeon-obsessed buzzards following me through town. There was a parking space in front of the shop but one of those twenty-minute types. I found a two-hour spot a block or two away. Don't know how Sausalito does it, but the fog that envelopes San Francisco is prohibited here. The sun seems always to be out. Maybe that's what Sausalito means.

I walked up the street past storefronts typical of a small town. A lawyer's office, a saloon, a for rent sign on an empty store which had been a used book shop. Tragic. Hey, don't try to tell me that the problem is not the proliferation of these new e-books. E-book? No pages, no paper, no cover. What the heck kind of book is that I ask. Who buys those things?

At Miriam's – she calls her antique store Miriam's Miscellany – I saw a pushcart out front with a selection of hardback and softcover books. The real kind. Small consolation compared to that out-of-business second hand bookstore. I stepped into the shop. Stuff everywhere. On the floor, on the walls, on shelves, hanging from the ceiling. A ratpacker's paradise. And the odor, a pleasant one that is unmistakable in a store like hers. Miriam was at the back of the shop talking with a man and woman who appeared to be paying customers. Miriam looked down the aisle at me and turned her attention back to the couple without acknowledging me. After a short time, the couple paid for something and left holding a few *objets d'art*, items I could not identify. All I can say is that they were not pottery birds.

"Jaguar Beault!" she lilted as she walked down toward me. She pronounces both names just the way I like and has stopped calling me Basil – most of the time anyway. She's a sweetheart in that respect. Miriam is perhaps four or five years older than I am and looks ten years younger. She is almost as pretty as a woman can be. She must come from a gene pool that could populate a beauty pageant studio. She was wearing hiking boots, Levi's, a sweater-vest thing and big gloves. Her black hair was fashioned into a ponytail. She leaned up and kissed me on my lips. I looked around hoping someone would see this gorgeous girl kissing me. No one.

"How is my favorite shamus, Jaguar?"

"Miriam, hello, and aren't I the only shamus you know?"

"Don't be so cocky." We hugged as old friends would. We would be married now if it weren't for the fact that she says no every time I ask her. What's more, Miriam is a Ph.D twice over. Pretty and smart. University of Wisconsin. Liberal through and through which makes her about middle of the road in Marin County.

"What brings you to Sausalito...besides that old car of yours and the great pleasure you get from crossing the Golden Gate?" She knows how I feel about the bridge. There's nothing like it. Driving across it, walking across it. A leisurely run. It's like when I was a kid in a department store riding up and down the escalators. Nothing like it.

"I've got a problem."

"Is that what you call it when you drop in and we, uh, you know?" I smiled that shit-eating grin you get when you...never mind.

"No, actually, I do have a problem."

I told her the story of the birds, of the thugs, of the pain, of Grenville's burglary...and at Grenville's name she burst out, "Grenville! How's that dear boy? I haven't seen him in months."

"Fine, fine," I said, "but back to the birds."

"He's such a kind man. He sent me a beautiful wish on my birthday."

"Yes, yes, he is a thoughtful guy, but..."

"You didn't."

"I didn't what?"

"Send me a beautiful birthday wish."

This was going nowhere good. She's worse than Emily when it comes to Grenville. So I went on about how there was a chance that pottery-ized birds – I'm no expert in the field, so that is what I call them – might just become sought-after items. Kind of like if one bird is suspected to be full of jewels, others may be, too.

She thought for a moment then said, "No. It doesn't make sense. Ceramic birds (Ceramic! That was the word I'd been searching for. I knew I could count on Miriam.) aren't repositories for valuables unless a one in a million shot. If these crazies went after Grenville's, it's only because of the connection between the two of you."

"That's what I thought, too."

"Well, you are a detective, you should arrive at these deductions. Me, I'm just a small-business owner with no detecting skills just making unfounded guesses." Zing!

"Ouch! You sure know how to hurt a guy." In a completely different way from Emily and that solar plexus specialty of hers.

"Just kidding, Basil. Just having some fun at your expense."

"We do have fun, don't we, Mir? Why didn't we get married? We'd be a good match."

"Maybe you didn't ask me the right way or at the right time."

"You mean..."

She smiled.

"Oh, Mir, would you please do me the great honor of becoming my wife?"

"No." There was no sense in debating it or debriefing it. At least she is consistent.

She laughed. "You want to go upstairs?" she teased. This just after getting turned down at the most important question a guy can ask a dame. Of course I said sure.

"Going upstairs" was a euphemism, a thing we did from time-to-time. After closing hours, not in the middle of the day. Well, what the hey, why not?

"How about the shop," I asked, "your customers?"

"It's been a slow day. Go lock the door and, here, put this sign in the window."

It was one of those fake clocks. It read "Back in Five Minutes." Five minutes! That's not very complimentary. In fact, it's damned insulting. And very inaccurate. I don't have to take that. I can go longer...well, I'll show her.

Traffic was slow on the bridge as cars were approaching the unattended toll booths. Too many people were still trying to figure out the no-cash pass-through system. Just keep driving I wanted to shout. Instead, I was going over what Miriam said about the birds. What it meant was simple: the problem was still in my lap. There was no widespread run on ceramic birds by jerks trying to corner the market. So my trip over to Sausalito was a success. On review, yes, I'll call it a success. All things taken together. However. However, yeah...did I hear her or did I imagine that I heard Miriam moan my brother's name? I was kind of busy at the time so I can't be sure. I could have misheard her. Maybe that's her way, on the other hand, of prolonging. Prolonging is important in this scenario. We all do it. I do it. I replay splash-hit home runs by Barry Bonds. Oh, yeah, so what do you do, buddy?

17

I was just getting off the shi...just finishing one of my daily duties when the phone began ringing. That was good timing. What's worse than having the phone ring when you are, well, doing that? Kinda hard to just get up and walk over to the phone. There is a worse time. When you are right in *flagrante delicto* with a bosomy doll and...no, not one of the blowup rubber dolls you see advertised in the back of those "art" magazines. I mean a bosomy doll made of flesh and smells nice and likes...oh, the phone.

"Beault." That's how I answered it.

"Oops, my mistake," someone said, "I was trying to reach Jaguar Beault Investigations."

"It's pronounced beault."

"You sure? It doesn't seem like it."

"Well, it is."

"What about all those vowels in the name?"

"It's my name, I should know how it's pronounced."

"Okay, if you say so."

"I do say so. What do you want?"

"Are you the investigations man?"

What is this guy's problem? "Yes, I am the investigations man. I am Jaguar Beault. That's why I said my name when you called."

"Hey, you don't have to get testy with me. I need to know I'm talking to the right person."

"You are, okay?"

"Good. Your ad in the yellow pages says you provide the whole range of investigation services. Is that right?"

"The ad doesn't lie, my friend."

"You will do anything?"

"I do it all."

"Can we meet so I can tell you what's going on and what I need you to do?"

I agreed. A paying client, whoopee. We set up a time at a place I know called The Will Cuppy over on Columbus. I asked him what his name is and he said, "Smith, John Smith." As if.

I like this bar. I like the atmosphere that says you are welcome here and nobody's going to judge you. I like the name – an obscure but terrific American humorist with no connection whatsoever to San Francisco. The clientele is not really a clientele, rather it's a scramble of locals who know a good thing when they see it.

I sat at one end of the long bar. I told you about my drinking background, though I do have an occasional glass of beer. I was looking forward to meeting this John Smith. I could use the money from a new case, one that would take my mind off the damn ceramic bird puzzle. Besides, I was curious about a new client who would start off by trying to slip a fake name past me. John Smith? Uh-huh, sure. He should have a talk with Phyllis Gunn or Covington or Goodbody or who knows what other new names she is inventing. Mr. John Smith could use some pointers. I'm a detective, a private one, yeah, so how could he think he'd be able to con me this way? I may up my fee on this guy.

It was just after three in the afternoon when I saw someone come through the door and look around. When he spotted me all alone looking back at him he walked over.

"Jaguar Beault?"

"That's me. John Smith?"

"And that's me," he said with a twinkle. He took the bar stool next to mine and surveyed the room. Smith, yeah right, Mr. John Smith, was past fifty and sported a high forehead dictated by a receding hairline. Slender but not skinny. He was dressed as if he had just come off a golf course. Not the spiked shoes, but casual, comfortably fitting clothes.

"I like it here," he said, "nice and quiet. Good place to do business."

"About that," I said, "I think we've already got off on the wrong foot."

"Oh no, what is it?"

"Your name."

"My name? What's wrong with my name?"

"I don't like it."

"What don't you like about it? It's common enough."

"Too common."

"I don't understand what you are talking about."

"I don't like to do business with people who are not up front with me, people who try to scam me, people who give me false names, say."

"Are you talking about me?"

"Yup."

"You think my name isn't John Smith?"

"Mister, I'm an experienced private eye. I can see right through this name thing of yours."

He reached around to his back pocket and came out with his wallet. He flipped it open to his driver's license, the one with his picture on it and slid it over in front of me. Name: John Smith.

"Mr. Smith," I said, "let me give you a real good piece of advice. You should never carry your wallet, or any valuables, in your back pockets. That's easy pickings for pickpockets. Put it in your front pocket."

I pushed his wallet back over to him. He looked at me kind of strange. Can't be helped. He's John Smith all right. Not everyone can be Lavernia Lavender or Phyllis Gunn or Alice Goodbody, names with some zip to them. Oh, and Marcel Lorenz.

John Smith ordered a beer.

"You need investigative work, Mr. Smith?"

"Let me tell you what's going on, and then I'll tell you what I need you to do."

John Smith was married to a woman who, he said, was running around on him. He was sure. Her excuses for things, her absences, her withdrawal all pointed to an affair or, even, affairs. He was at the end of his rope so he called me. I told him I felt for him, that I had seen too much of this in my professional life, that I know how to surveil and to come back with the evidence he wanted. I told him my rates – without hiking my usual fee – and said I could have answers for him in less than a week's time if she did not alter her furtive schedule.

"That's not what I want."

"You don't?"

"No."

"Then you want photographs, too?"

"No, nothing like that."

"I'm missing something. What is it you want me to do?"

"I want you to kill her."

I coughed, coughed again, reached for my pen, hovered it over a napkin and clicked it. "Excuse me?"

"I want you to kill my wife."

"Mr. Smith, I don't kill people."

"Yes you do."

"No I don't."

"Yeah, you killed that guy the other day."

"What guy?"

"The dead guy in your office."

"What the...where'd you hear that?"

"Around."

"I did not kill that guy. He was shot before he got to my place and dropped dead in front of me."

"The police think it's you."

"No they don't! Where does this shit come from? Hey, what makes you think I would kill someone?"

"You said you do a full range of private eye work. You said, and I quote, 'I do it all'. Right?"

"Jaguar Beault Investigations does not whack people."

"I'll pay you."

"Mother of God! You can't pay me enough. I'm not going to kill your wife. I'll follow her and do my fact-finding thing, but I am not going to snuff Mrs. Smith. Jesus," I exasperated.

"That's too bad," he said. "I'll have to take what I can get. Yeah, do your spying on her and bring me info about her and her lovers. Do you like irony?" he asked me. I said yeah, I guess I do. Then he said, "My wife gave me your name when I told her I needed some investigation work done for my job. Funny, right?" I did not laugh. "Hey," he went on, trying to get me to kill somebody, anybody, I thought, "if you find out who she's messing with, would you kill them?" I looked at him and could not think of a single answer to give him.

At the beginning of my tale I told you I turned down cases that appeared to be too screwy. This was one. However, I also told you I was not proud. This was one of *those* times. I took the case because I needed the money. I didn't see any income stream from that Madagascar Pigeon dead end, so that was going to be a financial bust – if I lived through it. I'll wrestle with my moral compass some other time. Like when I have enough money in my bank account. From my lawful practice. Kill his wife? What was he smoking? I wonder how much he would have paid me. Jaguar Beault, wife whacker. No thanks. A real hit man would probably go about fifty thou, think?

18

T he city was wearing its famous fog again as I drove back to my inner sanctum. To my home. I had a nice fat bundle of cash in my pocket, an advance from Mr. John Smith, a man who had it in for his wife. I couldn't meet all his demands, but at least I was going to be able to satisfy his morbid curiosity about his missus. Knowing for a fact that she was schtupping guys behind his back would give him the ammo he needed to take corrective steps, short of putting her six feet under. I feel pretty good that I had talked him out of that drastic step. Whacking her was an answer, I had argued to him before we left The Will Cuppy, but it wasn't *the* answer.

When I got in, I took the money from my pocket and put it in my safe place, inside a big collector's edition of *The History of Tom Jones, A Foundling*, by Henry Fielding. No one knows that's where...I...hide... Umm. Messages. Do I have any messages? The red light was blinking. I went to the bathroom and got rid of the beer I drank. Back at the phone I pushed the message button. It announced that I had ten new ones. Ten? People wait until I leave and then call knowing they won't have to talk to me? Is that it? What's up with that?

First message: Hello, Mr. Beault, this is Phyllis Gunn. I know you told me not to bother you, yet I am so anxious to get my souvenir. Please call me. Here's my new phone number. Beep.

Second message: You left your jacket in the shop. (It was Miriam.) You don't have to fake things like that to have an excuse to come back up to see me. It is a cute ploy, though. Bye, sweetie. Beep.

Third message: I'm pregnant, you jackass. You said that rubber would work. Now what? Wait'll my dad hears about this. He's going to like go all apeshit. We might have to get married. I can't get married, I'm only fifteen. This is Crystal if you didn't know. Beep.

Fourth message: Well, well, Mr. Beault, not there I see. I hope for your sake that you are busy retrieving the item you owe me. (It was The Pole's voice.) My associates and I do not make threats lightly, I can assure you of that. Ms. Wu, for example, sends her regards. Beep.

Fifth message: I expected you to be smarter, Beault, than to try to double-cross me. This is not likely to have been your first mistake ever, but it may turn out to be your last. (It was Clint Westwood.) The Malinese Mallard, where is it at and when do I get it, or am I gong to have to beat it out of you? Don't worry, I'll find you. Beep.

Sixth message: Gee, this is like really funny you thinking you knocked up a fifteen-year-old. I guess I called the wrong number when I said I was pregnant. (She's laughing here.) I could just see your face. Anyway, that numbnuts, Bobby, he called me and I figured out I called you by mistake. Numbnuts, I said. He ain't that, is he? (Still laughing.) He proved that. Unless (laughing again) it wasn't him and it was some-body else on the basketball team. Well, sorry about the scare. Say, you have a nice voice on your message thing. Hey, do you want my number? It's area code 415-368-xxxx. Beep.

Seventh message: Hello, Mr. Beault, this is Archimedes Pym, Emily's colleague at the college. Did I fail to mention that the Malinese Mallard has sometimes been confused with the Madagascar Pigeon? Oral tradi-tions being what they are, intersecting cultural references adding to the confusion, these things happen. I thought it was best to let you know this. You know, let you know there may not even be a thing called the Malinese Mallard. I'm not sure I discussed that fully enough with you last time we talked. I hope it's not bad news. Beep.

Eighth message: Oh, how awful, I detest these telephone record-ings. I, this is Lavernia Lavender, Mr. Beault, Phyllis Gunn's twin sister. Do you remember me? I came to visit you and told you she is a liar and a cheat and a thief and a dreadful sister. It broke my heart when mother would always take her side on anything that happened. Mother loved Phyllis more than she loved me. Where is the statue, Mr. Beault? It is mine and I wish for you to provide it to me immediately. Well, thank you for listening and have a nice day. Beep.

Ninth message: You know, Basil (ugh), you have tried this before. You leave a jacket behind and then you use it as an excuse to come back. It isn't going to work. You don't get in. Get my drift...you don't get in. Anyway, if you want this jacket I found here in my office at school you can buy it back from the Goodwill store on Lombard Street. It's such a great coat it will easily cost you two or three dollars. Ta-ta. Beep.

Tenth message: Oh, ah, leave a message, well, yes, if I must. This is Hugo Blankenship, Mr. Beault, and, well, it's very hard to say this, but I think my wife, that is, uh. I'm rambling and you want to know why I am calling. Sorry. What I need to tell you is that Mrs. Blankenship is... Buzzz.

The tape ran out.

19

Everybody tied into this bloomin bird blowup had called except the one person who could have made sense. I called Grenville.

"Hey, bro," he said, and it was music to my ears.

I told him about my message tsunami. "I learned that I am still under threat from a cadre of crooks, one of my jackets is now missing, Mrs. Blankenship is a...who knows what, and I may have to marry a fifteen-year-old who told me I fathered her child."

"Have you been drinking?"

"I had a beer at The Will Cuppy. Oh, that reminds me, I got a new case. There's money in this one."

"Good, maybe it will take your mind off this statue mystery."

"Guess what my new client wanted."

"What?"

"He wanted me to waste his wife."

"You can't do that, Basil, I think there's a commandment against it. I'll go and look up which one it is." Always with the comedy, good old Grenville.

"I'm not going to do it, Grenville, I'm out of bullets."

"You're a shitty shot and would have missed her anyway."

"Hey, show more faith in me. My aim is getting better."

We had a good talk. We always do. He also informed me that he had spread the word through the congregation about the burglary of the ceramic pieces at the church and he got wholehearted support for whatever action might be required. I'm glad I called him.

The phone rang just as I hung up. Probably Blankenship calling to finish his message about that crazy wife of his. It wasn't. It was John

Smith. "Look," he said, "I was thinking. I'll go as high as fifty large if you'll do my wife." Fifty thou? See? Just as I guessed.

"No."

"Shoot," he sighed. "Well, tonight she's out again. I gave you our address and a picture of her. Come by my house before seven o'clock cuz she'll be leaving right then. Park down the street and follow her. Stay a few cars behind so she doesn't see you. Then when she meets up with someone you find out who he is..."

"Mr. Smith, John," I raised my voice to him. "You don't have to tell me how to do my job. I've done this a lot. I'm good at it. She won't know I'm around. Trust me on this. I am an experienced detective, okay?"

A pause at his end. "Yes, okay, I see your point. Sorry," he said.

"What car will she be using?"

"The Mercedes. Always the Mercedes."

At about six-thirty I found a parking spot a few houses down the street from the Smith house – not because Smith told me to do it this way, but because that is how it's done, straight from the private eye textbook – and paralleled in. It was dusk and darkening fast from a soup of a fog rolling over the city. Nobody was out in this weather walking their dogs to let them shit in their neighbors' yards. I ate a 3 Musketeers even though I did not have Mexican for dinner. I needed a sugar loading for the job ahead.

Right at seven Mrs. Smith came out her door, flicked a remote, watched her garage door curl up, stepped into a car, backed out, checked to see the door came down to close off the garage, and headed south in a Mercedes. I swung around after she had gone down the street a ways. When she made a right turn I flipped on my headlights and hurried on ahead. She was driving west on California. I noticed we were hitting a lot of stop signs and red lights. Geary would have been more efficient, but then I didn't know where she was going, or why. I was always about three or four cars behind her.

Traffic was moderate so I knew I wouldn't be seen. At 25th Street she hung a left and then – ha! – she turned on Geary heading west again. All the way out to the ocean and south past the Cliff House onto Great Highway. Hey, this is how I get to Pacifica. "She going to Taco Bell?" I joked to myself. No. A moment later she pulled across opposing traffic into the Beach Chalet, a nicely restored bar-restaurant with a panoramic view of the ocean and across the street from a popular surfing beach. I drove on past her and made a U-turn to head back so she would not spot me. So far, so good.

The Beach Chalet has two decks. I eyed her upstairs sitting alone at a table. I moved in and located a spot at the bar where I would have an easy view of the room. I ordered a diet cola. Fewer than half the tables were occupied. A little early for dinner for San Franciscans, I gathered. There was an older couple together at the bar about midway between me near one end and another man sitting down at the other end. Mrs. Smith was reading a menu when two more women came in joining her after hugs and good wishes. What's this, I thought, they running in packs? Is it going to be an orgy night? Old man Smith is going to be mortified.

Nothing much happened. The older couple at the bar left, replaced by two guys who ordered beers and appetizers. More tables filled for dinner. The guy at the other end of the bar nursed a tall drink. Could have been a gin and tonic. Poor slob, all alone. Uh, oops, I was all alone. But I was working. Mrs. Smith and her friends ordered dinner and ate. When I asked for a refill on my soda, the bartender, a tall, handsome guy who obviously did a lot of surfing, said, "Whoa, slow down, mister, this is potent stuff." We both laughed.

In the mirror behind the bar I saw Mrs. Smith get up. I was on alert. When I saw she had her purse but had left her coat draped over the back of her chair, I deduced she was going to visit the ladies room. I turned back to the bartender. "Good surfing out there," I pointed, "do you surf?"

"No," he said, "I tried it once but I didn't like it."

"Same with me," I lied.

He was seeing to his other drinkers when I felt something against my shoulder and neck and heard whispered into my ear, "Hey, big boy, want to party?"

I about crapped, nearly knocked over my glass with my elbow and choked out, "Oh, Christ!" I looked. Mrs. Smith staring into my face inches away.

"Did I make you jump?" she said all pixie-like.

"Jesus," I said, "where'd you come from?"

Now here is where it gets interesting. I have described this whole scene from the Smith home to the Beach Chalet to show you how I do surveillance. The incognito private detective, that's me. The stealth tail. The one you hire for the hard jobs. My question, blurted out to her as I was recomposing myself, was mostly a rhetorical gagging. She answered anyway. "Why, Mr. Beault, you're the detective, you tell me."

20

"**C**ome over to the table with me, Mr. Beault, and we can talk." I followed and sat down as Mrs. Smith introduced me to her friends, Pearl and Yvonne. They were attractive women, looking to be in their late forties or early fifties. The three of them made a handsome tableau. One moment I am doing stealthy surveillance on a target, the next I'm sitting at her table, ordering another diet soda and ready to make small talk.

"You know my name," I said to Mrs. Smith.

"I do know your name."

"How do you know my name?"

"I am married to a compulsive-obsessive who is unable to conceal his mistrust in me. I have him followed. I've been on to you since your rendezvous at The Will Cuppy."

"But how?"

"See those two fellows who were sitting near you at the bar?"

"Oh, yeah, I had a feeling about..."

She paid me no attention. "Now look down to the end of the bar near the window. The sad-looking gentleman. His name is Frank Bodie. People call him Ping. He's a private eye."

"I've heard of Ping Bodie."

"He's working for me following my husband."

"Following..."

"The reason's not important. My husband's put a tail on me. I've put a tail on him. He thinks I'm cheating on him. You want to know something interesting? I gave him your name. Kinda ironic, no?"

"I don't understand."

"Not to worry, and it's not the first time. I think it's cute." She thinks it's cute? The guy wants to erase her. What would she say if she knew that?

"Did he try to hire you to kill me?" My mouth fell open and I looked from Mrs. Smith to Yvonne to Pearl. Those two giggled at the remark. "Don't be alarmed, Mr. Beault, he's tried this before. He always gets turned down. This is San Francisco after all. We don't tolerate such revolting behaviors, do we, girls?" Pearl and Yvonne were still giggling.

"But what if he finds someone willing to...who might...who doesn't believe in the proprieties of other San Franciscans, Mrs. Smith?"

"Mrs. Smith? Is that what he told you our name is? He's John Smith?"

"Yes, he..."

"Did you believe him? John Smith? Isn't that a little obvious?"

"He showed me his driver's license."

"Of course he did. He has a bunch of those. Same picture, but different names. Yvonne and Pearl were still laughing. They were getting a real kick out of either John Smith's doings or my gullibility. I was getting kicked right in the teeth, symbolically. Mrs. Smith, or whoever the hell she was, reached over and patted my hand. "Wouldn't you like something a little stronger to drink, Mr. Beault?" I didn't say anything to her in response because I didn't have anything to say. I was completely befuddled. Mrs. Smith nodded toward the waitress who came over.

"Yes?"

"A drink for Mr. Beault, please." She studied me for a moment or two and then said, "A Hennessey."

"Warmed?" the waitress asked. Mrs. Smith looked at me again. "No, straight up. Make it a double."

My diet soda was gone, but I was still holding onto the glass. Mrs. Smith said, "I don't want you to feel bad, Mr. Beault, my husband has pulled the wool over the eyes of a few private investigators he has hired. He is a clever man. And I have to say that at times I give him reason to distrust me. Let me assure you though that that does not include unfaithfulness. I just have business to attend to that cannot involve him."

I could barely follow what she was on about. All I seemed to hear was blah, blah, blah. How could I be having such a rotten day? I did hear myself say, "What does he do?"

"He's in the import-export trade."

Something correlated. "What's he import, what's he export?"

"Antiquities from all over the world. It's a lucrative field."

I perked up. "What, like furniture and Persian rugs and clocks and like that?"

"Sure that. But mostly ceramic pieces, statuary. There's a steady demand for pricey display pieces. Interior decorators are especially eager to locate them. They're hot right now. My husband is an expert in that field. He is always on the scent for them."

The waitress arrived back and plopped a snifter in front of me and reached for my empty soda glass. I was holding onto it so tight she had to yank it from my hands. I stared down at the double Hennessey. It looked like iced tea. I thought my heart was going to constrict and my veins clog up with this revelation about John Smith. Pricey ceramic display pieces, huh? Like the Madagascar Pigeon? The Malinese Mallard? Was I living in some parallel galaxy where everything that was swirling around me came back to that damn bird? Those damn birds?

I took a swallow of my first-ever Hennessey. It is not iced tea. I'll give odds that most of you knew that before I did. My throat cried out, my sinuses exploded open, my eyes teared, a shiver started in my hair and reached to my socks. This amused the girls. "Whew! What is this stuff?" I asked when I got my frame of reference re-calibrated.

"It's cognac. You should sip it." Now she tells me. Sipping it proved more intelligent.

I was hoping John Smith's profession of trading in ceramic antiquities did not intersect with my current non-revenue case of purloined birds. It was probably too much to ask. Moreover, I couldn't raise the subject with Mrs. Smith for fear of giving away information John Smith didn't need. Instead, we talked about this and that. I learned that Pearl runs an antique store in Tiburon and is acquainted with Miriam's store. When I joked that they may have met through the Junk Store Owners Association of Northern California, she seemed to enjoy the humor.

I learned that Yvonne held a master's degree in electrical engineering from the University of California at Berkeley. She now owns an upscale club in North Beach given to exotic dancing. "The money's not good," she started to explain, "it's great." I had no joke to make about her career choice. I did not ask her if she...danced.

I went to Cal, I told them, wondering if we had been there at the same time.

"Don't be coy, Mr. Beault," Yvonne said, "or are you just being gallant and trying to make us think we are as young as you?"

"I..."

"We freely admit, Mr. Beault," Mrs. Smith piped in, "that we are somewhat older, and we do not worry over such things anymore. Did you graduate?"

"No, I left early. There were circumstances."

"Circumstances? Such as?"

"I'd prefer to leave them unspoken. Nothing felonious...just, you know, circumstances."

"As you wish."

I got nosey. "How did you three ladies meet?"

"In college," Pearl said. "Went through the same fraternity at Cal."

"You said fraternity. You mean sorority, don't you?"

She looked at the other two then back at me. "You maybe went to college your way, Mr. Detective. We went to college our way." They got a big laugh out of that exchange.

I learned these things during my first and second Hennessey's. Doubles. On my third, still digesting all this information about John Smith's import-export business and trying hard to remain prudent in my speech so I would not let on that I, too, was involved in ceramic antiquities because of the dead guy on my floor, thugs against me, the cops, and the fact that I had a highly coveted treasure at this very minute, I asked Mrs. Smith, "You ever heard of the Madagascar Pigeon?"

Oops.

"I have," Mrs. Smith said, "Why yes, I have. That is one of the holy grails for...in my husband's industry. He's always looking for it. But it's like trying to win the lottery. You put your money in and your numbers never come up. What do you know about the Madagascar Pigeon, Mr. Beault?"

"I have it..."

"You have it? You have the..." she cooed.

I pushed my Hennessy away from me. "No, no, no..." I spoke through the cognac, "no, no, no. I have it, I mean...on good authority that there's a mob in San Francisco right now searching for it. Everybody in the mob claims it's theirs."

"Mr. Beault, tell me more. I...I think my husband will be thrilled to learn that the statue may be so nearby."

The Hennessey began talking and I listened to myself relate the whole bloody saga. When it looked to the women that I was finished, Pearl said, "You were pistol-whipped? I am shocked someone could do that."

"Well," I said, "it appears there are still practitioners out there. I don't believe they hold conventions or anything (I chuckled), but they are out there."

"Who did this to you?" I had kept that to myself – along with the secret that Captain Kluszewski had handed me the Madagascar Pigeon. – during my recital of the saga.

"It was Marcel Lorenz."

"Oh, yes, one of the bullies you told us was looking for the statue. Was he arrested for that attack on you?"

"No, he's dead."

"Dead?"

"Yes, he was shot," I admitted.

"Mister Beault!" Pearl proclaimed. "You shot him? You murdered him?"

"No, someone else did." Pearl looked at me skeptically, I thought. Mrs. Smith and Yvonne sat silently as they listened.

Mrs. Smith intervened. "Did you tell any of this to my husband?"

"No."

"Good. Let me do that, please. I want to see the look on his face when I tell him the private eye he hired to kill me is cheek-by-jowl with the Madagascar Pigeon. Oh, this is just too precious, what you've told me tonight." She got up and went to the bar where she spoke to the bartender for several minutes. When she returned to the table she sat down and said, "We've had ourselves quite the night, Mr. Beault. Private eye shenanigans, obtuse husbands who can't get a hit man to off his wife, world-famous ceramic pigeon, and, maybe best of all, you were introduced to the Hennessey experience." The grin on my face told it all. We gabbed for a while longer about things I didn't remember later on. Then the bartender came to the table.

"Your taxi is here, sir."

"My what?"

Mrs. Smith said, "You didn't think we were going to let you drive home, did you?" I dunno. "It's my treat, Mr. Beault, for such an illuminating evening and, of course, for safety's sake." A taxi took me home.

21

That night I dreamt that I was gripped on the shoulder by the talons of a giant bird which carried me out of the Taco Bell and flew me into the dark expanse of a strip club where Emily punched me repeatedly in my solar plexus. Twice I got up to vomit, once to pee. Hennessey's dark little secret. Inevitably, I began to recover and I made the usual resolutions about drinking never again, shaved and showered, and then set about to see where I was in my professional life. A little voice said your professional life smells, you nitwit, aren't you proud? I'll have to think about that. So I took that day off. I was, you know, hung over.

The next morning I put on the coffee, hurried around the corner to buy a small box of donuts, hurried back and poured a cup of Joe. I checked for phone messages. Not blinking. That's funny, it should be shouting at me after all those previous messages carried familiar omens. Aaah, the blasted recorder tape ran out after all those other calls came in. Nuts. I forgot that happened. How many calls have I missed? I went back over the messages on the phone machine to make notes on the calls before erasing the tape. (It's not a very modern recording machine.) Not much there except some people who are pissed off at me, some who may want me dead, some who are just weird, and Emily, who made my mid-section go pitter-pat. And poor lost Crystal. I called Grenville and asked him to help me fetch my car still marooned at the Beach Chalet.

I hung up from talking with Grenville and my phone rang.

"Jaguar Beault Investigations," I answered.

"That's a crock of shit, you jerkoff,"

Blough. "Hello, lieutenant, and how are you today?"

"Never mind that. Where in hell ya been? I've been callin.'"

"I've been ill. I was bedridden."

"You come down with a dose of the clap from the sluts you gotta pay for?"

"Please, lieutenant, I haven't been around your wife in months." Grrrr is what I heard.

"That's it, you prick, I'm sending a unit to your place, and they're gonna drag your sorry ass downtown. I got questions for you about the thing that Kluszewski guy gave to you. I get answers or else."

"Did I miss something, Blough? I did. I missed something...no, it's you, and I think I know. You missed that class in your cop training about warrants."

"I did not...hey, shithead, I don't need no fucking warrant to haul you in."

"Interesting. Can I quote you on that when I sue the department?"

"There won't be a need for suing the department, Beault, you're volunteering to come in, you're such an upstanding guy."

"Why not, Blough, only you'll need to send something bigger than a unit."

"What for?"

"I'll need room for my two lawyers, a neighbor of mine who writes for the Chronicle, a girlfriend of his who covers the city on TV, her cameraman, and that fella who attends every Supervisor's meeting demanding more transparency in the San Francisco Police Department. We'll want coffee, too."

"Uh."

"What time will the bus be here?"

"Uh."

"Not sure, is that it? You let me know when you can have one pulled out of your motor pool. In the meantime, is there anything else I can do for you?"

"Uh. Look, Beault, you're taking this whole thing all wrong. I'm working a murder case on this Kluszewski character, and now this Lorenz dude is tied into it to make a double homicide, and all I hear is that you are right in the middle of it because you got some expensive bird statue or something and you're holding out on a bunch of suspicious misfits. All I'm asking for is the truth."

"I'll tell you what I know, lieutenant, now that you're asking in such a nice way and because I like doing my civic duty. Kluszewski shows up at my office and drops dead on the floor. A lady with a half dozen names claims a bird is hers – theirs. A giant redwood and his two shadows come by making a threatening claim on something I don't have. A few days later Lorenz shows up at my office and tells me to give him some sort of thing I don't know what he's talking about, and when I tell him I don't have what he wants, the fat bastard pistol-whips me. He's dead now and I can't say I'm not too happy over that.

"It doesn't make any sense."

"Why not? I just explained it to you in simple English."

"No, it's not that. Why's everybody so certain you have it? And if you don't, where is it?"

"Now you are asking the right questions. If Kluszewski did have it and then didn't when he got to my door, that can only mean that it got separated from him by force or by chance or by just bad luck. My guess is it happened close to my building because he got all the way to me. Probably all by adrenaline. Maybe somebody on my floor intercepted him. Maybe he was looking for somebody else than me. That Bevalaqua (here I had to quash a laughing spell) has always looked a little crooked to me."

"Who?"

Still stifling a laugh, I told Blough about my neighbor, the tax man. Please, please, lieutenant, pay a visit to that horse's ass, I prayed silently.

22

This morning I walked the three blocks to a local bakery on Balboa run by a nice young couple. I hope they have a lot of success. I had a big glass of orange juice, a cinnamon roll and a coffee. People in San Francisco drink a lot of coffee and eat a lot of sweet rolls. The walk felt good, something I haven't done much of since this bird statue silliness started.

Back home, I sat down when the phone rang, moving me to answer in my usual pleasant tone.

"Jaguar Beault Investigations."

"Is this Mr. Beault?"

"Yes."

A pleasant voice said, "You don't know me, Mr. Beault..."

"If that is true," I interrupted, "then already I am a big fan of yours."

"Pardon me?"

"No need for a pardon. I am just exalting in the good fortune you bring me by not being one of a chorus of babbling idiots who are orbiting around me at present."

"Did I call at a bad time?"

"Far from it. It is a brilliant time. Can I help you in some way?" I stated, ready to serve.

"This *is* a bad time, isn't it?"

"No, no, I am just venting some positive vibes. Go on."

"My name is Nadine Berry. Perhaps you have heard my name."

"Uh, no, I don't think so, should I?"

"I'm a television reporter. I do the news on KSFG."

"Oh, yes, are you that pretty blonde on channel what is it..."

"That's sweet of you, Mr. Beault. Yes, I suppose my face is well known across the Bay Area to the station's viewers."

Your face and blonde hair, my dear woman, and I mean no disrespect to you or any of the others who in the same mold are so pervasive on television that it begs the question as to whether you are required to be so coiffed in order to read the news on the screen or interview coaches on the sidelines of football games. I did not actually say this out loud to Miss Berry, but I sure thought it. It is something that has been on my mind.

"Anyway," she continued, "I have a problem I hope you can help me with."

"Solving problems is my business, Miss Berry. What is it that is troubling you?"

"My boss, my editor is what he is called, has started harassing me, and I..."

"Harassing? Do you mean sexual harassment?"

"Yes, that's it."

"I'm not tuned in too close as to how big companies work, but I thought you had a, what, a hot line you could call or a human relations department that would squelch that kind of behavior."

"That's true, yes, except I feel they are listening with only half an ear. They ask me for instances, and when I tell them, they think I am exaggerating or not interpreting it right."

"They afraid of a lawsuit?"

"I don't know."

"Are you building up to a lawsuit?"

"No. I need this job. I have a daughter who's only two years old who I am responsible for. I went to my minister..."

"Minister?"

"Yes. I live in the Castro. He is the minister of the Congregation of Brotherly Love in the Name of Jesus Christ. His name is Grenville Protherington..."

All right, there it is. Now you know. My name is Protherington, Basil Protherington. Do you even have to ask why I go by the name Jaguar Beault? How much faith would you have in the Basil Protherington

Investigations Company? Oh, maybe to track down a wayward poodle or to get your cat out of a tree, but face down an armed hoodlum? No. For that you call Jaguar Beault.

"...And he suggested that if I had some solid evidence, I could...Mr. Beault, are you okay? You seem to have tuned out."

"Oh, sorry, I was miles away. Yes, evidence."

"In fact, Minister Grenville recommended I call you."

"He'll no doubt want a finder's fee."

"I'm sorry?"

"Just joking, Grenville's my brother."

"He's such a dreamboat, too, and...ooh, that came out all wrong. It is not at all what I meant. I mean he is so supportive of his congregation."

"Don't worry, I hear that all the time. Every girl who's ever crossed his path has gone goo-goo over him. It's something I've learned to live with. Now you, too."

"Oh no, not me."

"Well, you're married so it is a bit different."

"I'm not married."

"Divorced then?"

"No."

"But your daughter."

"She's adopted. My partner and I adopted her. Her mother was only fifteen when she had the baby."

"Your partner?"

"Yes, I'm lesbian. My partner decided she wanted something new and different, meaning she didn't want a child. She left me."

"You are on a run of bad luck. But hold on, what kind of idiot is your boss – a man, I am assuming – if he's hitting on a lesbian?"

"He's a he, yes, and he's twenty-six going on sixteen. I guess he doesn't believe I am gay. Or he doesn't care or he thinks he's just too cool. I haven't had trouble from anyone else at the station. Only him. He's just so immature. I may be overreacting, but as I say, I need this job."

I accepted the case. I had two reasons. One, Miss Berry was agreeable to my fee and, two, Miss Berry did not know the first thing about the Madagascar Pigeon. I interviewed her to be satisfied she wasn't in that crowd which had crawled out from under rocks to discombobulate my life over that bird statue in my gym locker. Okay, I had a third reason. Nadine Berry is an eleven on a scale of ten, a gal you could look at all day and never turn away, a beauty any red-blooded, God-fearing, tried-and-true American, post-pubescent lad would give up his soul in exchange for a mere smile of her least recognition of his paltry existence and his future in which she would have absolutely no part. "She smiled at me" would be his lifelong mantra.

Yes, it was a phone call. I had, to tell the truth, actually seen her on the television.

I thought I better call Grenville. We talked a little. Gab, gab, gab, yeah, yeah, yeah. Then, "Thanks for recommending Miss Berry. I have decided to take the case," I told him.

"You did, did you, because her case merits the solid detecting abilities you are qualified to bring to bear and to right the wrongs of that man who is causing her so much discomfort?"

"Wha.." I got out.

"She's kinda cute, isn't she?" he added. "You've seen her on the tube?"

"Yeah, she...you think so?"

"Bas, I may be gay, but I'm not blind." My brother is full of surprises. "Just remembered," he said, "some of the fellows in church are planning a football game. You know, just for fun. Why don't you think about playing, too? No date set yet. Think about it."

23

Owing to my busy schedule of hangovers, getting my head bashed in, quarreling with horse's asses – really just one of these and you know of whom I speak – staring down the barrels of guns, evading arrest, getting solar-plexused, oh, you name it, owing to all this, important responsibilities were not being met by yours truly. I made a grocery list.

I didn't make it to the grocery store for the critical fact that I did not make it to my car. I tossed some invoices I had prepared into the mail box in front of my building hoping for some income from my scant list of clients, turned to go to my car only to see The Pole and his two whatevers. "Get in our car," he threatened.

"Why?"

"I have a question for you."

"So ask it here."

"No. Get in." The gun again. I got in.

"With gas prices so high," I volunteered, "wouldn't it be cheaper to just walk around instead of driving?"

"Shut up."

The city was sporting fog again this day giving gloom a good name. It dampened the windshield as we drove. The Pole at the wheel hit a button or something every few seconds to wipe off the dew. The minion sat up front with The Pole, Ms Wu beside me in the back. She was accompanied by a gun. The Pole went over old territory about me and the bird. I answered his questions and his threats with mostly truths. Why not? I didn't give away anything about the statue, but the rest was easy to admit to. Ms. Wu scowled at me just for practice.

"I don't get it," The Pole repeated. "You say you don't have the statue."

I nodded.

"Then why did the captain travel all the way to your door if he did not have the statue to give to you?"

"Now you're talking," I agreed and nodding even more. "Now you're talking like the police who asked me the same question. You're not a cop, are you?" I teased. No answer. I went on. "This is really central to the mystery. Miss Gunn, if you can believe anything she says, says the captain was paid to bring the package to me. With four bullet holes in him he may have been distracted about the whole mission. On the other hand, he was probably in search of some life-saving assistance what with all those bullets lodged in his frame. Also, it's possible that someone in my building intercepted him and took the package." As an aside, I lowered my voice and said, "I wouldn't put it past that tax man I told you about who works on my floor." I saw The Pole take note of that and I smiled inwardly. Take that, Bevalaqua.

The Pole, his strange sidekick and Ms. Wu fell silent for a while trying to decide, I guess, whether I was lying through my teeth or just a sad, unfortunate victim of idle circumstances who should be patted on the back, apologized to and set back as a free man. The looks on their faces told me they didn't really have any useful thoughts on the matter. Individually, they appeared quite desperate. Collectively, they appeared quite clueless.

"I just love these daytrips around the city," I said.

"Shut up."

The Pole drove back to where I do the business of the Jaguar Beault Investigations Company. "Get out the car," he cried. Then from the window he said, "What's his name?"

"Whose name?"

"That taxidermist you mentioned."

"Taxidermist? Oh, you mean tax man. It's Jason Bevalaqua." I didn't add "the horse's ass." The Pole will figure that out in due time. He drove away.

I reached for my key to go upstairs to my place and out it came along with my grocery list. That's right, I remembered, that's where I was going when The Pole and his nice friends so kindly took me on a scenic tour of parts of San Francisco. The city has it all. Coit Tower, cable cars, grocery stores. Off I went to do my shopping. Even us sophisticated, danger-defying, dare I say handsome, ruggedly handsome, private eyes have to do some grunt work.

I carried my groceries in to my kitchenette using my non-plastic, non-paper, reusable, eco-friendly cloth bags. I have about twenty of them. You can't turn around without some organization foisting one on you to promote its name and civic commitment. I puffed out my chest feeling pride in my contribution to the efforts to preserve Northern California's untrammeled beauty. I had left my shoes at the door because I had stepped in a pile of dog dirt.

In my stocking feet I went over to the message machine because the light was blinking. I pushed the button to activate the playback and returned to the kitchen to make dinner. A p.b. and j. on toasted sourdough because it is the all-American sandwich. Smooth peanut butter, not that senseless crunchy type used, I always believed, only by Communists.

My attention went back to the messages when I heard "...is John Smith, Mr. Beault. My wife told me about your involvement with the Madagascar Pigeon and that she told you of my own interest in the item. She fell under the impression that you have the item yourself. No doubting she also told you that it's more than a mere interest I have in it. As a collector, oh, and as a dealer of appealing ceramic pieces, I would be willing to offer you a very fair price for it." His tone changed when he said, "I am known as a successful businessman, Mr. Beault, because I am a determined one." Then his tone changed back as he said, "and I am glad that you declined my first proposal regarding Mrs. Smith. Otherwise, I would still be unaware of my being so close to obtaining a prize, a minor prize, in ceramics. Please don't do anything with it until we have talked face-to-face and I can persuade you to deal with me." Beep.

Second message: Hey, Bas. I'm getting a great response to the football game idea we're planning. We plan to do it in the park at Kezar. We've done that before and it should work fine. Beep.

Third message: Phyllis Gunn here. You are avoiding me, aren't you? You owe me the statue. Call me and we will get together so I can have it. I still owe you fifty dollars. Here's my new number...Beep.

Fourth message: This is Crystal, Mr. Jaguar Beault Investigations. Turns out I'm not pregnant, one of those false positives (she's laughing, naturally). God, Bobby almost creamed his pants he was so relieved. What does that mean, Jaguar Beault Investigations? You investigate stuff? Like what? How do you do it? You got a nice voice. So I figured I'd give you a buzz. Whyn't you call me back? Here's my number. (I tuned that out.) Beep.

End of messages.

For you good people who haven't followed my advice about getting to San Francisco, by "the park" Grenville meant Golden Gate Park – a wow of a destination – and by Kezar he means the venerable old Kezar Stadium. I am going to have to send a bill to San Francisco's visitor's authority for all the promotion work I am doing here on behalf of the city.

24

I was back from a sweet roll and a coffee and a second sweet roll and turning the key at my door when Bevalaqua yelled down the hallway from his end, "Beault, you dirty son of a bitch, why'd you sic the cops on me?" I smiled inwardly, and to myself I said, "Blough, you magnificent bastard, you did it."

Outwardly, I straightened up and asked, "Whatever do you mean?"

"You know the fuck what I mean. Those two cops came here asking a bunch of questions and making a bunch of accusations about me and that Gunn woman you sent here. They think I have something to do with that guy you killed."

"Did they take your gun to run it through ballistics?"

"Gun? No, I don't even own a gun. What would I do with a gun?"

"Well, for one thing, use it for protection in case of when a burglar breaks into your place here or where you live, or, and this is more likely, when a client of yours comes back all fire and brimstone because you wrecked their income tax return."

"Real fuckin funny, Beault."

"I wasn't finished, Bevalaqua. You also could have used your gun to kill that guy who died on my floor. You were only fifty feet away."

"God damn you, I don't own a gun."

"That's your story and you should stick to it."

"Never mind about that. Why'd you tell them to see me anyway? I've got nothing to do with your detective doings. And what is all this shit about a statue of a bird? That doesn't make any sense to me."

"Are your fingerprints on it? They can test for that you know. They dust for prints. They use it for evidence during the trial." I could hardly contain myself.

"What trial? Hey, I don't know squat about a statue or a bird. My fingerprints aren't on it."

"Good, you were wearing gloves, right? That's smart."

"Jesus, Beault, I'm telling you I don't know anything about it. I never saw it." Here he agonized, "Why would you do this, why did you tell them about me?"

"I didn't tell anybody about you. Those guys are cops. They talk to people of interest who may know something about a crime. Especially murder. You hire a lawyer yet?"

"A lawyer," he screamed, "what'd I need a lawyer for? I haven't done a damn thing." This was just too delicious. He was squirming like a worm in warm water.

"Well that's good. I'm sure the cops believe you. Did they have a warrant to search your place?"

"A warrant, oh God. No they...oh, shit, my files," he shuddered. "I gotta go." He went. I felt so good I decided I owed myself a chocolate chip cookie. There's a bakery...no, it's been a long day and I'll just bask in the success of it.

I felt so good about yesterday I decided I would put in some time at the gym. Some cardio on the bike, some free weights, a few crunches, work on my hamstrings, which have been giving me some uncomfortable signals, sounded like the right thing to do. I'll watch carefully so I am not followed.

As I went out my door, Westwood jammed a .45 in my ribs. "Come on, let's go."

"Shit, Clint, you scared the crap out of me. What is your problem?"

"I have no problem, Beault, you're the one with the problem and it's me."

"It's I."

"No, it's me and you'll soon find out why."

"No, it's not me you should say, it's I."

"I'm the one who knows what I'm saying, so shut up." He shoved the gun into my side for emphasis. I cut the grammar lesson short. "Down the stairs, my car's out front. Don't do anything stupid."

"Stupid is my long suit, Clint." Again with the shoving of the gun. "Hey, that hurts." He shoved again. I suspended further blarney that might be interpreted as stupid.

We were alone on the street when we got to his car. He pointed with his gun for me to get in. "I'll shoot you if you try anything, Beault, so remember that."

"You going to drive with one hand?"

"I'll manage."

"Okay, but highway safety is tops on my list, Mr. Westwood." He glared at me. "Where are you taking me?"

"That's none of your concern." None of my concern? If not mine, then whose? He pulled out and drove two blocks, turned left and drove two more then found Geary where we turned east.

We drove all the way on Geary until King and then O'Farrell where it hits Market. Then north on Grant into Chinatown to a Chinese restaurant open early with just a few customers sipping tea and reading newspapers.

In a booth near the back sat John Smith. Well, well, well. "Good morning, Mr. Beault," he greeted me. "Join us for some tea and pastry." We all sat. "Thank you, Mr. Westwood, for accompanying Mr. Beault here." Westwood grunted. "I hope this hasn't put you out any, Mr. Beault, but I believe it is time we had a talk." I looked at him and then at Westwood. Casually, I brought out a pen and doodled on a napkin. Then I clicked the recording button hidden on my pen gadget.

"You are surprised at our relationship, I see. I'll explain." He told me how he had hired another private detective to tail me once he heard from his missus that I might have the Madagascar Pigeon. In the process, the private eye saw Westwood lurking around me at all hours. Confronted, Westwood revealed his interest in the statue. That is once he was convinced he was not looking for the Malinese Mallard but rather the Madagascar Pigeon. Joining forces seemed the right path to follow. Why the right path? Because Smith had the helpful contacts to extract the best price for the bird, he boasted. Left unsaid was that Clint Westwood couldn't tie his shoes without help.

"Now all our cards are on the table, Mr. Beault. You know where I stand on the matter. What's more, I have the means and the resources to make it happen forthwith." He paused. "And profitably for us all. What I do not have is the item itself. My wife..."

Here I inserted, "A charming woman, by the way."

"What? Yes, I guess she is. My wife, as I was saying, is a perceptive woman. She believes that you are in possession of the Madagascar Pigeon." He watched to see if I gave away anything. I held my poker face. "Ah, you do have it," he said quietly but confidently.

My poker face. I recovered. "Actually, I do not. I did, only not now. Oh, it's safely out of reach of all those other pests who want it. You see, I have, it is, well, it..."

"Cough it up, Beault," Westwood elbowed me.

"Mr. Westwood, enough of the rough stuff," Smith admonished. Westwood backed off. "Take your time, Mr. Beault," Smith encouraged me.

"The statue," I started, "is my get-out-of-jail-free card and valuable to me only as long as I hold it."

"What does that mean?"

"I've been threatened (I looked at Westwood) but no one is likely to kill me because I would take the location of the statue to my grave. If I give it up to any of you without guarantees, I may lose out on potential proceeds. The cops, too, are increasingly interested in its whereabouts as their murder investigation moves on. They have arresting powers I respect. The lead investigator on the homicide case already hates my guts."

Smith drank some tea and said, "Good points. A cogent argument. The key in there was your phrase 'without guarantees' and I can accept that."

I nodded. "That may be. Truth is I liked the part when I brought up the fact that I can't be killed." Smith smiled. Westwood grunted. He must like that sound.

"My fear," Smith said, "is that the others may try to coerce you to their side by using measures you cannot stand up against. I figure them to be uncouth. I would be on my guard if I were you. I, on the other hand, believe the most powerful leverage is the one that has driven the human animal since the Big Bang."

Sex? I thought.

"Greed, Mr. Beault. Money." Oh, that one.

"Yes," I agreed for no reason at all.

"Let's leave it at this, Mr. Beault, we will consider ourselves in alliance. I will make inquiries with some contacts I have and other associates. When I have satisfied myself that the time – and the price – is right, I will call upon you for you to do your part." He waited for my response.

"It appears I have much to think about," I mumbled.

"Indeed you do."

"Well, thank you for the tea and pastry, Mr. Smith. Please pass along my regards to your wife, and to yours, too, Mr. Westwood, if there is such a thing." He grunted.

All their courtesies ended right there. I had to hire a taxi to take me home.

25

I paid the cabbie and walked upstairs to my joint. Oh, wonder of wonders, just what I need, a visit from my two pals. I hadn't seen them in days. She was standing next to my door, tall, elegant, and even appealing if you hadn't ever had to speak with her. But which one of the two personalities, Phyllis Gunn or Lavernia Lavender? Time to detect. I put my interrogation training to work. "Oh, hello," I said, "here to see me or Mr. Bevalaqua?"

"Why, you, Mr. Beault, I have no reason to see that man again." Phyllis. Okay. Got that straightened out. I unlocked the door and left it open for her to follow me in. She did and closed the door.

"I thought we had a deal, Miss Gunn. You would leave me alone in exchange for my assurance to you that I would call if I ever saw your East Asian souvenir."

"Aren't we way past that charade? Captain Kluszewski is dead and with him is the answer to where the statue is. That is, if it is not already in your hands."

"Is that where things stand? I've been so busy gawking at guns, getting my head bashed in, and going on unwanted automobile trips that I have lost my bearings. How about you, what have you been up to besides checking out of hotels on a daily basis?"

"That's for my own protection. People are after me. They want to take from me what is rightfully mine."

Yeah, yeah, yeah. Tell me something you haven't told me before, you whacko, I thought. I said, "You mean The Pole and his friends and..."

"Yes! Them. And Lavernia. Ooh, Lavernia, that awful...she will stop at nothing to get it from me."

"Really? Do you have it now?"

"No, no, I am just saying...oh, what's the use. You have it, don't you, you wicked man?" Out came her gun. Why not? "I'll shoot you right now, Beault, if you don't..."

She should have backed up. I flicked my hand out and around her wrist turning the business end of the pistol away from both of us. I twisted the gun hard and it came out of her hand. She yelped and tried to hit me. I blocked her arm and slapped her backhanded across her face. She put her hands to her head and cried out, "You brute, you hit me. You awful brute."

"I'll hit you again if you don't clam up," I growled at her. She began crying. Her gun was a revolver. A .25 caliber, not a .32. I emptied out the six cartridges and tossed them in a drawer. Miss Gunn had slouched into a chair a bit theatrically I observed. When women are crying around me I don't know what to do. There's no good action to take. Wait, don't take that the wrong way. Women aren't crying around me so often that I've come to this conclusion. No. It's happened a few times, that's all. I was saved by a knocking at my door. Who the hell's here now? Another bird aficionado, no doubt, and with a gun as doubtless. That's how my life was going. Could be anyone. Well, anyone but Lavernia Lavender. She was sitting in my chair with her twin sister.

I opened my door. A man was standing there. "Are you Jaguar Beault?" he asked.

I looked at him. I looked at my door. I looked back at him. I looked back at my door. "That's what it says right there," I pointed. "Jaguar Beault Investigations. That must be me."

"I'm Hugo Blankenship." The Gunn woman heard that and let out a scream that sent electricity up my spine. Hugo jumped back away from the door.

"Don't let him in," Miss Gunn shouted, presumably to me. "Don't let him come in here," she repeated loudly.

I heard her the first time. People across the San Francisco Bay heard her the first time. It's my office and my home, I can let anyone in whom I please. Is it "whom" or "who"?

"I'll kill him if he comes in here," Miss Gunn shouted. She appeared to be upset. Lest I forget, she also carries a gun. Fortunately, I had already taken that from her. I wondered what else she might use to smoke Mr. Blankenship, so I grabbed her purse. I looked and saw nothing of a weapon sort. That was reassuring.

"Come on in, Mr. Blankenship," I invited him. Miss Gunn whooped another scream. "Oh, for pity sake, please stop that bellowing," I told her. Miss Gunn, who had stood up, slunk down into a chair and turned her back on us. "You can sit there," I told Blankenship, pointing to another chair. Hugo was short of thirty years old and about as tall as the twin sister in the room. Hugo wore glasses that didn't detract from a virile face. "Well, now, isn't this cozy?" I tried to ease the tension.

"I came here about that matter we spoke of on the phone. I didn't know she would be here," Hugo said.

"I thought married couples shared with each other like what their plans are."

"Married couples? What are you saying?"

"You and Mrs. Blankenship here."

"Are you nuts? That's not my wife. I'm married to Lavernia, her sister. Her twin sister."

Miss Gunn piped in. "Lucky her," she said, painting her words in sarcasm. Hugo tossed his head up.

"Hold the fort," I said, "let me get this straight." I shook my head to make the image go away. I was overacting. "You are not married to this woman, we'll call her Phyllis, you are married to her sister, we'll call her Lavernia?" They didn't catch on to the scorn I was pitching.

"Of course. What did you think?"

"You and Lavernia, huh?" is what came to mind and what I said. Then, "Do you have kids?"

"No, we have not been blessed."

"Oh yes, yes you have," I sneered. It was fun making fun of these dingbats.

Miss Gunn, the unmarried half of the tall, slender women, spoke up. "Somebody would have to be crazy to marry you," she spouted towards Blankenship. Bingo, I thought. There's enough crazy among the three of them, excuse me, between the two of them, to populate an entire loony lockup.

Hugo ignored his sister-in-law and said to me, "Phyllis and Lavernia have never gotten along. Something in their childhood caused a rift that has never been settled. It's a sad thing, really. Do you know I've never seen the two of them together. That's how sad it is."

Where I come from, from my genetic makeup and my life experiences and my environment and who had influences over my critical thinking development, where I come from when we rubbed up against somebody this stupid, me and my friends, etc., we would run like hell away. It was good policy, one if I followed now would mean these two would be left alone in my office and my home. So they had to go.

"Say," I said, "this has been just so much fun and I am sorry you have to leave now. But life goes on and I have to..."

"Our business isn't finished yet, Mr. Beault," Blankenship said. "I've come for the statue."

"Don't you dare give it to him," Miss Gunn yelled, "it belongs to me, not to him or anybody else."

"Shut up, you female-only aperture," Hugo exploded, only he used the c word. It floated in the room.

Miss Gunn shot him a look and cried out, "Fuck you, you peter eater," only she used another c word and that one thundered in the room and stopped me cold. The tiff was reaching new depths, so I decided it was time for Jaguar Beault to use some c words.

"Children, children," I cautioned, "let me counsel civility."

"Civility, my ass," Hugo responded. At which time, naturally, out came a gun. Well, why not again? This is Jaguar Beault's office and his home. It is a shrine to the inalienable right of all visitors here to draw a weapon and point it at me. Or worse. Whatever happened to just bringing along a fruitcake? I like fruitcake. I'll even share it with you. A gun didn't appear to be quite so friendly.

"Where's the goddam statue? I want it and I want it now," Hugo shouted. That same old refrain I've got from a chorus line of gun-owning felons over the past week or two bent on separating me either from the Madagascar Pigeon or from my life. Until John Smith, each time I had denied that I had it. For the first time since I heard this demand, it occurred to me – even though I knew what the answer would be – that I had not asked any of them the obvious question.

So here goes. I said, "Why?" It stumped him. It tickled me to see him thrash around in his head how to answer. I almost volunteered the answer for him: It is valuable and I will sell it and get rich. He hemmed and hawed as the saying goes.

As if it were fifth grade, Phyllis came forward when little Hugo didn't answer teacher's question. "He'll sell it and make a lot of money." She may be a repeat customer at the nut counter, but she has a good handle on lost ceramic birds. Apparently, Hugo agreed because he said, "Yeah."

That being settled I launched into my soliloquy about Kluszewski arriving empty-handed at my door, etc., etc. etc.

Hugo was unimpressed and began making unhappy gestures. "I'll shoot your ass, Beault, if you don't fork it over."

"Won't help if I'm dead, eh, Hugo? Suppose I really do have it."

"Then I'll shoot her and put the blame on you."

"Shoot Phyllis? That will not go down well at all with Lavernia."

"Ha, they hate each other."

"There is a symbiosis there that you may not want to tinker with, let me assure you."

"What in hell is he talking about?" he said to Miss Gunn.

"How the hell should I know, you twerp."

"That is fucking it," Hugo exploded, "I have had all I am going to take from both of you. Either..."

A knock at the door. Two knocks, boom-boom.

I liked the sound of that. "Get rid of him," Hugo whispered.

Boom-boom. "Beault, open up." San Francisco Police Department Homicide Detective Lieutenant Joseph Blough. I liked it even better now. Oh, and probably Sgt. Headley, too.

"It's the police, Hugo. They won't take no for an answer."

He put his gun away and shriveled into his suit. "Shit," I heard him say.

"Beault!"

"Coming," I said.

"Please come in, lieutenant, oh, and the effusive Sergeant Headley. Nice to see you both. Let me introduce you to Mr. Blankenship. He is here in hopes of my helping him find a missing, what, we called it an heirloom, yes. This is Lieutenant Blough and Sergeant Headley. And this is a client of mine, Miss..."

Before I got out one of the roster of names she had confessed to already, she smiled and said, "Cordelia Lear, how nice to meet you."

If the introductions meant anything to Blough and Headley, it didn't show. "We've got police business, Beault, so maybe these people are done with you."

That was cue enough for Blankenship who held his jacket closed over his gun and went to the door. Cordelia Lear said, "Well, I never!" but got up nonetheless and followed Blankenship out.

"How can I help the department today, lieutenant?"

"You can't but we'll talk just the same. Tell me about the bird."

"What bird would that be?"

Outside, there set up a screaming and yelling and an exchange of some really unattractive language when used between a man and a woman. Blough went to the door and opened it to see my erstwhile guests toe-to-toe in a spitting match. "Get the hell away from him, from her, or by God I'll run both your asses in for disturbing my peace. Got it?" Things quieted down. Where's there a cop when you need one? Right here in my home.

Blough came back in and shoved his hands into the pockets of the MacIntosh he was wearing against what I presumed was a fresh covering of the city's famous fog of which I have remarked to you. Or else he liked the image he projected in a long overcoat. "Let's cut the crap, shall we? I know there's a trophy in the middle of my homicide investigation, a statue of a bird people think has some big-time value. Let's not do some stupid dance, just you tell me what you know, okay? Just like old times." What old times would those be, I asked myself. Oh, well.

I told him almost everything I knew and what had transpired until now. I held out that I had the bird, and I didn't try to avoid accusing any of my new acquaintances with criminal intent. When I was finished, Blough said, "So, you *have* been holding out on me."

"Oh, my God, that's it? I give you chapter and verse on the whole heart of your investigation and all you can say is I've been holding out on you? This isn't about me. You have two stiffs and a whole boatload of possible killers, me not included, and they're all looking for this damn bird statue and telling me I'm dead if I don't give it to them. One after another. Shit, I wish I did have it. I'd a given it to the first one who asked me for it if it would have sent all these pricks somewhere else. It seems to me it's a good thing the statue is buried somewhere because if one of these creeps comes up with it your murder case will evaporate as quickly as they all disappear. While it's still here in San Francisco, and it probably is, they'll all stay right here hoping they'll come across it. Isn't it true that the best link between the dead guys and the killer or killers is the gun? You have good ballistics on that."

"Yeah, that's right."

"So you want those guns in your jurisdiction, not in some other state or some other country. The key is the bird, not because it's valuable but because it keeps the killers here."

"Maybe."

"By maybe I'm guessing you mean 'that's right, Mr. Beault'."

"Okay," he said.

"Just like old times," I told him.

"Don't push it, Beault."

"Right."

"We gotta find a way to flush the killer out," Blough said.

"Very true. I've been working on that. It's sketchy right now, and I need a little more time to bring it around full circle. I've got some more poking around to do. Some more legwork. Hard work by the private sector, lieutenant."

"I doubt that, shamus. Exactly what are you doing?"

"Ah. About that...there's just a slight chance that my plan would raise an eyebrow or two with a judge when the evidence is combed. My approach is a little different from the one that you and the sergeant might take. Need I say more?"

"Nice seeing you, Mr. Beault, the sergeant and I will be saying good-bye."

"Good-bye, lieutenant, sergeant. No, hold on, you went to see my neighbor, Mr. Bevalaqua. Did that turn out to be helpful?"

"Not in this case. I am considering passing him on to our Fraud Division. That guy's a real horse's ass."

"He is? Gee, I hadn't noticed that."

Then Blough said, "Her name is Cordelia Lear?"

26

The dramatic climactic scene in the drawing room where all the suspects are collected to hear the hero reveal the way the case unfolded and, alas, who murdered whom that I hinted to Blough about was still a long way off. I had to lay some groundwork and put some pieces together first. This was going to require careful planning and some more detecting. I'd wait until later to find a drawing room. My little place wouldn't hold everyone. I knew where to start. I called Grenville.

I brought him up to speed on how things had progressed. "She said her name was Cordelia Lear? That woman has spent too much time with her head in a microwave oven."

"You're right about that...a quick-cooked brain."

"How can I help?"

"I got a little list, well, not so little, of some help I can use over the next week or so from folks in your congregation if they are available."

"Shoot."

"A computer expert for audio recordings."

"Bas, holy cow, a bunch of those."

"One with, uh, some discretion."

"You betcha."

"How about a locksmith or someone who can crack a bird?"

"Let me think on it."

"You told me you minister to two retired NFL linebackers. They still around?"

"Not two, three. They are going to play in the football game at Kezar."

"Terrific. That game is going to come in pretty handy, I believe."

"You are sounding very devilish, Bas. I like it."

"Good, here's what I'm thinking."

Ring-ring. The phone. Is this my lucky day?

"Basil Protherington Investigations, Inc." I answered.

"Very funny, Mr. Beault, are you working under cover today?" I recognized the sound of the voice, only I couldn't put a name to go with it.

"No, I..."

"This is Mrs. Smith."

"Oh, Mrs. Smith."

"What are you doing?"

"I don't know, I mean nothing. I just got off the phone."

"What I mean to say is what are you doing right now? For example, are you free for lunch?"

What the heck was going on, free for lunch? "Yeah, well, I guess so."

"Such enthusiasm, Mr. Beault. It overwhelms me. Maybe you have already had a better offer."

"No, not at all. You just...you just surprised me, that's all."

"I'm full of surprises, Mr. Beault. You know the Beach Chalet, where we met and you went home in a taxi?"

"I do know it. And I do remember some of that night."

"Oh-ho. Yes, and I wish to apologize. I should not have allowed you to overindulge in the cognac."

"What's done is done. I did take a valuable lesson away from it."

"What is that?"

"Stick to the lessons about liquor I learned in my salad days."

"You have history with the booze, do you?"

"A short history, but plenty enough to have known better."

"I'll be waiting at the restaurant." She hung up. Okay, I'll go for lunch. I went to the bathroom to, uh, to go to the bathroom. While in there the phone rang again. Shoot. I won't be able to pick up. I'll let the machine get it.

"Hello, hello, is anybody there? Gee, mister, you haven't called me. Why not? Oh, this is Crystal. Whyn't you call me? Here's my number..."

That kid needs counseling. If not a leash. After erasing Crystal's message, I hurried out the door to escape the damn phone.

I saw Mrs. Smith sitting at the same table as on our previous meeting. Nothing had changed. Pearl and Yvonne were there, too. Cautiously, I scanned the café and bar. I did not see Ping Bodie.

"Hello, ladies, nice to see you again." We did the greeting things all around, discovering that we were each fine or good. The waitress took our drink orders. The ladies asked for coffee. I got an iced tea. A real one. To Mrs. Smith I said, "I don't see Ping Bodie. I hope this means he's not tailing me any longer."

"Just because you do not see Mr. Bodie, Mr. Beault, or Mr. Protherington, if you will, does not mean he is off the case. Frank Bodie is good."

"Yes, but..."

"Don't worry yourself, you are on your own now," she chuckled.

"Protherington? You're name is Protherington?" Yvonne directed at me.

"That's how he answered his phone when I called him this morning," Mrs. Smith answered for me.

Yvonne said, "I know a guy by that name. He runs a church in the city. Big handsome guy. A real doll. I've had the biggest crush on him since I met him when he helped out at a food bank me and girls sponsored in the Tenderloin. I guess he's married or has a steady girl because I shook everything I had at him from these down to this and all I got was that beautiful smile of his. It really fractured my confidence."

Pearl said, "Yvonne, you dear thing, if he runs a church in the Castro, do you think it's just possible that his head is turned by an Adonis rather than a Venus?"

"You mean he's...he's gay?"

"Way to go, Sherlock."

"Damn, I never thought of that. How can I find out if this is true?"

"Ask his brother," Mrs. Smith suggested.

"He's got a brother? God, I hope it's a twin. But who's his brother?"

Mrs. Smith pointed at me. I'll use a sports analogy to describe the way Yvonne reacted when she learned that I was Grenville's brother and, obviously, not his twin. Down the peninsula from San Francisco sits Palo Alto and in Palo Alto sits the campus of Stanford University. Perhaps you've heard of it. Stanford is well known for its sky-high educational standing. Kudos to Stanford. Stanford also fields a football team each season. Yvonne's disappointment that I was Grenville's non-twin sibling was written on her face in the same way the Stanford student section would react if their quarterback fumbled the ball on the last play of the game as the team was attempting to score the winning touchdown with no time to spare.

Yvonne sagged into her chair, reached for her coffee cup and held it to her lips without drinking. Pearl laughed at her. I must have had a pathetic look. Mrs. Smith patted my hand. A silence descended on the table. I broke the silence after an uncounted interval. "Grenville's gay. Has been all his life." Yvonne lifted her eyes to me. I take comfort in the fact that she did not ask, "Does Grenville have any other brothers?"

"Protherington?" Pearl inserted.

"It's our family name. It has a long proud history if you forget to include a few generations of horse thieves and arsonists, anti-Royalists who met their ends in the Tower of London, Royalists who met their ends out in the countryside, colonial tyrants, seamen expert at impressing. You know, your typical English forebears. Let me assure you, though, that once the family immigrants reached the shores of the USA, their outlooks looked up and they decided to operate in a law-abiding way. More or less."

Yvonne put her coffee cup down. "No other brothers, though?"

There it was. "Only me, Yvonne, I am sorry to say."

She eyed me forlornly and said, "No sweat."

No sweat? Only no sweat, not you're okay, too, Mr. Protherington. Just no sweat? I really didn't care all that much, but come on.

To Mrs. Smith I said, "You did not seem to be put off by my last name."

"Mr. Bodie is a resourceful investigator like yourself. He uncovered this for me."

"What's so interesting about me to you? You got Bodie watching me and now this lunch business."

"Fair question. It's the Madagascar Pigeon. I..."

"You want me to give it or sell it to your Mr. Smith. I see, but I don't..."

"No, I want you *not* to give it or sell it to him."

"Hmmm." Her explanation was somewhat circuitous only because I didn't fully understand all of it. It was as if she didn't want me to understand all of it.

I drove home not needing the use of a taxi this time. Iced tea will do that for you. Thirst-quenching and sobering.

27

Nadine Berry, my new fee-paying client, and I had devised a plan to capture evidence of her boss's ignorant behavior. She would go to a bar near where she works, a nice one she knew about where the clientele was mature, professional and usually obliging about people's space. A destination she knew her boss – his name is, get this, Xerxes, Xerxes Stone – would follow her. I would have a seat not far away and within range of my digital directional audio recorder. My pen. I also would be armed with my tie tack camera for graphic evidence. My gadgets are really cool.

Sure as shootin, Miss Berry was sitting at the bar no more than two or three minutes when Xerxes came through the door. She had given me a brief description of her boss: about five feet ten or eleven, around a hundred sixty-five pounds, pitch black hair and looking to be way too young to be legal in a California-licensed drinking facility. She confided in me that he loved to get carded. Twenty-six going on sixteen was what she said earlier about him. I was seated a few stools down the bar wearing a cream-colored blazer, dark glasses, and a funky old hat.

Xerxes bided his time for the very good reason that Nadine Berry had nearly frozen the men in the place when she first came in, something she undoubtedly does to men whenever she enters a room. A few had migrated toward her, offering hellos and drinks or whatever they could devise to earn a spot near her. She was gracious to one and all as she let them know she was waiting for a friend.

At the first little seam between the suitors near Miss Berry, Xerxes slipped through, greeting her as if he had no idea at all that she was here tonight. I flipped the button activating my recorder toy. I manipulated the tie tack so it was aimed at the two. Miss Berry declined his offer of a drink since she already had one. He ordered his own and stood there. He told her that he was impressed with the work she had done today, a piece on the opening of a pocket park devoted to mothers and/or fathers pushing baby buggies. It was the idea of the local San Francisco Supervisor, a project financed in part by a federal grant. When he said he was going to tell her cameraperson to do more tight shots on her, she objected. He said, "You're the star, Nadine, and I like looking into your deep blue eyes. Close ups on you sell ratings and they drive me to wild fantasies. Want to hear them?"

"Xerxes, please, I have asked you not to talk this way."

"It's only talk, how about if we move on to action? We have all night. We could go back to my place and leave talking at the door."

"No, Xerxes, no. I've told you before that I am not looking for that from you."

"I can make things very easy for you at the station, you know."

"You're my boss and you should not be acting this way toward me."

He put his arm around her waist. "I can also make things hard for you, too. Know what I mean?"

"Xerxes! Please don't do this."

I slid off my bar stool and, carrying my drink and acting like I had one or two too many, shuffled toward Xerxes bumping into him hard enough to get a response.

"Hey, jerk, watch where you're going."

"You watch where I'm going, jerk," I mumbled like a drunk. I tipped my glass and it ran down his coat and pants.

"Oh, shit, old man, look what you have done. I ought to kick your ass."

"Oh, yeah, you and who else, you pussy," I slurred.

"I don't need anybody else."

"Maybe you better ask the lady to help (hic, I burped) so you can make it even."

"Get lost, asshole."

The bartender spoke up. "Take it outside, fellas, before I get Security."

"Mr. Gutless here's too afraid to deal with this old man outside," I tempted.

Xerxes, beyond any hope I had put into my spur-of-the-moment scheme, slapped his glass on the bar and looked up and said, "Let's go." I don't know why just a few people came outside, Nadine included. I thought afterward that most of the drinkers figured the whole mess would dissolve into a non-event. Young stud vs. a drunken old man.

I shambled along behind Xerxes. We got to the patio entrance where he turned and threw a punch at me. He was right-handed. I heard Miss Berry gasp. I raised my left arm and blocked the punch and brought my left fist down onto his right eye. Xerxes cried out and put his hands up to his face. He should have quit. I was pretty glad he didn't. He tried the punch thing once more. I dodged that and put my right fist onto his nose. He went down to his knees. I looked at Miss Berry who stood there in shock or disbelief or something. I was hoping it was admiration. At least appreciation. Hard to tell. Things had happened fast.

"I'm sorry about your boyfriend," I slurred some more. "But he's not very nice." I walked away.

Have you guessed yet that Miss Berry and I had not met in person up to this point? Yes. We had done all our planning by phone. She didn't know me by sight. I am not a celebrated face in television like she is. Moreover, I do not sufficiently resemble my brother – as so many other women have let on recently – so she had no touchstone to say, ooh, that handsome dude is Grenville's good-looking brother. I called her number when I got home and left a message saying I got plenty on Xerxes and would have it on a DVD in a day or two for her. I added that I hoped that misunderstanding between Xerxes and the drunk didn't lead to anything ugly. Then I called Grenville and told him what happened on condition he not reveal my Rambo act to Miss Berry.

"You did good, bro, though I do not condone the violence. I preach peace and you should practice that."

"Like you've always practiced peace and non-violence?"

"That was my wayward past, Bas, not who I am now."

"Right."

"So you bloodied his nose, huh?"

139

"All over his shirt, you shoulda seen it. And he won't see out of his right eye so good for a week or two."

"Naughty, naughty."

"Hey, he's a top-rated butthead."

I made arrangements for Grenville's computer expert to fix up the audio and graphic evidence on Xerxes. "I'll pay him," I said.

"Damn right, you will."

28

Boom, boom, boom, the door resounded. Dang, are we having the big one? I mean The Earthquake.

"Beault, open the door." That would be Detective Lieutenant Blough. I recognized his friendly demeanor. Boom, boom, boom.

"Hold it a minute, I'm coming," I shouted. Blough pushed his way in with Sergeant Headley in his wake. After they were both in, I said, "Please come in, gentlemen." They didn't see the ready wit in that nor the irony.

Blough spoke. "You're coming clean with me, Beault, the whole nine yards, or I'll sit on your ass so hard you'll..." I had started laughing at that image. SFPD detective sitting on the hindquarters of a licensed private eye and a free citizen to boot.

"What's so funny?"

"Sorry, nothing." It was here that it occurred to me that Blough and Headley never flash their badges. Under the circumstances, Blough, being on edge, I let it slide.

"I got a picture I want you to look at." He reached back to Headley who passed him a folder. "Lookit this." It was a picture of a dead guy lying on a slab at the morgue. "Know him?"

"Yeah, actually, I do. He looks different here. Like he's not alive."

"Good detection, shamus. How do you know him?"

I told Blough how I knew Clint Westwood, the dead guy in the picture. How he interrupted my dinner, how he'd threatened me over the statue I didn't have, and how he had teamed up apparently with Mr. Smith. Blough listened. Headley, I presumed, listened, but that was hard to know for sure.

"How come you're asking me about him?"

"We found your card on him," Blough said. "He threatened you, yeah?"

"Well, sure, that's the new national pastime ever since the dear departed Captain Kluszewski expired on my floor. People coming out of the baseboards like cockroaches telling me to turn over a bird statue I don't got...or else. But if I went out and killed everyone who's threatened me lately you wouldn't have enough body lockers down at the morgue. So to answer the question you are about to ask, no, I did not kill him. How was it done?"

"A .32 behind his ear."

"Oooh, mob style."

"Shit, this isn't mob doings. There's three dead bodies and all tied directly to you. And, I gotta guess, that bird statue you say you don't have, which I'm bettin you do. Where is it, Beault? You put it in a locker down in the bus station?"

"Whoa. You've been watching those late night movies, haven't you? No, it's not in a bus station locker. It's somewhere between the boat Kluszewski came in on and my front door, just like I've told you before, a bunch of times," I lied again.

The phone rang.

"Let it go, Beault, I'm not finished."

After some unanswered rings, the machine activated and a voice came on. "Hello, hello, oh, I missed you again. You still haven't called me Mister Jaguar Beault Investigations. I think your voice is cute. Whyn't you ever call me back? Oh, yeah, (giggling) this is Crystal if you didn't figger that out by now." I started to walk over to the phone to cut off the connection, but Blough stopped me. "Let it go on," he ordered. Crystal was going on. "...Because I'm only fifteen you don't think I know my way around. Well, I do and I could...oh, fuck, here comes my dad." Beep.

Blough was staring at me and Headley was laughing.

"I can explain that, lieutenant, only I am convinced you wouldn't believe a word I said."

"I oughta arrest you right now for being a deviated son of a bitch."
Things went downhill from there before they departed. I erased
Crystal's message.

Clint Westwood dead as a fence post, joining Captain Kluszewski
and Marcel Lorenz in the Choir Invisible. Blough is right, too, that all
three are connected to me and to the Madagascar Pigeon. Where does
that put me? Am I on the hit list? Does asking this make me selfish? You
bet it does. And tuff toast to you if you don't like it.

I called Grenville to fill him in on the latest crapola and get a little
sympathy, underscore little.

"Be careful," he told me.

"Dead guys all around and I'm smack dab in the middle of this mystery and all you can do is quote Emily and her colleague and say be
careful," I said, trying to sound mad.

He said, "This is what brothers are for." He's the comic in the family.

I immediately set out to be careful. You hear it from one person and
you can blow it off. You hear it from a second person and a third, you
better listen up. I'll rifle through my mail. It has stacked up a bit for a
few days. The usual junk, the usual unsolicited offers, the notices of
overdue bills (okay, okay, I'll send it to you).

After I finished sorting through my mail, I headed to my gym. I made
it this time without being diverted at the end of a gun barrel. Nobody
followed me unless it was the invisible Ping Bodie. The workout was
refreshing. By that I mean the heavy breathing on the slider didn't lead
to a fainting spell, and the fire in my muscles from the weight machines
didn't set the gym ablaze. It takes about two years of steady and uninter-
rupted sessions at the gym to reach a decent level of being in shape. Lay off
for a week or so and you can guarantee breathlessness and flaming body
parts. What's more, I pay a monthly fee for this pain. I hunched around my
locker door to make sure no one could see the pet bird I had hidden in it.

Before going home I swung by a Japanese restaurant on Balboa and
had sushi and tempura and rice. No sake. I put sake in the same category as Hennessey. I had two pots of tea, which meant I had to pee like
a racehorse when I got to my door.

That's when I heard Bevalaqua come storming down the hall yelling at me, "You did it again, didn't you, Beault?"

I raised my hand. "Time is out, Bevalaqua, while I go to the bathroom." Nothing was going to interfere with that, not even a moment of glee needling my floor mate.

"You sent one of your deadbeat cronies after me," he started up again after I came back. "What the shit are you up to?"

"All this means what?"

"That tall creep and his two creepy friends. They asked me all sort of questions about that dumbass bird statue. I thought they were going to kill me. It's your fault. First the cops and now these, these, what the hell is that guy anyway, a fuckin freak? I was scared shitless. What'd you tell them?"

"I may have mentioned your name once or twice. They were holding a gun on me, too."

"Jesus, what have you gotten me into? I've got nothing to do with you or a bird or anything. Keep me out of it, for Christ's sake."

"I'll try, you know I will, but, gee, when there's a guy pointing a gun at me, what should I do?"

"Keep me the fuck out of it, that's what," he shouted.

"Yeah, but when bodies are piling up all over the place you have to cover your behind."

"I don't need to cover my...what did you say?"

"The cops found another dead guy. And guess what, he's been searching for the bird just like those others. You'll love this. His name is...was...Clint Westwood. Isn't that a scream?"

"Was he, oh shit, was he, oh God, was he...was he murdered?"

"Sure. What else? A .32 behind his ear. Mob style. Is your gun a .32?"

"No. No! Jesus, no. I mean I don't have a gun."

"That's a good alibi. It should work."

"Alibi? No, no, it's the truth."

"I believe you. You don't look like the gun type to me. Say, did you hire a lawyer yet?"

"No, I...no! I don't need a lawyer."

"That's very brave of you."

"Holy God, what is happening to me?"

"This is a real puzzle, isn't it? Do you have a solid lock on your door?"

"Oh God," he moaned as he hurried back down the hall.

Beault, you are a scoundrel of the first rank of scoundrels, I told myself. The horse's ass.

29

Two phone calls made me feel darned good. The first was from Grenville to tell me the photo and audio discs his congregant transcribed for me were ready for pickup at the church. They had Nadine Berry's evidence of the harassment by her shit-for-brains boss-editor, the one with the black eye and broken nose.

The second call was to Miss Berry who was pleased to hear I had the discs for her. I told her I could come to her station and give them to her, a regular service provided by the vice president of transportation of Jaguar Beault Investigations. No. She said it would be better if I did not come to the station. Instead she said to see her at the same bar where Xerxes donated blood. All right if that's what you want, I agreed. Tomorrow night after the dinnertime news hour was over. All this talk of dinner reminded me that I was hungry. I had no breakfast this morning and I don't remember why unless it was my empty food pantry. That would account for no meals at home under even the best of circumstances. I went out for lunch.

Let's get real about the went-out-for-lunch remark. This is San Francisco. Going out for lunch demands your full attention. You need to perform a self-assessment on the types of taste treats you want. There's an unlimited array of ethnic cuisines in the city's forty-nine square miles. And that's even if you don't add in the rest of the entire Bay Area. Once you have settled on a country or regional favorite for the day, you then have to consider how far you want to walk or drive and how much you can afford. Not to mention the ambience you will require to fit your current mood. Oh yeah, and what view do you want from your dining venue. Loads of decisions to make from so many choices. I chose Fisherman's

Wharf where I planned to have a chowder (white) and a salad (Caesar). As I was ordering I was trying to think whether the parking fee up here was just under or just over my monthly car payment from the old days.

After I ate I ransomed my car from Wharf parking and headed out. My cell phone rang. Yes, I carry one although I mostly have it turned off. The primary reason I carry it is to be able to reach a tow service. I love my car, it's paid for, but it is a temperamental old thing with different opinions about providing reliable service.

"Yes," I answered.

"Mr. Beault, John Smith."

"Hi, listen, I'm in my car and I'm driving..."

"We have to meet."

"As I was saying, I'm in my car and I'm driving, and as it is illegal in this state to use a car phone, unless of course it is hands free, I don't want to get a ticket. I cannot afford the big fine. I'll call you later."

"Where are you?"

"Just leaving Fisherman's Wharf."

"You're not far from my house. Come over now." Click.

All that was true about car phone use, the high fine for violating the law, and how close I was to the Smith manse. What the hell, why not? The Smith front door came open before I could push the doorbell. "Come on in," Smith beckoned. Not friendly, not unfriendly. "Wanna drink?" I declined. "Over here, sit down." Not friendly, not unfriendly.

He was about to say something when I said, "Usually you send Mr. Westwood for me." I left it at that. His face went all funny.

"God, he's dead," he said.

"He is? How awful, and don't call me God."

"Real fuckin funny, Beault. This is serious. Westwood's been shot. Didn't you know?"

To lie or not to lie, that was the question, whether to... "Yes, I guess I did hear something like that. Who killed him, you?"

"Me? No, hell no. I'm no killer." This from the guy who asked me to ice his spouse.

"Oh, that's right, you just hire it out."

"Never mind about that. Westwood's dead. This just got too close to me. I need you to do something about it."

"I can't do anything about it. Call the cops."

"Oh, Jesus, no, not the police." A pause. "You can do something about it. I know who killed Westwood. And the other two as well."

"You mean Lorenz and the sea captain?"

"Yes, them, who else? They are all part of the Madagascar Pigeon mess. I'm afraid. I'm afraid I could be next."

"Oh, self-preservation. An admirable act of human self-interest."

"I'm serious."

"You sound serious. If you know who killed Westwood, you have to go to the authorities."

"I will not go to the authorities. As soon as I think to do that, she'll kill me for sure."

"She?"

"Yes."

"She?"

"Yes! My wife."

"Mrs. Smith? Don't be absurd. She's really a very pleasant lady."

"Don't be so gullible, Beault, everybody said the same thing about Lizzie Borden."

"Well, I don't see it, all I can say...wait, what, who? Lizzie Borden?"

"Lizzie Borden, Beault! God, haven't you ever heard of her? Here, let me say it: *Lizzie Borden took an axe and gave her mother forty whacks. When she saw what she had done, she gave her father forty-one.* The hatchet killer. Fall River, Massachusetts. She's famous. And here's the thing. Everybody said she was a pleasant lady. It didn't prove she couldn't fillet a couple of people. Her own parents, for Christ sake."

Had Mr. Smith gone off the deep end somewhere? Lizzie Borden? Forty whacks? Is he a branch on that Gunn-Lavender nut tree?

"I just don't believe it," I said. "You know what I think, I think you're just letting your jealousy get the better of you. I followed her and I didn't see any clues about seeing other men. What makes you think she's a killer?"

"She goes out all the time, and when she's home she's been asking me a lot of questions, delving into my financial affairs, bank accounts, life insurance. She's really changed. She makes me jittery."

"I am not a married man, Mr. Smith, so it is hard for me to judge what you are saying. I just figure a man and a wife discussing topics like money is a common thing."

"What? I don't know...maybe...anyway here's the thing. I'll up the payoff to a hundred grand."

"What payoff?"

"*The* payoff. The one we talked over recently."

"You mean..."

He looked around. "Yes," he said in a lowered voice, "one hundred thousand dollars to kill my wife."

"No."

"I'm desperate, it's either her or me, and I just know that."

"I don't off the wives of my clients as a general rule, Mr. Smith, it looks bad on my professional *curriculum vitae*. Know what I mean?"

He sagged into a chair. "Yes, I see, I know. But what can I do? Wait, do you know anyone else who...no, you wouldn't tell me if you did."

"I wouldn't tell you because I don't know anyone, as you say, who..." With absolutely nothing resolved for this poor sap, I took my leave. When the front door closed, I clicked off my recording gadget. These are great things.

As I went toward my car, Mrs. Smith came around from her garage.

"Why, Mr. Beault, this is a surprise. You were visiting?"

"Yes, with your husband. I'm just leaving. I am sorry to say he is quite distressed about Mr. Westwood's death."

"Westwood...yes, I suppose he is."

"Well, nice to see you," I said taking my leave.

"Mr. Beault, would you do me the favor of another get-together? I would be grateful if we could have dinner, say tomorrow night?"

"Dinner? Uh, well, okay, but not tomorrow. I have a..." I almost said date, why, I couldn't say. "I have an appointment. The next night?"

"Thank you, yes, that would be lovely. At the Beach Chalet? We both know it."

"The Beach Chalet. Sure."

"I'll see you there at eight then." Two dates. One with a killer beauty (Nadine Berry, my lesbian client) and one with a killer killer, according to her husband.

30

Before my big date with Nadine Berry, that embodiment of beauty who makes the dullest news stories sparkle on the television screen, I went over to Grenville's church to fetch and pay for the DVDs capturing the infantile behaviors of one Xerxes Stone. I left a check for the computer dude who transcribed my audio and photography work. Grenville asked me what I was up to. I explained that tonight I was delivering the discs to Miss Berry.

He said, "Isn't she a beauty?"

I said, "Oh, do you think so? I guess she has a kind of beauty."

"Yeah, bro, a kind of beauty, you know," Grenville was saying with a huge twinkle in his eye, "the best kind." This from my gay brother.

But enough of this talk of whether Miss Berry is the most beautiful woman in the world or just in the top five. (I bet you can't name four others.) She is just another client who will get the same professional, skilled performance as the next person who may not even be gorgeous or famous.

"You be nice to Nadine, bro, because remember this, I am very protective of my congregants," Grenville said as I was leaving.

"What is that supposed to mean?" I said, trying to sound offended.

"It means what it means," he said, and there was this really weird look on his face.

"Is there something I don't know? Is she dying of cancer or on the lam from the Cosa Nostra? You getting a thing for her? What?"

"Just remember what I said."

"Sometimes you can be a real wicked witch of the west, you know that?" Saying that used to piss him off in the old days. I didn't say it but once or twice back then because I knew I'd get a good ass-whooping from him. Now he just laughed it off.

I got to the bar and annexed a stool, and when I ordered a root beer I was told by the mixmaster, who was the same guy from the last time I was there, that he didn't stock root beer. I was about to defend my choice as a very popular and delicious drink when he turned back to me from the TV set and said that no cocktails he was familiar with contained root beer and, thus, he didn't have any. As a professional and experienced private investigator, I was fully accepting of his description because he was also a professional and experienced craftsman of his trade and would know what beverages to stock and what not to stock. I had to applaud that. I didn't in actuality. Giving a round of applause to a bartender in a bar for telling me to order another drink would have drawn unwarranted attention.

The bartender turned back to the TV after he delivered my second choice. On it was a reporter, quite a pretty girl herself, but not in Nadine Berry's league by any shot. This blonde was dramatically telling viewers that a street demonstration had blocked traffic in the financial district, disrupting workers trying to get home by car and public transport. The demonstrators were demanding more equality for everyone and everything. San Francisco!

"Say, why not flip it over to KSFG," I said to the bartender, "they do a real good job covering local news."

"Nah, they'll probably have that dyke on there showing her true colors."

"Dyke?"

"Yeah, that Nadine Berry. That blonde bimbo. She comes in here. I can't stand her."

"Because she's a dyke?"

"Well, yeah, sure."

"How'd you figure she's a dyke?"

"Oh, I can tell, and people talk."

"You aren't from San Francisco, are you?"

"Huh, what, no, I moved here from Houston. You been to Texas?"

"No, I couldn't get a visa. My IQ is above eighty." I got a real strange look from the guy. Now I was extra glad I didn't applaud him earlier. I turned and put my back to the television – and the dickhead barman – and watched the bar slowly fill.

Uh-oh, here came Xerxes. Shit. He'll see me. His head was cocked to one side so he could see where he was heading, still operating with only one functioning eye. He got to the bar without colliding with anybody or any tables and took a stool two over from me. I rotated slowly to give him no more than my profile. He ordered a Manhattan, which the bartender provided, not having to say he didn't carry all the ingredients. The jerk. Xerxes looked up at the TV, head sideways with the good eye aimed forward.

"Loog at her and dat fat dose of hers," he said to nobody in particular, his critical eye – one eye – assessing the competition.

I couldn't resist. "You don't think she's good looking?" I said staring at the TV.

"Do. Loog at her. She's got bwonde hair, bud I bed her roods are bwon."

"Are you okay? You got a cold or something?"

"Do, I rad indo a door and busted by dose."

"Sorry to hear that."

"Yeah, whadever." A moment later Nadine walked in. I could tell because the normal buzzing in the bar shifted noticeably. Xerxes and I turned to look. Well, I looked, he looged. Xerxes waved at her and she somewhat reluctantly headed over. The stool between Xerxes and me was unspoken for and that meant the beauty would sit down next to me.

Didn't happen. Xerxes jumped off his stool and onto the one next to me. Miss Berry sat down and ordered a ginger ale. The bartender didn't say a word to her. Xerxes pointed at his Manhattan as if to say hit him again. The ginger ale came along with his drink, and Xerxes said put both on his tab. Miss Berry winced. The bartender scoffed.

Miss Berry and Xerxes traded small talk. She on news and TV topics, he with real small tog that matched his broken dose and his intellectual altitude. Interspersed were some of the most idiotic advances a bar has ever heard. Miss Berry on several occasions was heard to say,

"Xerxes, please, don't say that." When she finished her ginger ale, she said she would be back in a moment from the powder room. Xerxes motioned the bartender over and ordered another Manhattan and told the asshole barkeep to bring the lady a ginger ale and vodka. What he said was, "a giger ale and bodka."

I leaned into him without turning my head and said, "That's a beautiful woman."

"So whad," he sneered.

"Oh, I just think it's too bad about her."

"Whad's too bad?"

"Oh, come on. I overheard you talking. You're in the news business. You have to know."

"Do whad?"

"Her and her story, come on, don't kid a kidder."

"I dode do whad you're togging aboud."

"Look, everybody knows she's been trying to get past that ugly event in her life."

"Huh?"

"Okay, I'll pretend you don't know and play along with you." I had my hand up against my face so he couldn't easily recognize me. The bartender set down the two drinks. I said, "A few years ago – how long you been with your station here (he said two years) – about three years ago before you got here, some dude got real pushy with her and she snapped. Went all postal on him. Said it was self-defense, but you know how that goes. He just kept hitting on her and worse until she got him where she could do some harm."

"Harb?"

"Yeah, get this, now he's not able to sire children (Xerxes' head snapped up sideways), but the good thing is he can sing soprano in the company choir."

Xerxes swallowed his drink in a couple of gulps, tossed some money on the bar and, head cocked to one side, aimed his way out of the bar.

Miss Berry was back and sat on her stool looking at the empty one next to her. The bartender sidled over and looked at her then at me. "I don't think that yarn of yours was true," he said smugly.

"Nobody asked you what you think."

"I can have an opinion."

"Good, then get one that isn't horse shit," I scoffed.

"Mister, I got a good mind to run your ass outa here."

"If you had a good mind, you wouldn't be from Texas."

"Okay, that's it, I'm coming around there and..."

"If you come around here," I said, "I'll announce to your patrons in the bar how you view the gay and lesbian lifestyle. As this is San Francisco, I am willing to lay down my one hundred bucks to your five that one or more of these folks will tear you a new orifice."

After a short contemplation, he said, "Aw," and moved down the bar.

Miss Berry had been watching this. She reached for her drink.

"Don't drink that," I said.

"It looks like it's paid for," she claimed.

"Your boyfriend, before he remembered he had an engagement someplace else, ordered your ginger ale with a potion of vodka. He called it bodka, by the way."

"He's not my boyfriend, Basil, and I think you knew that."

My heart went skyrocketing and my inner me started shouting, "She knows my name, she knows my name."

"How do you know my name?"

"Grenville told me."

"Grenville told you? When did Grenville tell you?"

"When he recommended that I see you to do the investigation work for me. I told you I go to his church. We're friends. He thought you could help me. He seems to like you."

"Ha, he has to, since he's my brother."

Neither of us saw him coming when a guy about six feet five and about two hundred fifty pounds put together like a heavyweight boxing champion sat down on the stool between us, his back to me, facing Miss Berry.

"Hi, gorgeous," he said. "I've seen you on TV."

Without missing a beat, Miss Berry said, "The man sitting behind you I am interviewing for a segment on our station's True Killers program. He is a homicidal maniac. Tonight he's on his medication, only I don't know if the pills will be enough. He is armed and he might just shoot you in the back as not. You see, I get the feeling from him that he doesn't like interruptions. You are an interruption." Without looking at me, the giant rose and edged away.

The bartender had been listening. He said, "You're armed, huh? Well, I'm going to call the police and see your sorry butt go right to jail. What do you think of that, you loser?"

Miss Berry sighed. To him she said, "Take this drink away and bring me a ginger ale, ginger ale only. While you're doing that (and here she pulled out her phone) I'm going to call our Hot Scene correspondent who likes to rate restaurants and bars around town. I'll tell her about the drug dealing in the powder rooms here, the watered-down drinks you serve, the lax carding you do, and the amateur bartender who looks a lot like you. Then after you've done what you're supposed to do about my drink and you come around to check to see if this man is armed, I'll call 9-1-1 and have an ambulance standing by to take you to the emergency ward." We got the idea that the bartender got it. The it being to close his flap. He walked down the bar in a snit and in a short time was back dutifully setting down a ginger ale.

"Miss Berry," I said, "I am quite convinced that if that gentleman came out here to pat me down for a gun, he'd have had to go to the emergency ward not from anything I might have done but for what you could do."

"As we like to say, don't mess with Texas."

"You're from Texas?" She smiled her answer. "So is he," I pointed.

"From Houston, am I right?" she said. I laughed. "If I am going to call you Basil, you are going to have to call me Nadine." My heart did that skyrocketing thing again. I get to call my lesbian buddy and my client by her first name, I silently shouted.

The envelope with the evidence discs I owed Nadine was on the bar top this whole time. I pushed it over towards her. She moved to the stool next to mine to retrieve it. She said thank you and put it in a valise she carried. My assignment for Nadine Berry was over. She said she was grateful for my work. We talked for a while. Then she said, "You clocked Xerxes pretty good with just two punches the other night...and you being so drunk at the time. That's very impressive."

I didn't know what to say. You know how some guys, well, most guys, can be ignoramuses? Yeah, well, that was me. I fell in love with an avowed lesbian.

31

The gym was crowded with all the pre-work fanatics who like to get to their jobs, I assumed, sweating. None of my new friends trailed me there. I usually don't go this early. I patted the bird in my locker. Most of the machines out on the floor were busy, so I missed out on some of my favorites. It was a decent workout, not one of my best. The day was starting off iffy. Things improved when I got to the Favonius Tearoom, a pleasant place on Balboa Street offering a variety of good-for-you treats as well as decadent ones to go along with your hot drink of choice. I chose tea and decadence. Why not? I drove down Balboa and turned onto my street, got lucky finding a parking spot not too far from home and walked toward my building. Out front, parked quite illegally, almost desperately, was one of those trucks you hire to do your moving on the cheap. Wonder who, I wondered. Half way up the stairway to my second floor paradise, I was nearly run over by a file cabinet belted on a dolly.

"Hey!" I offered as advice regarding courtesy.

"Get out the way," a voice behind the cabinet hollered. Bevalaqua's voice. Clump, clump, clump down the stairs he went.

"Bevalaqua," I exclaimed out of habit.

"Look out, Beault."

"Whatchya doin, Bevalaqua?"

"This is all your fault, Beault. I wouldn't have to move if it wasn't for you and your criminal cronies. Look out!"

"You're moving?" I asked all innocent like. "Where?"

"Tell you? No way, no fucking way. I don't need you and those assholes around me anymore."

Down the stairs and out the door he went. It appeared out of my life also. Bye-bye, you horse's ass. For the next half hour I heard scraping and fumbling along the hallway finally giving way to quiet. I listened. It *was* quiet. Ah, the bliss of it. The horse's ass. Just to show you how precisely nice a person I am, I did not call the police and report the illegally parked truck to have them tow it away. I thought about it, but you know me, I wouldn't kick most guys when they were down. If anybody was down, it was that horse's ass.

My day did start off iffy with that average workout at the gym, got better from the treats at the tearoom, and struck gold when Bevalaqua trucked his life out of my life. Ahead were the chores even lesser private eyes than I had to do. So I did my laundry and went shopping. I refilled my pantry and frig and tossed my keys next to the phone on my desk, which rang. I answered it. The phone, not the desk.

"Professor Pym, how nice to hear from you." Archimedes Pym, Emily's colleague at the college and the expert on the bird statue branch of study whose call reminded me I was still in the thick of a conundrum.

"Can we talk safely, Mr. Beault?"

"Sure, what about?"

"Your phone is not tapped, is it?"

"Tapped? What are you suggesting?" Where was this going?

"I don't want our conversation overheard by anyone."

"This is starting to sound scary. What's up? Oh, and yeah, my phone is not bugged. I have a gadget that scans for that type of thing. I just swept it yesterday. I love doing that."

"Good then. I don't want to alarm you (too late for that, pal) when I tell you that I have had two very unexpected inquiries about the statue you hold."

"That's strange."

"In some ways, yes, but remember that I have a reputation in the field. The inquiries were odd in one way and that was the interest of the two callers was toward the statue's whereabouts rather than in its fame and dubious value."

"Uh-oh. Dang. Well, I suppose I have to ask who called you."

"Neither identified himself or herself."

"A man and a woman?"

"Yes."

"Double dang."

"I was put off guard by the calls, Mr. Beault. To repeat, they were most unexpected. I fear I did not convince either of them that I had no knowledge of where the statue is."

"Oh my."

"Not that I revealed anything, you understand."

"Okay."

"However..."

"However what?"

"I am of the opinion that you should move the statue. You can't be sure that some slip of the lip might not lead to the wrong person getting his hands on it. I say that with a twinge of envy. A relic of the ilk you have belongs in the right hands, Mr. Beault."

"You make a lot of sense, Professor. I guess I oughta move it."

"Yes, well, maybe."

"Maybe?"

"What I mean is that if these ruffians suspect that you have it, and Emily tells me that's the appearance of things, then perhaps one or more of them might follow you and intercept you with the statue."

"You are absolutely on target, Professor. You should have been a detective."

"Oh, mercy, my life is in the academy, Mr. Beault, not on the mean streets."

"Well, thank you for this information and for the excellent counsel."

"It's the least I can do after my naïve deportment on these two phone calls."

"Don't beat yourself up over it, Professor."

"You are too kind." And the famous San Francisco shamus, Mr. Jaguar Beault, headed back to the mean streets. Where'd Pym come up with that one? Reading the old pulp fiction, was he?

I did not look at this next decision with any relish. Be that as it may, it had to be done, so...*twas well twere done quickly* to paraphrase some

163

poet or other. I drove to the college and waited outside Emily's office. I knew she wasn't in there because I knocked. Twice. I also did not stand near the glass in her door so that if she was in there she could simply ignore me. I saw her when she was coming down the hall. My God, I thought, she's killed someone. She was holding a skull. No, not a homicide. She's an anthropologist. She uses it as a prop in class, I surmised. If I looked closely, however, I am sure I would have found my name scratched into it.

"You here again." A statement of obvious fact and no warmth from my old flame. Before I had a chance to greet her, she went on. "Don't make a habit of it."

I moved straight to the business at hand, careful to keep a safe distance from her right hand and to ignore that creepy skull. "I need your help."

Nothing. She unlocked her door and went in. I followed, keeping that halo of safe distance from her.

"I think you'll like my plan." Nothing. She dropped her books and checked her phone recorder. "I want you to take the Madagascar Pigeon and hold onto it for safe keeping."

This stopped her. She looked at me. "No."

"But why not?"

"Because it's you, you dickhead."

"Emily, there's already three dead guys and if I'm next, well, I'd want you to have this thing."

"Tell me why you want me to take it. Isn't it safe in your locker?"

"Yeah, until somebody puts a .32 behind my ear. Then when my gym membership runs out from lack of dues paid, some twenty-year-old part-time employee gets assigned to break into the locker to clean it out where he finds an ugly statue which he tosses in the trash or gives to his aged grandmother who donates it to her church's monthly rummage sale..." I stopped. "Mentioning the possibility of a .32 behind my ear didn't really upset you, did it?" No answer. Then I told her about Professor Pym's call and the counsel he gave me.

"Okay, I'll take it. If it's to be in anybody's hands, it should be in mine."

"Okay? Oh, good, swell, that's great."

"Give it to me."

"I don't have it with me. That's too dangerous. I'll tell you how to get it. No one else will know, and the damn thing will be in a safe place of your choosing."

"Tell me."

"It's in my locker at my gym, like I told you. You can go over there and get it. Put it in a gym bag and no one will be the wiser."

"Just walk into the men's shower and steal something?" she said.

"Yeah, no, oh, I..."

"I'll do it. Give me the key to the lock."

"There is no key. It's a combination lock. Do you want to know the numbers?" I asked with a smile.

"Of course, unless I should stand there and try every permutation."

"Try every what?"

"Permu...oh, too big a word for you. Sorry. Just tell me what it is."

"It's 38-23-34."

"That sounds, that's...those are my measurements!"

"I know. That's how I remember the combination. I couldn't forget that."

"Get the hell out of my office before I put you on the floor."

"Thanks for your help," I said over my shoulder as I hurried away from her and into the hall beyond the range of a solar plexus attack. I walked to my car with my head up high, not bent over from the effects of a punched-on mid-section. Score one for the private eye.

32

My chariot needed a refilling of fuel, which I accomplished south of the park in a gas station I have been going to for years. A creature of habit, I am. Besides, the mechanic there has performed miracles on my car for ages. I pulled out and headed west, turned north up to Lincoln Way and turned west again. I'd go to Great Highway, turn right – or north – and be on the road to my date with Mrs. Smith at the Beach Chalet. I had given it some thought and could not arrive at why she wanted to see me. It hadn't been a thing where sparks flew between us. She didn't need my detective services. She had old Ping Bodie who seemed to be perfectly acceptable to her. She wasn't going to ask me to whack her husband. That was his *modus operandi*.

So what was... Kaboom! Pop! Pow! Holy crap, somebody's shooting at me. What in hell. Boom! Boom! I looked in my mirror and saw a fancy sedan about six or eight car lengths back. An arm out the driver's window with a gun. Had to be a semi-automatic. I was just at the light at Great Highway and I snapped a quick right turn. The sedan slowed, then turned left. Holy crap. The sun had dropped below the water's horizon out on the Pacific making it hard for me to get a clear sense for the attacking car, its type, its color, its driver. Only a fleeting glimpse. What the hell. I floored my poor tired car and sped on north to the restaurant looking in my mirror where I saw a few cars but not the sedan. Holy crap. I parked my car, jumped out, looked all around and ran into the Beach Chalet. I went straight to the men's room downstairs and took a leak, checking to make sure I hadn't wet myself all over my pants. Holy shit. I walked upstairs to see if Mrs. Smith had arrived. The same bartender was on duty, and when he saw me, he tipped a hat he wasn't wearing. Whatever. I saw the table and Mrs. Smith smiled in my general direction.

"You were shot, oh my," she said when I blurted out what happened.

"Shot at," I clarified, "I wasn't hurt."

"Oh my heavens." A lotta good that does. "Did you see who did it?"

"No, not really. Just a big sedan or something."

"Oh my stars." That was no better. The waitress came by and I ordered a ginger ale. If a ginger ale is good enough for Nadine Berry, one is good enough for Jaguar Beault. Or even for Basil Protherington.

"Do you think he followed you here?"

"I hope not. He turned the other way out on the highway. I didn't see him coming this way. I don't think he'd try anything here." Holy crap, I did not add.

"You need a real drink, Mr. Beault, to settle your nerves. Let me order you a Hennessey."

"Good lord, no. That would knock me on my a.. on my backside. Besides, I've sworn off Hennessey for reasons you will remember and appreciate."

"I do remember."

My mind was not on what drink to drink, rather on why anyone would want to shoot me. Like I didn't know the answer to that. That damn pigeon.

"Did you say a dark sedan?" she asked.

"Sedan, dark, light, I don't know. Yeah, probably dark."

"My husband drives a dark sedan. A Cadillac."

"Holy crap." This time out loud. "Are you telling me your husband is out to get me? What the hell for?"

"Actually, he's probably out to get you scared. To frighten you into letting go of the Madagascar Pigeon. To him."

"I thought he told me he didn't own a gun."

"He doesn't own a gun, Mr. Beault, he owns many guns. All different. He's got a fixation. Our house is full of them." Oh great. A fixation on shooting me because I did not shoot her? Aren't I the lucky one?

A funny look fell on Mrs. Smith's face as she looked up past me. I turned and stared up, way up into The Pole's narrow head.

"Just what I needed," I sighed, "another precinct reporting in."

The Pole's minion was standing behind him, and Ms. Wu, looking typically enigmatic, meaning murderous, was off a little to the side. "You seemed to have escaped the assassin, Mr. Beault. How fortunate for you," The Pole said.

"You saw that? Did you see who it was? Where in hell were you?" I asked excitedly.

"I was behind you, behind him as well. No, I did not recognize him. You are lucky he is not a sure shot."

"Maybe."

"Maybe? No, I think you are very lucky."

"What I mean is he may not have been shooting to kill me but to warn me. You know, like all those threats that have been made to me lately. From people like you."

"State your business, mister, and then get out of here," Mrs. Smith said coldly.

The Pole looked at her then at me. Ms. Wu edged in closer. The minion barely moved, which looked as though it would have to be an athletic feat for him. The Pole started into his tired old refrain about the Madagascar Pigeon.

Then we all heard the unmistakable sound of a shell being pumped into the chamber of a shotgun. We all looked. The bartender, my new best friend, said, "The lady and the gentleman are about to dine. Alone. Move it on out of here." My new very best friend.

"We'll only be a moment longer," The Pole argued. Then we all heard the unmistakable sound of a shell being pumped into the chamber of a shotgun. We all looked. Ping Bodie out from a shadow.

"You won't last long enough to spend that moment," Bodie rasped. The Pole bowed slightly, rotated around his skinny axis and led the other two out. Bodie slipped back into a shadow and the bartender went back to his post.

"It's a dangerous game you play as a private eye, Mr. Beault," Mrs. Smith told me.

"All in a day's work," I said to her, grateful that I hadn't browned my britches.

We ordered dinner and ate and talked about things I don't remember. I don't know what I ate either. Finally, I said, "You have me at a disadvantage, Mrs. Smith. You seem to know why we are here tonight having dinner under such entertaining circumstances, but I don't. Are you ready to tell me now?"

"Very well. Do you recall when my husband entered a conspiracy with Clint Westwood to obtain the Madagascar Pigeon?"

"Yes."

"Then how he tried to coerce you into the same conspiracy?"

"Yes."

"Does it trouble you that whereas at the start he was prepared to obtain the statue for himself alone but decided he needed Mr. Westwood to help, which would reduce the payout from any profits in the matter perhaps by half, then to ask you to join in the bargain and thus further reduce the expected profits and then to learn that poor Mr. Westwood met an untimely end and you yourself were a target only this evening?"

She said all that without hardly taking a breath.

"Does it trouble me?" I repeated. "Well, it sure as hell does now," I admitted.

She held up her hand, raised a finger and said, "One, my husband. Two," another finger came up, "Mr. Westwood. Three," another finger went up, "Mr. Beault." Then, dramatically, she lowered one finger, "Mr. Westwood." She lowered another finger, "Mr. Beault." Only one finger remained up. I thought about that. Holy crap.

"You are saying your husband is the killer."

"I am saying follow the clues, Mr. Detective."

"You know, don't you, he suspects you?"

"Oh, that's nothing. He suspects me of everything."

My date with Mrs. Smith is not likely to be inducted into the Romance Hall of Fame, not that I had any designs or expectations along that line. Nor, I concluded, did she. On my way out, I tipped the hat I wasn't wearing to the bartender. He did the same back to me. My new best friend. Mrs. Smith, I presumed, left with Mr. Bodie.

I got all the way home and nobody shot at me, nobody threatened me, nobody, I was pretty sure, followed me. I locked the door and made a mental note to get another deadbolt installed. It's not a shotgun, but it can't hurt. My phone message light was blinking. I poured myself a glass of milk and pushed the button.

Message One: Oh, yeah, uh...oh, okay. Well, shit, Mr. Investigations. God, my dad almost heard me talking to you. That woulda been one big scream, right? He woulda turned purple. You haven't called me. This is Crystal calling. Call me, you dreamy man. Beep.

Message Two: Call me, you big shithead. Beep. (Emily.)

Message Three: I coulda killed you, Beault, with those shots tonight. Next time I will if you don't take them as a warning to lay off Phyllis Gunn and Lavernia Lavender. Or just Phyllis...and Lavernia. She wants the statue you have...oh, don't try to tell me you don't have it. Everyone this side of East Asia knows you do. It's hers...theirs. I have a special interest in it...in making sure the statue is put into my...the rightful hands. You better get smart, Beault. I'll be in touch. You're in my crosshairs. Beep.

Message Four: This is Phyllis Gunn, Mr. Beault. Here is my new phone number. (I didn't write it down.) Beep.

End of messages.

I looked at the clock and said no way would I call Emily at this hour. She'd go off on me in ways I did not want to think about. I also decided it could wait until morning to give Grenville a report on my evening. And there was unequivocally no way I would dial up Crystal. That girl needs a hormone-ectomy

33

What a night last night was. Target practice on my car, The Pole looking meaner than ever, shotguns left and right, Mrs. Smith telling me Mr. Smith, in her estimation, is the leading suspect in a series of homicides. That, of course, was contrary to the view held by Mr. Smith that Mrs. Smith, herself, was the murderess. Just the sort of case a private eye could sink his teeth into for the flavor of the adventure and excitement his – or her – profession brings. But if I asked you to name how much money I should be getting for all the adventure and excitement compared with the fifty dollars I got from Miss Gunn, what would you say? That is, what would you say after you laughed at me for an hour. Fifty dollars! Apparently, James Bond I'm not. He gets a handsome paycheck from the Royal Treasury and he gets the girls, while I get fifty lousy dollars and shot at. Holy crap.

I just talked myself into a sweet roll and a cup of tea. My phone calls would have to wait.

Out the door, down the hall, down the stairs, onto the sidewalk, down the street, around the corner to Favonius because sweets were in order. I leaned down to look into the glass display counter considering the virtues of the pleasing variety of doughnuts, Danishes, scones, brownies...when a strange shadow edged over the glass. Long and narrow. The Pole. I straightened and looked up, way up.

"You don't have your friends to protect you this morning, Beault, like you did last night. We have something to do. The Madagascar Pigeon. I want it. Where is it?" He was not being discreet. He was hot under his way-up-there collar. His minion was, as usual, just behind The Pole and just to the side. It was as if he was always ready to catch his unusually shaped mentor in case The Pole, losing his grip on per-pendicularity, tipped over. Ms. Wu, a few steps back and a few steps to the side, today was wearing an even more enigmatic look than I had seen before. I could tell that something was on their minds and their appearance here was telegraphing trouble.

"You are going to cough it up, Beault," The Pole proclaimed.

Then we heard the unmistakable sound of a shell being pumped into the chamber of a shotgun. You don't hear that sound and have the first thing to come to your mind be, "Oh, gee, I've won the lottery." Nor do you hear that sound for the third time in the past 12 hours and then tell yourself that life is an ocean cruise of relaxation and stops at exotic ports of call.

The entire clientele of Favonius put down coffee cups and forks and newspapers and looked up from laptops and iPads to where the sound came from. It was...where...over there where Mr. Hui was aim-ing his weapon at The Pole and his two frozen associates. In a string of Chinese, he seemed to offer his opinion on the inadvisability of the presence of the three people causing a scene in his establishment. A very unwelcome presence if the look on Ms. Wu's face was telling an accurate translation. She pulled her hands free from her pockets and whispered something to The Pole. Minion, who looks to have excellent hearing, spun around without falling and was out the door of Favonius. The Pole nodded to Ms. Wu and the two of them made a non-stop exit of their own. Mr. Hui muttered a comment to the departing trio and uncocked his shotgun.

"Motherfuckers not come to my shop and push that shit," he said.

"I think you mean pull that shit," I corrected him.

"Okay, Beaurt, I no good at English." That's how he pronounces my name.

"You're pretty good with a shotgun," I complimented him. He bowed slightly and went back behind his cash register. Mr. Hui's clientele went back, too, to their coffees, sweet rolls, newspapers and computers as if the floorshow was over. San Francisco, you just have to love it. I took my nourishment in the café, thinking The Pole was coming to the conclu-sion that everybody in the city packed a scattergun.

I walked home and no one cornered me or blocked my entry into my own place. The bad guys must be holding a conclave somewhere else. I called Grenville and told him about all the cool things that had been happening to me.

"I thought I warned you to be careful," he said when I was finished. That was true enough. He did warn me.

"I'll try harder the next time I'm at the trailing edge of a fusillade."

"No joke, Bas, this doesn't sound good. You need protection."

"Protection? Like a bodyguard?"

"Why not?"

"I can see how that would go over at the next scheduled coffee klatch for all the private eyes in San Francisco when someone blurts out about Jaguar Beault, the private eye, hiring a private eye to, well, protect him. Grenville, the humiliation."

"Basil, what about the humiliation of your picture on the Internet or on television with somebody announcing that a local private eye was transformed into a slab of Swiss cheese?"

We talked a bit more about it and nothing got resolved even with two brilliant minds tilling the soil for an answer. With enormous self-control, Grenville didn't repeat the be-careful thing. I did tell him about Crystal and her phone messages. He laughed so hard I thought he was going to spit up.

"I didn't tell you this to make you laugh. Where'd you get your sick sense of humor?"

It wasn't a question, it was a zinger, or so I thought. He answered anyway, "From Pop."

Putting off my next chore any longer would be a failing of good common sense. Even in her best frames of mind, she took it for granted that Jaguar Beault was a hopeless moron. That's another one of those direct quotes from Emily. She even spoke of me like that to other people. As a college professor, with all the authority and experience she was wrapped in and an anthropologist to boot, these other people sucked up her opinion of me like the foam off the top of a caramel latte. I called Emily. After close to nearly a dozen rings she picked up.

"Yes!" Oh, good, yet another mood.

"It's Jaguar."

"No it's not."

"Yeah, it's me, Em."

"No, it's Basil (ugh), you fake."

"Okay, if you insi..."

"I told you to call me."

"I am calling you, that's what I'm doing right now."

"I didn't tell you to call me and then say whenever you feel like it."

"Geez, I was a little rattled last night when I heard your message. Someone shot at me."

"You hit?"

"No, I was..."

"Missed you, eh? Well, send whoever it was over here and I'll give him some pointers."

"Not funny. It's all because of the Madagascar Pigeon."

"That toy of yours, huh?"

"Yeah, did you have any problems at the gym? Anyone try to stop you?"

"Hell no. I just walked in like I said I would. There were six or eight guys in the shower. You know, Muscle Beach types, built pretty good, too."

"God, how embarrassing for you."

"For me? That's a scream. I wasn't embarrassed. You should have seen how those guys tried to disappear. You know what was funny, all those guys with every muscle group on their bodies big as all get out? Their wankers are real little. You know, tiny itty-bitty ding-dongs." This is from my friend Emily, the cultivated college prof. Wait, there's more from her. "How come," she went on, "they don't have one of those body-building machines to develop their dongs?"

"Jesus, Emily, the way you talk."

"What? I'm just saying. Big pecs and little peckers."

"Emily, where'd you learn that language, in a pool hall?"

"Oh, chill out, you wimp." That one hurt. I'm no wimp. I am one of the top two hundred and forty-seven private eyes in practice in the greater Bay Area. So there.

All I said was, "Well, that's done then. Thank you...and don't tell me where you put it."

"I can't put it anywhere. It wasn't there."

"What wasn't where?"

"The Madagascar Pigeon bird statue was not in the Basil locker at your gym."

"Come on, no kidding on this."

"I'm not kidding. I wasn't surprised, though, because I figured it wasn't beyond you to send me on a wild goose chase. You're such an asshole. Archimedes was furious."

"You're serious? You're telling me the statue was not in my locker? What in hell could...oh, crap, you took Pym with you? Why in hell for?"

"He's interested in the object. It's his field. I thought you knew that."

"Yeah, I knew that. I thought this was our secret."

"That's what you thought, did you? Guess what, you thought wrong. But don't worry, I haven't told anyone else."

"Where did it go? Who could have taken it? I mean, what is going on here? This is incredible. I'm up shit creek. It's the only thing standing between me and a bullet. Oh, shit. Emily, are you sure? You looked all through the locker?"

Because the answer was self-evident to Emily and then, after a second, to me, too, she decided not to answer.

"Sorry," I said, "I'm just panicking."

"You're not going to cry, are you? If you're going to cry, I'm going to hang up." Her and her tender side.

"Hold on," I said, "did you see any evidence of who might have taken it, how it got out of the locker? This doesn't make any sense."

"What, like fingerprints?" I stopped myself from saying yes. "I didn't have my dusting kit with me, Mr. Private Eye who is in the business of solving mysteries like this one. Archimedes said it might have been an inside job. Someone connected to the gym. You got any enemies over there? Somebody jealous of your dick whose got an even smaller one than yours?"

177

"Emily Birch-Aspen, you are unrelenting, you know that? And, no, I have no enemies over there. Shoot, they all think I'm just right for the place. I'm the gym's poster child for Before.

"I gotta go," she said with a click ending the call.

34

This called for action. I had been shot at, my car full of bullet holes, testimony to a determined new jerk in my life. I had been threatened yet again. I had been burgled and the Madagascar Pigeon was now a goner. I had several options. One...oh, never mind. My best option was to move to some backwoods up in Idaho or someplace. No forwarding address. That option was full of inarguable logic and an extraordinary display of maturity. It would, however, take a coward to choose that way out. I couldn't do it. The real reason is that I just didn't have enough capital to relocate. It's expensive. So I did what I always do when I want to make it look as though I'm fairly smart. I jumped in my car with its new free-form airflow modifications and headed towards Grenville's church. That's after I checked to make sure The Pole and his, his...what are those two people who hang around him? They weird me out...to make sure they weren't lurking in some hiding place ready to leap out at me with guns drawn.

Heading east on Fulton on the north perimeter of the park, I could see the spires of St. Ignatius Catholic Church up at the University of San Francisco. One of the city's terrific sights. Then...whoop, whoop, whoop, wee, wee, wee...and red lights. The cops. What did I do? I didn't do anything. My seat belt was on, I wasn't texting, I ran no stop signs. Maybe one of those shots got a brake light. I pulled over. From the police unit's loud speaker: "Get out of the car with your hands up." I did. "Face down on the pavement." I did. "Hands stretched out away from your sides." I did. "Spread your legs." I did.

"Beault, you are the sorriest sack of shit this side of the Rocky Mountains." Blough. "Get up, you dork." I did. "See, Mr. Private

Detective, we at the San Francisco Police Department do have a highly developed sense of humor. See all those good citizens watching us? They got a good laugh out of this. Our little dividend to the taxpayers." All this was over his unit's speaker.

"Glad I could participate, lieutenant. Am I free to go now that our pantomime is ended?" I asked when we were all on our feet.

"No, I got some questions."

"Shoot."

"That's a good one. In fact it's my first question. Did you see who shot you last night?"

"No, it was too dark. How did you know what went down?"

"I'm a real cop, Beault, we get results. So why do you figure you got shot at?"

"It was a warning. I got a phone message says I gotta give up the statue everybody has been bugging me about. I wish I had the thing. If I did I'd put it on eBay and sell it to the highest bidder. Hell, I'd sell it to the lowest bidder if it meant getting it out of my life."

"Who was it?"

"He didn't leave a name. It's a new player in this pile of shit."

"You been lyin all along, haven't you? I bet you have the thing socked away someplace. Judging from last night it's going to turn out to be the death of you, Beault." He said it without any tinge of regret. San Francisco Police Department Homicide Detective Lieutenant Blough, in all his officialdom, asked me some more questions, and I answered them all with the truth, except about the statue. When we were done, he told me to leave. "Oh," he said, and I thought he might be ready to say something like "be careful," but all I got was, "if you are gonna get shot at again, do it outside the county."

Heading south on Castro in the neighborhood where Grenville's church is located, you don't see tall spires on his church like you do when you see St. Ignatius at USF. I quickly concluded that two different architects had been at work here.

Usually quick with a joke, Grenville was subdued when I pulled into the parking lot next to his church. He came out and easily saw the damage done by the bullets.

"You might have been killed."

"He claims they were warning shots. If he's that good then when he doesn't want to miss me, he won't."

"He wants the statue?"

"That's the message he left me." Inside the church, I told him what Emily said. Not about the small wankers on the guys in the gym, but how the statue was missing from my locker. "You don't seem surprised," I said.

"What, oh, yeah, no, I am surprised. I was just thinking that this could be a good thing. Sooner or later Lieutenant Blough is going to show up with a search warrant. When he opens your locker he won't find what he believes you have had all along."

"But without it, do I still have any leverage over this crowd of scum who've been badgering me to give it up?"

"They don't know it's missing, do they? They'll still believe you have it. So the only ones who know it's gone are you and me and Emily."

"And Professor Pym."

"Who?"

"Emily's colleague at the college. Archimedes Pym. Didn't I tell you about him? He is some sort of expert in this ceramic antiquities field. A peculiar sort."

"How did he get involved?"

"Emily clued him in when I first told her that I had the statue. She said he knows a lot on the subject. Seemed harmless enough to me at the time."

"He'll be harmless enough if he keeps his mouth shut."

We chattered on and then I took him to lunch. Try as we did, we couldn't unscramble who the new character in this mystery was. The one who shot at me. Husband? Lover? Accomplice? Psychiatrist? Pen Pal? Haberdasher? We got nowhere.

We were walking back from the lunch counter where we ate when Grenville asked, "So what's with the statue of the pigeon, it's full of jewels and gems and such?"

"Naw. That's what the legends are all about if you want to believe them. Professor Pym throws cold water on that, but I guess the only way to find out is to open the bally thing. And now I don't even have it."

"Did you try opening it when you heard it might be full of jewels?"

"I looked it over and couldn't see any way to do it."

"I have guys here at the church who could fiddle with it. Not that my church-goers are criminals, you understand."

"That's a great idea. Oh, time out, we don't have the pigeon, do we?" I said full of bitterness.

"Well, yes, that's right. I meant if we did have it."

"We? What, are you bucking to become a private eye?"

"No," he laughed, "just trying to be helpful. I'll leave the detecting to you."

"That's smart because your calling is a lot safer. Nobody is likely to strafe your car with you in it because your Sunday sermon disappointed one of your gun-toting congregants."

"I hope you're right. No gunfire, but my collection plates would be lighter after that disappointing sermon you refer to." We both laughed about that knowing it was not true. The people Grenville served in his church were very generous with him.

I went a little out of my way home so I could ask a few questions at my gym regarding an item missing from my locker. I got no useful answers. The manager was shocked and apologetic, but he added that it was unbelievable that anyone on his staff would do such a thing. I wasn't making an accusation since I had no evidence and only a slight suspicion. The manager said there had been reports of a woman skulking around the men's locker recently. He couldn't account for it except as rumor.

Thus it was back to Emily and Grenville, the only ones who knew where I had hidden it. Grenville did not have to steal it from me. If he said he had reason to take it, he would have merely asked for it. Emily, on the other hand, would gladly steal from me just for the simple plea-sure in doing so. Still, I discounted that because she, too, would have asked me for it. If I had said no to her, she would have used the oppor-tunity to sock me in my solar plexus just to give her the simple pleasure she takes in that pugilistic moment. Then there was Pym. What's his story, I began to wonder.

35

I got no answers at the gym, just more questions. Keeping an eye out for anyone following behind me either to take me by the scruff of my neck or put bullet holes in my car, I headed home. Unaccompanied. When I opened my door I heard scraping. Someone had stuffed a thick envelope under the door. Letter bomb? No, too clean...I prayed. Then I saw it was from Severino Carlusconi, my favorite bail bondsman. He throws business my way, the kind of business I like least. Skiptracing, or bounty hunting. I do it because it is good money. My phone message light was blinking. Screw that, I'll get to you later. The envelope contained all the usual documents authorizing recovery of the bad guy who bombed out on his bail, including a photo of Pablo Pedro Perez and the names of his known associates and preferred hangouts.

Number one on the list of locations was The Top of the Bottom, a sleaze joint in the Hunter's Point area. Senor Perez was listed as five feet nine inches, two hundred sixty pounds. He has already spent a third of his life as a tenant in state-run accommodations, which means he's pumped iron for close to ten years. Oh, goody, an easy one, eh, Beault? But the money is good. I hope it covers a possible broken jaw. Never fear, I thought, because I remembered something that is ripe for this one.

"Grenville, Bas."

"Hi."

"Remember about two years ago I had to collect that bail skipper and you and some of the boys lent a helping hand? Our charade? Worked like a charm? Piece of cake? Skated on ice?"

"Do you want me to answer or do you have more clichés?"

"I was really going there. Anyway, I'm sure you remember. I got another one."

"Okay."

"I was thinking next Thursday night. I want to stop shaving for a few days."

"Thursday afternoon is our basketball game. After that?"

"Perfect." We set it up. I think Grenville really likes doing this quasi-cop stuff.

The blinking light on the phone message machine demanded attention. As I reached down to push the button to start the replay, I said to myself I wish that someday I had the cajones to let it go, just leave the callers in a telecommunications limbo. Two counter arguments won the day for the phone, one, that if Emily had called and I ignored her, I'd be in for a flurry of right hands to my mid-section, and, two, if Miss Berry had called and I ignored her I would hang myself.

You have four new messages.

Message One: Basil, this is Nadine Berry. You must have the magic touch. My editor has been the paragon of nice. He's almost afraid of me. I can't imagine what you said or what you did. Are you willing to share that with me? Here's my cell number. (I wrote it down.) Beep.

Message Two: John Smith, Beault, and just a quick call to assure you I had nothing to do with that shooting. My wife told me all about it and how she implied it was a car like mine. No, sir, it was not me. Where does she come off trying to push the blame on me? What have I ever done to irritate her? Beep. (Well, you did try to hire an army of assassins to put her six feet under.)

Message Three: Hi, Basil, it's Miriam. I had an unusual visitor in my shop today. She asked about a pigeon statue. If you are going to be across the bridge anytime soon we can talk about it. Otherwise, you know my number. Beep.

Message Four: Shitall, Mr. Investigator, whyn't you never called me yet? I do all the calling. My friends say, Crystal, you got a boyfriend who won't call you, that's so...oh, fuck, my mom's here. Beep.

End of new messages.

She left me her cell number. The lesbian I'm in love with. Just another sailing of the shipwreck of my love life. I'll call her because that's the kind of guy I am, an amiable one, sociable-like. Nadine's good bud.

"Berry."

"Hi, Miss Berry, it's Jaguar Beault."

"Hello, Basil, thank you for calling."

"My pleasure."

"You heard my message, I guess, and you know your efforts for me are more than I hoped for."

"I'm glad for that."

"If it's not a trade secret, can you tell me how you managed it?"

"Let's see, what can I say? I kinda stretched some boundaries of the truth, said some things that got Xerxes attention. As I elaborated within my fictional scenario, his attention became undivided. I got the impression he acquired a new appreciation for your wiles."

"What did you do, did you threaten him?" she gushed.

"No, not exactly. I did hint that he could come to harm at the hands of somebody else."

"Me?"

"Yes, I told him you had a history of successfully resolving problems with aggravating men."

There was a pause. "Uh, Basil, has Grenville said anything to you?" she asked with a little angst in her voice.

"About what?"

"About me."

"Just that you have a real yo-yo for a boss and could I help."

There was silence for a bit before she said, "Well...okay. Then can I ask for details about you and Xerxes?"

"Now we would be getting into my trade secrets."

"You're a prince, Basil, and I owe you. I'll be sending a check to pay you as agreed. How about payment and a cup of coffee?"

"With me?"

"Yes, you."

"Well, sure, anytime." That was easy to agree to.

"Towards the end of the week, Thursday would be good for me. After work," she offered.

"Great. I'll...oh."

"Not good?"

"I'm working a case Thursday night. Picking up a guy who jumped bail."

"Sounds dangerous."

"Sometimes, but I've got some special assistance behind me."

"Basil, the bounty hunter."

"Not my favorite type of case, but it butters my bread."

"I just had a thought. Capturing a desperate guy would make for great television. Can I come along and cover it for the news?"

I was flabbergasted. My gast was flabbered. "I...uh...I...I don't know."

"Tell me how you are going to pull this off. I can plan around it."

I told her.

"Basil, this is priceless. I can see this going to the network, national. You'll be famous."

"If I don't get my teeth knocked out."

"Even better!"

"Wha..."

"Only kidding. I don't want that to happen. Besides, your plan has you covered."

"It had better. On the other hand, remember what Shakespeare said about plans going wrong."

"And Burns, too, who said they *gang aft agley*."

"Hmm?"

"I don't understand it either. Let's have that coffee before Thursday and get everything arranged. I'm excited about this," she said.

36

A date with a lesbian. You talk about plans ganging agley, huh? Well, you play the cards you're dealt. I drove across the Golden Gate Bridge, a thrill each time I do it, whether it was shrouded in our famous fog or if I was running across on a clear day. I found my way to Miriam's junk store in Sausalito. A lot had happened since she and I talked last – and gone upstairs – so I brought her up to date on my misadventures, my brushes with death, the crazies I was dealing with, the missing Madagascar Pigeon, everything. Then I listened as she described the shop visitor who asked about old statues, bird statues, and finally the Madagascar Pigeon in particular and where it could possibly be. She hadn't seen Pearl in a long time and had forgotten they were in the same line of work. Soon, she said, the light came on and she remembered.

"It was irritating the way she flitted around her real interest," Miriam said, "so I did the same, offering up no real help to her. She finally admitted that she had met you through this Mrs. Smith. Clearly, she was here as a surrogate for Mrs. Smith. You've got your hands full, Basil. I hope you are being sensible about this business."

"That's me all over, Miriam, Mr. Sensible."

"I'm serious, Basil, she...there was something foreboding in the way she phrased her questions and comments."

"I'm sorry you got involved with this."

"Don't worry about me, I can take care of myself. It's you I'll worry about. What's next? Do you plan to look for the statue?"

"I don't know where to start. I've got my eye on Professor Pym, but I'm not sure why. He's a puzzle."

"Well, be careful." That again. I got up to leave. Neither of us mentioned going upstairs.

"Tell me about the Berry woman."

"She's a newswoman at KSFG. I handled a problem for her. Grenville recommended me to her."

"Yes, I have seen her on the news. She's a beautiful girl, isn't she?"

"Oh, do you think so?"

"Don't get coy with me, Basil. You have a crush on her, don't you?"

"If I did, it wouldn't matter. She's a lesbian."

"Ah-ha," she snickered. "There you are and here I am, you, a confirmed hetero, in love with a lesbian and me, an in-training spinster, in love with a gay guy. We both drew the short end of the romance stick, my friend."

"Yeah," I agreed.

"Give my love to Grenville, won't you?"

"I always do."

"Basil, here, take your jacket." We laughed and hugged.

I cruised above California's Golden Gate on the fabulous bridge of the same name and made a quick right turn and then joined Lincoln Blvd. taking me through the Presidio toward home. A phalanx of fog floated over the Pacific Ocean frowning at the city with an intimidating stare. "Give us your best shot," I shouted. "We can take it."

Halfway up the street from my office-home, a car was just abandoning a parking spot. Bless the luck of the Protheringtons. I pulled up to take possession of the space only to see the car back in again and the driver turn off the engine. Expletive! That's not very civil, I determined. Five minutes later walking toward my address from the substitute parking spot, two people emerged from the car I had cursed. Hugo Blankenship and his wife, Lavernia Lavender. Where was that murky mountain of fog now when I could have hidden in it from these two loons? Luck of the Protheringtons, eh?

"We have business, Mr. Beault, let's go inside," Hugo told me. When I reached for my door key, I clicked on my recording gadget as usual in a circumstance like this.

"I'd offer you a drink or some coffee, but I'm not in the mood to be nice," I said to them.

"I hope you are in a mood to be cooperative," he retorted.

"Cooperate how?"

"I, we, we want the Madagascar Pigeon."

"Why?"

"Why, he asks," he said to Lavernia who stood there with a look on her face that said, "Duh."

"Because, Beault, it belongs to us."

"Do you have a document showing your ownership like people do with a deed to a home or a pink slip for an automobile?"

"Don't be disingenuous, Beault, we're in a hurry."

"I wouldn't be dis, uh, disingenuous. I don't even know what it means."

"Just hurry up, you ass."

"Haste makes waste, Hugo."

"And this gun makes holes, deadly holes, Jag-u-ar."

"Oh. I won't argue with you on that."

"Where is it?" Hugo pressed.

"It's in the trunk of my car, hiding in plain view from all of you perps who lay claim to it. Wait here and I'll go get it and be a better man for relinquishing it."

"Do you think that I am an idiot?" He stopped and considered something. "Give me the key and I'll get it. Verna, hold this gun on Mr. Beault until I return. If the statue is indeed in the trunk of Mr. Beault's car, we may let him live. If it is not, we will need to kill him."

Miss Lavender took the gun and pointed it at me. Blankenship left for my car with directions from me where it was parked. I sat down.

"Do me a favor and don't point that thing at me," I said to her.

"Screw you."

"No, what I mean is you may get an itch, and I don't want you to pull the trigger accidentally. I didn't put on my bulletproof vest today."

"Bulletproof vest? Do you really have one of those?"

"It's a figure of speech, Lavernia. I just want to be sure I don't get shot for no reason."

"I'll shoot you if there is a reason, you can count on that."

"Well, there you go," I said before adding, "he won't come back, you know."

"Yes he will."

"You know by now the statue holds a fortune in precious stones."

She smiled and asked, "What is your estimate at their value, just in round numbers, twenty-five, fifty thousand?"

"More than that, Lavernia." I could have said Phyllis.

"How much more...no, wait, how do you know?"

"I opened it and had the stones assayed. The number blew my mind."

"How much?"

"Just under a million." That was not a lie because I did not know the truth. It was just a joke. The real value is zero. A million sounded pretty good, though.

"A million? Oh, gad. A million."

"And those are a million reasons why your Mr. Blankenship will be long gone once he opens the trunk of my car. He strikes me as an enter-prising and free-thinking man. He's been so intent on getting his hands on the statue, I'm in the camp of those who believe he knows exactly how much those jewels are worth. Isn't he the one who uncovered the bird in China?"

"Shut up, you bastard. He will be back."

"Come to think of it, you are right. He will need your car. He sure won't take my old heap. Where will he go, I wonder. North to Canada. East to Reno. Loads of fences in Nevada to unload the jewels with all that gambling available. South to L.A.? No! South to Mexico. Does he speak Spanish?"

"Shut up, damn you."

"Sorry. Just making conversation while we wait. Let's see, my car is just two minutes away and he's been gone for what? Eight or ten?"

She swung the gun around and looked at the door. "If you like," I said, "we could go down and wait by your car – if it's still there."

"It's still...how far...where is your car parked?"

"As I said, only a moment or two away, just around the corner."

"What should we do?" A growing panic in her voice.

"One option is to wait here for the requisite seventy-two hours for a missing persons report to get the police looking for your husband. Except he would have a long head start that way. I think the best option is still the one where we go down and keep watch on his escape, I mean keep watch on your car. A million dollars is a lot of incentive to get out of Dodge."

"We'll go down to the car. No funny business, Mr. Beault, I have a gun."

"So I noticed. Let me put my jacket on. We're due for a foggy afternoon."

I put it on and turned up the collar. "You probably think I have a gun in this jacket. I don't. For your peace of mind and so you won't get trigger happy, pat me down like the police do so you know you can trust me."

I raised my arms. The moron did as I said.

"You fucking animal," she screamed at me as I grabbed her gun and twisted it from her hand. "You son of a bitch," yelling again.

"Keep quiet, please, or I will use this on you. Sit down!" She sat down and began sobbing. I refrained from laughing at her. In a moment Hugo came back and pushed the door open. He saw me sitting in a chair with my arms folded across my chest. My own gun was concealed. Miss Lavender was holding Hugo's now empty gun. Hugo looked pissed.

"You are in for it now, Beault. The statue..."

I raised my gun. "The statue was not there, is that what you were going to tell me? I know. I lied. I'm terrible that way."

"What in hell happened?" Hugo screamed at his Verna.

"He tricked me."

"He tricked you? You have a gun."

"It's not loaded."

"Of course, it's loaded. Do you think I would use an unloaded gun?"

"He unloaded it."

"How in hell did he unload it? Did you hand it to him?"

"Stow it, both of you," I interrupted. "Sit down, Hugo, and put my key on the table. We should talk."

"About what?"

"About..." is all I got out when Lavernia jumped in with, "He says the jewels in the pigeon are worth a million dollars, a million!"

Hugo's face flushed. "A million?" he said almost licking his lips.

"Is it my turn?" I asked, "Okay I'll say it, too. A million? There now we've all said it."

"Where'd you get that number, Beault?"

"He opened the statue and had the ice assayed. He just told me that," Lavernia answered.

"You don't assay ice, you nitwit, you assay ore. Shit! You had a gun on him. You're about as useless as that stupid twin of yours."

"Fuck you, Hugo."

"Fuck me? Fuck you."

"This is dreamy, everyone having such a good time. Tell me something, Blankenship, where did you plan to fence the jewels?"

"What difference does that make?"

"Humor me, please. Over in Nevada?" I looked at Miss Lavender and raised my eyebrows. "I hear it's easy to do." I raised my eyebrows at Lavernia again. No answer from Hugo. "And no state income tax. As if you'd pay taxes on the deal, eh?"

"Well?" Verna urged him.

"What? No, I don't even have the damn things. He's got them."

"You were going to take the statue and leave me, weren't you? You bastard." She threw Hugo's gun at him. He ducked just in time.

"I was not. We're a team." Miss Lavender, to my undying appreciation, stood up and flipped Hugo the bird, the one with her middle finger. It was a riot.

"So, Hugo, do you go to Nevada much?"

"My work has me traveling a lot. To lots of places."

"And Mrs. Blankenship, this half of the twins, she travels a lot, too, so you don't spend all your time together?"

"What's it to you?"

"I'm just curious. It's funny, though, how both of the twins seem to push their way into my life over this stupid statue, yet you don't see Miss Gunn, your own sister-in-law. That doesn't make any sense to me. Does it make sense to you?"

"It's how I, we, prefer it, Mr. Beault," Lavernia said, "Phyllis is not welcome in our lives. It is a personal family matter, which I do not want to discuss. Hugo feels the same way."

"Okay, Beault, it's your turn to answer a question. What do you plan to do with the statue and the million?"

"Ah, yes, the contraband. Well, there's no million."

"Not that much, is that it?"

"Haven't got a clue. Couldn't open the thing."

"You told me you opened it and..." Miss Lavender objected.

"I lied about that."

"But the jewels?"

"Same thing, no idea. An expert I know says there are no jewels. Only a stupid bird. I lied about all that. Been doing a lot of that lately. It's your fault, you know."

"Mine?" she said.

"Well, not you exactly, your, um, sister. Twin, isn't she? Ever since you, she, showed up here with that fiction about a trashy souvenir from East Asia, I've been exposed to lies from a platoon of liars. I got exposed to the germs and I caught the virus. Liar, liar, pants on fire. That's me."

Fog put siege to all that one could see, darkening the day and reminding me that I was up to here with these two fugitives from a loon circus.

"Time for you to get the hell out of my sight. I am done with you."

"There is still the matter of the Madagascar Pigeon, Beault. It belongs to Lavernia, to us. We want it."

"Phyllis Gunn tells me it belongs to her."

"She's a thieving liar!" Miss Lavender shouted. "She stole it from me."

"Hugo, Hugo, Hugo, please explain how that could be. I'd love to unravel that tale."

"I wasn't a part of any of it. I only know it's Lavernia's, ours, and it's only fair that you give it to us."

"Fair? You want me to play fair now that you don't have a gun on me? That's goofy. But that's just you being you, I've come to expect."

"Ha-ha."

"Tell you what. You come up with a pot of cash – American cash – and if I see it's a persuasive amount, we could do business."

"But..."

"Oh, please, Hugo, let's be adult about this. You go liquidate your assets and stand by for my instructions. I'll tell you when and where to show up with the money. Remember, cash only. Which hotel are you in now? It's so hard to keep up with you."

"Verna is hard to please." This from Hugo with a look at his wife that could crack a mirror.

"Okay, folks, you run along now."

"What about my gun?"

"I'll keep hold of it for the time being. They're very dangerous in the wrong hands."

"But..."

"Again with the buts. Get the hell out of here!"

37

My appetite was all the way back if you grant with me that it hadn't gone very far in the first place. A taco salad down in Pacifica sounded pretty good. Eating alone did not. I called Grenville who blew me off with some lame excuse about an evening counseling class he has conducted weekly for the past seven years.

I hung up and the phone rang.

"Beault."

"Hello, Basil, it's Nadine. I owe you a coffee," she said. I died and went to heaven. Only it was bachelor heaven. "I'm off work now and if your schedule is free, I could meet my obligation."

A schedule? I don't need no stinking schedule. "That sounds very nice. I'm sure I can break free," is what I said.

"Meet me at the station in an hour?"

"Okay."

Miss Berry stepped out of the lobby of her building into that fog we San Franciscans boast of. We were both wrapped up against the damp and cold. "I propose we get a bite to eat with that coffee if you care to," she offered.

I would hunt down the game, clawing my way through marauding beasts to put a dinner before you, given the chance. I didn't say that out loud. What I said was, "That will be nice."

"Let's walk. I know a place not far from here."

The place was John's Grill on Ellis, notable as the haunt in the old days of Dashiell Hammett, he of the popular detective novels. I had heard of him. My first thought was I can't afford dinner here, two dinners, unless I saved up for a few weeks or so. This was as bad as Harris'

Restaurant. Was Miss Berry going to order like Emily does? My second thought was I'd make the sacrifice and go without lunches for the next six months. At the door, the friendly hostess said, "Good evening, Miss Berry, always a delight to see you. And Mr. Beault, welcome to John's Grill. We have a table waiting for you." Oh, suffering Satan, I thought, they've got me pegged for a whopper of a bill.

Another nice lady led us up the stairs to a table in a corner on the second floor. I wasn't surprised when every head in the restaurant turned as Nadine passed along. Did I tell you she is rather handsome? I was surprised – no, astonished – when at the top of the stairs I was staring right at a bird statue. I almost lost consciousness. So that is what had rankled me early on in this dead-end mystery. I'm not the only one who has had to contend with the terror of coming to grips with a strange bird replica. I wonder how the unlucky bastards in that case fared. Probably babbling in a straight jacket behind locked doors right now.

As we sat down, a waiter placed a glass of wine in front of Nadine and asked me if I would care for the same, a Chardonnay from the Ernest Dowson Vineyards in Sonoma County. I nodded my thanks. Like I was going to argue.

My wine arrived seconds later. "Here's to friends," she toasted, "who cherish friendship." We raised our glasses and we tinked them together.

Well, okay, that is quite nice, but why not, "Here's to a night that never ends, with a wine that oils the passions of love, and the two of us naked..." I did not say that out loud.

"Basil, did you disappear?"

"What...no...just admiring the surroundings and this wine."

"I am glad you like it here. My station will be pleased. This table, you see, is one that they hold for KSFG when it is needed. The station, by the way, pays for the evening. Isn't that sweet of them?"

Sweet, huh? More like life-saving. Again, not out loud. "That is nice," I managed.

"We'll have that coffee I owe you after our dinner."

I was beginning to relax, thank the angels above. We talked some about Grenville. Nadine likes him. She is grateful for his counsel and his friendship, which she called companionship. We talked about his church where she took services when her unpredictable schedule permitted. I asked her about the news business. She had fun telling me how the process was the same every day, a team of reporters and writers out and about to fill a couple of hours of air time. How the content was sometimes just a mirror from the day before – local news, sports, traffic...geez, the traffic...fires, murders, the inevitable San Francisco street protests and occasionally the off-the-wall, exciting, almost unthinkable. "I'm hoping Thursday night falls into that last category," she offered.

"Oh, yes, our scofflaw on the run."

She asked me about the private eye business. It was a treat to tell her. Though with my not-so-full appointment book, it didn't take long to outline.

"What about you? Tell me about you," she asked me.

"I just did."

"Not really. Tell me about Basil Protherington."

Okay, I thought, why not. "I am a lucky person despite some real heartaches. Great parents and a great brother. We had a wonderful and loving upbringing. Grenville and I are about eighteen months apart so we've been real close. I got a scholarship to Cal. Baseball. I'm no Babe Ruth, but I was pretty good. Then the bomb dropped. Two bombs. Mom died of cancer when I was a freshman at Cal. Dad owned a successful print shop down in San Mateo. One night about a year after Mom died, a couple of guys came in to rob the place. Dad apparently resisted. He was shot and died. It crushed all of us. As the older brother I thought I was going to have to be the new dad. Hell, Grenville was so much more self-assured than I was. We had a long talk. He went to live with an aunt of ours and he started college. He wound up with a degree in Sociology and a Master's in Philosophy from San Francisco State. Me? I quit after my sophomore year and joined the Navy. Three years as an SP. Shore Patrol."

Nadine stared.

"After the Navy I went to work with a security firm. Learned some stuff the Navy didn't teach me. After a few years I got cocky and quit to hang up my own shingle. Jaguar Beault Investigations. I liked the name. I still do. I get clients from time to time. Enough to keep me off the dole."

"Never married?"

"Married? Me? Uh, no. Somehow women seem to see through me."

"To where?"

"Ha. Don't know. Haven't figured that out. Now if I had Grenville's looks and his brains and his character, it might be different. Grenville got all the good genes."

"Don't sell yourself short, Basil. And don't be jealous of Grenville."

"Jealous? No. Not ever. Just as proud of him as a person can be. You see him on his job, his calling. You know how competent he is, how he enfolds his congregation. And his energy."

"You like him," she said quietly.

"Yes."

The waiter stopped by after we each sipped a second wine. "Miss Berry, what would you like tonight?"

"Do you mind, Basil, if I choose something for you?"

"Not at all."

"Mr. Beault will have your filet mignon, medium, with the baked potato and tonight's veggies. I'll have the halibut and the veggies."

Before I go on I have to tell you. I know this lady – a special lady – who has had the filet at John's Grill. She has told me it is the best darn filet she ever had. I had to concur. Wow. Thank you, KSFG.

After dinner we declined dessert. Miss Berry said, "It's time to pay you that cup of coffee I owe you, Mr. Beault, unless you want something else from the drinks menu. Oh, I know, let's have a cognac. A Hennessey. Just a splash."

"No! I mean, no," I protested then calmed. "Coffee will do just fine, thank you."

"No Hennessey then? Grenville tells me you recently took on a new appreciation for it." She was trying to act quite serious.

"Very amusing, the two of you. I suppose he had a grand time telling you."

"He did," she admitted.

"Is there anything you two don't share?"

"No. Is there anything you two don't share?" she asked me.

I thought about that. "I guess not."

Coffees arrived. "How old is your daughter?"

The question made her face light up. "She's twenty-three months, two weeks, and three days. Her name is Alana. She is why I exist."

"Do you have a picture of her?"

"Basil, I am ashamed of you. Do you think I am one of those mothers who carry a picture of her kids in her wallet? I do not have *a* picture of her, I have about a hundred."

That made me smile. She is so proud of the girl who became her own. She pulled out her fancy phone and one by one she showed picture after picture of Alana to me. I was about to say how Alana took after Nadine, but I knew how crass that would be. Alana is adopted.

"Where is she now?"

"I'm lucky. My mother baby-sits her when she can. Also, and this is another reason why I love that brother of yours, he has helped me by getting a number of his parishioners to pitch in. He doesn't like that word parishioners and I tease him with it. The thing is, some of the guys – and the gals, too – have time away from work and they're great with children. I'm very lucky."

We talked more about Thursday night, how things might unfold while I was playing bounty hunter, and, I warned, how she and her crew should be on their guard.

"We go into some challenging situations to get the news, Basil. Been there done that. And we are always on guard, like you say." I had no answer for that.

We left John's Grill and walked back to Nadine's station. We shook hands. She kissed me on my bearded cheek. I drove home in San Francisco's legendary fog. No one shot at me.

38

The pounding on my door at seven a.m. woke me from a dream about which I am going to tell you nothing because it is none of your business. It is between only me and a psychiatrist if I think I have to go down that road. Blough! Only Blough announces his unwanted-ness by trying to demolish my door.

"Wait a second! I'll be there in a minute." Ooh, a mixed metaphor.

I opened the door to Blough and his mute partner when who to my wondering eyes should appear but The Pole and his two lackeys who pushed their way in. He started right in on the same old subject.

I stopped him. "I just got up, Pole, and I have to take a leak. I'll be right out. Don't make yourself at home."

"If you come out of there with a gun, we'll shoot you." Here all three flashed pistols.

"If I come out of there with a gun and you are still here, I'll shoot myself, you rodent."

I slipped a robe on over my flannel pajamas, my sop to San Francisco's fog and the cool dampness that accompanies it. Ms. Wu seemed uninterested in my relative immodesty. It might be she was not interested in men. That's a new theme in my life. It might be she was more interested in shooting me. That is another new theme in my life. It might be she thought I was ugly. I hadn't shaved in a few days getting ready for my gig on Thursday night. She was pretty stoic. The other one, the minion, seemed simply uninterested or maybe not even knowing where he was. His gun suggested otherwise, however. The Pole was just mouthing along about "the statue...give it him...where is it...or else...I'm serious..."

"Anyone for coffee," I interjected, "I can sure use a cup?" It was unanimous. No. "Look here, Mr. Pole, you've had your say and a splendid oratory it was. I am impressed. I'd be more impressed if I hadn't heard it on previous visits from you three charming people. No, let me finish. I'm getting the mental picture that you want something you believe I have. I can appreciate the sincerity in your belief. You seem like nice people (I was still in my lying mode), so I'll make you a deal you would be crazy to turn down."

"No deals, Beault."

"See? Crazy. But who's counting? Listen. You know there are valuable stones in that bird." I could see the first stirrings of emotion in the minion's face. "The price on them could go real high." Ms. Wu faintly reacted. "Here's how it works. I want to get rid of the damn thing. It's been nothing but misery for me since Captain Kluszewski dropped dead right here on the floor. But I want something in return. You go away and put together a sack full of money – cash money only – and I'll let you know when and where we can do some trading."

"No way, Beault, I want it now. Hand it over."

"No can do, it's not here."

"Then we will all go and get it so I don't have to spill your blood on top of Kluszewski's."

"If you insist, but I have to warn you that it is being guarded. Say, I think you know who it is. Remember the guy with the shotgun?"

"What, that bartender?"

"No, not him."

"Who, the Chinaman?"

"No, not him either. Whoa, there were a lot of shotguns pointing at you now that I recall. No, it was the other guy at the Beach Chalet."

"That old guy? Ha!"

"You do remember. Yes, him, the old guy, as you say."

"He won't be a problem. We'll take care of him."

"Good, because I can get back the hundred and a half I had to pay him for stopping him from blowing you away."

"What's that supposed to mean?"

"He shoots first and doesn't even pretend to have any questions to ask. He's kind of single-minded that way. We wouldn't even get within a half mile of him and that pigeon."

"Shit."

"Please, there's a lady present. Let's be respectful." The Pole paused. "My deal looks righteous now, doesn't it?" I said to him.

"How do I know you'll come through?"

"Oh, good question. I guess you won't know. Except this, Pole, I want to be as far away from that thing as possible. So take it or leave it at that."

"How much?"

"How much what? Oh, for the statue. As much as you can put together. I'd advise you to make it a persuasive figure. Who knows, one of your competitors might come along with a satchel full of cash and make me a whore."

"Shit."

"Leave a phone number on the table. I will let you know when and where."

"Shit."

As he was leaving, I asked him how tall he is.

"I'm an inch over seven feet."

"That's mighty tall."

"Shit."

I tried to picture him on a prison bunk.

I needed sustenance. I walked over to Favonius for a coffee and a roll or two. On the way, I congratulated myself. My plan may work. Tempt all these knuckleheads with the supposed riches in the statue and get them off my back while they scrounge up the money for a pigeon's ransom. Get them all nervous enough about their compulsions for the treasure and maybe, just maybe, the killer will do a dumb thing and reveal himself. That would be a feather in the Beault chapeau and a zinger in the craw of a certain homicide detective in town. What a darn shame that would be.

What a brilliant detective I am. I am going to have to start advertising: "Jaguar Beault Investigations. Brilliant Detective on Staff. Makes All the Right Moves. Call for an Appointment with the Brilliant Guy."

What, you ask, makes me know this? Only the fact that my phone was ringing when I got back from Favonius sated with cinnamon rolls and caffeine.

"Beault."

"Hello, Mr. Beault, this is Pearl, Mrs. Smith's friend."

See? Don't you see...another player in the Madagascar Pigeon sweepstakes? My plan was unfolding like a charmed, uh, plan.

"Hello, Pearl, nice to hear from you," I said, smiling to myself knowing full well that here was another chance to suck in a suspect. She'll want me to snoop on Mr. Smith. Mrs. Smith has already made it abundantly clear that her spouse has designs on the statue.

"I am going to assume, Mr. Beault, that your friend Miriam has told you that I went to her antique store in Sausalito and pressed her on the Madagascar Pigeon."

"Go on," I said without revealing anything.

"It is important that I find it and take possession."

"To put in your own store for sale."

"Oh, dear me, no. I'm looking for it... I'm acting as a proxy for someone else."

"Indeed, yes. Mr. Smith then, right?"

"Hell no, not for that blob. Why would you think that?" Pearl snapped

"Because..."

"I am doing it for Mrs. Smith. She has a very special interest in the item."

"Special interest. I think there's an echo in my phone, Pearl. That's the second time an individual has said that same thing to me about the Madagascar Pigeon."

"Who? Who was it?"

"Actually, I don't know. Except that he took a lot of shots at me the night I had that pleasant dinner with Mrs. Smith at the Beach Chalet. He left a message on my machine advising me he has a special interest in the statue. Maybe he's in league with Mrs. Smith. Shared special interests by the both of them. Did I say advising me? Well there you are. It was, my dear Pearl, a threat. The kind I respect."

"You can't give it to him. It must go to Mrs. Smith. You must see that."

"What I see are the bullet holes in my carriage. Not a swell car but mine own. Those holes got my attention."

"Mrs. Smith – we – will do whatever it takes to get the statue. What will it take, Mr. Beault?"

My plan was back on track. "As anxious as you are to take possession of the Madagascar Pigeon, I am even more ready to dump it. You and Mrs. Smith, you put together a fee, a persuasive amount – oh, in cash only, let me be clear – and wait for me to tell you when and where and then we can see if it's enough."

"But...but that won't do."

"If Mrs. Smith is so keen on getting it, she'll have to do it my way. My ass is in a sling over this bloody statue, and I am going to get rid of it my way. Her and you and Mr. Smith and, I'm guessing here, Yvonne, too, you all could form a compact, pool your money. Who knows, your bribe...your bid may win the day."

"Do you mean to say there are others you will sell it to?"

"Brilliant plan, don't you think?"

"This is terrible. The statue has to go to Mrs. Smith. There is a special reason."

"And so it will, Pearl, if the amount you bring persuades me. Very simple."

"I'll talk to Mrs. Smith and one of us will call you."

"Negatory. No more contact until I call you with the when and where. Have a nice day, Pearl."

I hung up. Mrs. Smith? What kind of name is that? And her friends really call her that? You know what I think? I think that is not her real name.

Let's forget about Mrs. Smith or whoever she is. And Pearl and Yvonne. I've got my eye on suspects with real motives. Mr. Smith for one. He's already admitted he'd be willing to kill even if it was his own wife. Phyllis Gunn, when she is in that guise, who started this whole mess. Who else knew about Captain Kluszewski? Answer me that. Professor Pym, too. I've been troubled by him since the day we first

205

talked. Another question: who knows more about the Madagascar Pigeon than the same Professor Pym? And its purported valuable contents. He strikes me as a sly dog. The Pole and those two things who hang around him seem hell-bent on shooting someone, anyone. And Hugo Blankenship, the type of person who could go off the deep end at the snap of your finger. Now we get to the one who pumped my car full of holes. No beating around the bush with him. He's got a gun and he uses it. What's with this special interest he talks of?

One of them is a killer and it's up to me to pin the crime on him. The key is the statue, the Madagascar Pigeon. The statue I have misplaced. Up poop creek without any toilet paper. Jaguar Beault, the brilliant detective. I am going to hold off on that advertising campaign I was considering. Holy crap.

My plan was under way. Time to push it along. I called Mr. Smith and Professor Pym. I had their phone numbers. Mr. Smith was appalled that I would require a bagful of money to pass the statue to him. Out of the question, he claimed. Had no money, he confessed. Except the lucre he would have used to pay me to whack his wife, I asked. He bought in.

Professor Pym was downright intrigued with the opportunity to obtain such a storied treasure for the museum. He thought he would never ever have such a plum fall into his lap. All for the good of the preservation of antique arts, he asserted. A boon to future generations of students and researchers into yadda, yadda, yadda. What a load of rubbish. He's as covetous of the true value of the prize as anyone. Probably more. Remember how he tried to make a red herring of the stuff and nonsense about how the jewels are just urban legend? How he said these first mythmakers were such comedians? Yeah, sure, I buy that. Bottom line? He said he would try in real earnestness to assemble a modest amount of museum money to acquire the statue. I'm really starting to dislike this guy. He wants me to believe he doesn't own a gun, too. Horse manure to that. Everyone else in this mystery owns one.

Two more suspects to scheme on and they were Phyllis Gunn and the shooter. I call him the shooter because I don't know his name. I guess you knew that. You probably also know I don't have his phone number which means I can't call him. Miss Gunn, our itinerant psychotic who cloned herself into her twin sister, leaves me a new number almost every day. Talking to her is like shouting down an oilman's dry hole, drilled five thousand feet deep to where there's only dead air. Like between her ears. The thrilling life of the private eye. A plan is a plan and must be obeyed. If you have to call Phyllis Gunn, call her. Rip that bandaid off your sore, tear that splinter from your finger, pour that iodine on your open wound. Tell Mike Tyson to his face that he is ugly.

"Hello." A woman's voice.

"I am trying to reach Phyllis Gunn."

"This is she."

"My good luck. I couldn't be sure that it might not be you but rather your, uh, sister."

"Don't confuse me with that liar and cheat," she bellowed.

"Yes, God forbid there is any confusion surrounding you and Miss Lavender. This is Jaguar Beault and I have information to tell you."

"You have the statue. How wonderful."

"Hold on a tick, lady, that's not it." I explained the Jaguar Beault plan to her, she gagging and choking.

"You can't."

"I will."

"I paid you fifty dollars."

"Blood money runs a lot more than that, honey."

"The statue belongs to me."

"And it's yours if your offer tops the others."

"The others? What does that mean?"

"Miss Gunn, you have my conditions."

I hung up and wondered which one of her would show up. "Lavernia" was already on notice. That girl is a freak of nature.

39

I do do some investigating, you know. Look at my company name: Jaguar Beault Investigations. It's right there in the title. It's not just a loss leader, it's what I do. Sometimes the effort pays off as I think it did in this case, my pigeon case, where I am still only $50 to the good, which is like a two-cents-an-hour rate. Whoopee. Not exactly a proud memory to share with the grandkids I'll never have. Miriam won't marry me; I am not masochistic enough to ask Emily; and my new girl buddy is a lesbian. Is this another digression? Sorry. Anyway, for some time now, I have been getting eye-opening info at the County Registrar's Office, from the state's gun registration files, and from U.S. Customs on passport activity by some of these people in the crowd who are all too eager to get hold of the Madagascar Pigeon. I had called in some chits, or, more likely, officials just felt sorry for me.

And if it takes a big man to admit he may have made a few false assumptions along the way or, more likely, was way off target, then I am your big man. What I deduced from the evidence I collected that got me pointing in a helpful direction is how this mess came to be and fell into my lap and, here's the really cool thing, who the killer is. Clear as a bell. Plain as the nose on your face. Open and shut case. Well...a suspect anyway. Evidence really helps in situations like this. I've even heard Blough say the same thing. Must be true. That is, if you read the evidence correctly. Yeah, if.

The consummation devoutly to be wished at this point was to get my solution in front of the authorities, meaning Blough, without having someone put a slug in me. "Shoot the guy with the big mouth" is not what I wanted to hear shouted on Saturday when I had the dramatic scene all set for curtain up at Grenville's football game at Kezar. I checked the Weather Channel and saw that no rain was forecast. There was a chance of fog. The weatherman's little joke. That's like telling San Franciscans that liberal politicians are likely to win in the next election.

I still had things to do orchestrating the big climax. I made a few phone calls to entice more participants on Saturday, made important arrangements with Grenville, and wondered if I was going to hear from my trigger-happy shooter who seemed bent on seeing how close he could come to drilling me without actually killing me. One huge loose end was out of my control. Where did the Madagascar Pigeon fly off to?

Last night was Wednesday, which makes today Thursday by my calculations. I'm almost never wrong about these calendar matters. Twice burned, once warned, I learned from a brace of times I missed important appointments due to calendar malfunctions. It cost me money. I'm more attuned to what day it is now. I bring up last night because it was about six o'clock when I called The Top of the Bottom bar and asked for Pablo Perez. "Pepe? Naw, he don't get here till after nine so's he can mooch beers offen his drunk buddies. Call back then." I did not call back. I called Grenville and told him what I had learned. Two things, really, Perez's usual arrival time and his handle. I called Miss Berry at the TV station and alerted her.

You can ask me why I didn't just go to Pepe's front door and stick a .45 in his face and take him into court-ordered custody. You can ask and I'll answer that I didn't know where he lived or stayed or flopped or what. The only constant was the dumb shit's need for recreation at The Top of the Bottom. The downside of apprehending him there was a bar full of like-minded bail jumpers. They treated it like an Olympics event. It rarely cost them a dime since bail money usually came from somebody else, like their mothers or their girlfriends.

Starting with a pair of scuffed-up Alpine-style hiking boots, I had on a pair of old Levi's, loose-fitting to conceal my ankle holster holding my little pea shooter. Next I had on an old flannel shirt and an Oakland Raiders jacket concealing my shoulder holster with my Police Special. Topping off a five-day beard was my "Serge's Disciples" black ball cap.

If you don't know who Serge A. Storms is, you are not living in the same good ole U.S. of A. as I am. I had a set of handcuffs in my jacket pocket.

I parked a block away from The Top of the Bottom in an industrial tract where an old car studded with bullet holes was not going to be out of place. When I got to the bar at seven there were half a dozen guys and a few girls outside smoking. You don't smoke indoors around here anymore so you can be in compliance with the laws on the books to protect people from second-hand smoke. You know me and smoking. I'm for this law. Yet indoors at this piss pot you can drink enough alcohol to strip the paint off a semi-trailer truck and go home a law-abiding citizen. Go figure. The cigarette smoke from this gaggle was indistinguishable from the San Francisco fog. One of the tougher looking smokers stared me down. She said, "You new here?"

Cleverly, I answered, "I'm new everywhere I go." I know it didn't make sense, but it was all I could muster.

Her girlfriend blew smoke my way and announced, "You smell like a brewery."

My comeback to her was equally senseless. It was, "I smell like this everywhere I go." What I had done was splash some beer on my shirt and pants to disguise my sobriety and suggest a wastrel. Having disarmed the ladies, I stepped into The Top of the Bottom.

It looked like shift change. The late afternoon crowd of construction crew guys and city employees were slowly exiting while the night shift bikers, ex-cons, sailors, pre-cons, San Jose State sophomores and juniors, and self-employed women were filling up the joint. A sprinkling of Grenville's recruits sat and stood here and there minding their own business. It's a fairly large saloon with a big horseshoe-shaped bar and a dozen or more tables. Two pool tables, tucked into an alcove near the restrooms, resonated with the clicking of cue ball on pool balls. The music favored the 1990s. The jukebox favored the near-deaf.

Unmistakable above the bar was a sign. It read, "Management Reserves the Right to Refuse Service to Anyone." Over the years, the notice was crudely amended with a sign below announcing, "This means you if you..." and here was a list of additions. They were: "Are ugly; Don't like Willie Nelson; Are Don Drysdale; Are a guy with a boyfriend; Are a gal with a girlfriend; Shoot the TV, unless Oprah is on; Don't blame George Bush." American freedom of expression on its Constitutional pedestal.

Somebody I recognized saw me approaching the bar and got up ceding his stool. I sat down. One of the two bartenders ambled over and tossed a coaster down in front of me. "Whada ya need?"

"Give me a minute."

"That ain't a drink we serve here, bud." Honky-tonk humor.

The guy sitting next to me spoke up. "Give him one of these. He'll switch to Hennessey in a while."

The bartender walked away. "I'm off Hennessey now," I said to the fellow.

"That's what I heard." One of Grenville's plants. The drink arrived and I sipped it. I detected no alcohol in it.

"These will help us keep our wits," the fellow said.

The waiting started. Pepe Perez wasn't up to bat for more than an hour. I scanned the bar. Grenville and another big dude were playing pool. Across the horseshoe I saw Ping Bodie hunched over a drink. He was wearing a duster that made him look like Jesse James' father. Then I remembered he owned a sawed-off shotgun, which, if he chose to, he could disguise beneath the overcoat. I bet he was in hog heaven. I'm glad I called him. He seemed glad I called him.

The music drove me nuts. I daydreamed that Bodie got up from his bar stool, whipped out his cannon and blew the innards out of the juke-box into the alley out back, if there was an alley. The stable of drinkers got uglier as the clock marched toward nine o'clock. Pepe Perez was going to walk into a bevy of friends, or at least acquaintances. Every so often the guy sitting next to me got up to be replaced by another guy who I was pretty sure took his divine guidance at my brother's church. These guys knew what they were doing.

Nadine Berry had arrived with a cameraman and a soundman. She dressed conservatively. She let it be known that they were doing a feature on the hot nightlife spots of San Francisco and tonight they were filming The Top of the Bottom. The bozos in the bar ate up the chance to be on TV. She went around to the patrons pushing her microphone into faces and asking questions, smiling at the answers, probably breaking a lot of hearts.

At a quarter to nine Pablo Pedro Perez, my bail jumper, came into the bar. A bigger guy than I had anticipated, husky looking, a product of all the iron pumping in jail. My quarry, and what fun this will be. He got a few greetings from some other big guys. Some guy I recognized pushed a beer into Pepe's hand. He knocked back a big gulp. The same generous guy jockeyed Pepe toward me and at the same time the guy sitting next to me got up and told me loud enough for people to hear to go intercourse myself. Pepe sat down and looked at me.

"What'd you do to him?" Pepe asked me.

"I didn't do nothing to him."

"Looked pissed."

"Did he?"

"Yeah."

"Good for him. Now he's pissed someplace else. Okay by me."

Pepe finished his beer. "Buy me a beer," he said. I looked at him then shrugged and raised a finger to the bartender.

"Pancho here needs a beer."

"Who the fuck's Pancho?"

"Ain't that you? Thought I heard them call you Pancho when you strolled in."

"Pepe."

"Pepe? Your name's Pepe? Thought that was just somebody's nickname."

"Yeah. It's mine. I'm Pablo Perez but they call me Pepe."

"I will call you Pepe."

"I ain't seen you in here before."

"That's because I ain't been in here before, Pepe. Been away. Guest of the government for a while."

"You did time?"

"Something like that."

"Where?"

"Not here. In I-raq."

"I-raq? Where's that, upstate?"

213

"Yeah, that general direction."

I saw Grenville and two others meander over to our place in the bar. I swore to myself that the two others had NFL linebacker experience written all over them. They were sure the right size for it. Nadine leaned in and Pepe about spit out his beer.

"Hello, honey," he flirted. She smiled and asked us if we would like to tell her what we liked about The Top of the Bottom for a television show she was producing.

Pepe said, "Sure, wanna talk it over with me in private?"

Nadine said the whole idea was to put him on TV. He blurted some drivel about free beers, horny senoritas and free beers. She put the microphone in my face and asked me what my favorite thing about The Top of the Bottom was. I stared back and said, "Nobody bothers me" and turned away.

She stepped back. Pepe looked her over. Dressed as she was in a pants suit, she was revealing little, but Pepe found plenty to imagine. Then he made a remark in Spanish that did not need translating. He turned back to me. "You didn't want to talk to her?"

"I don't need no bright lights shining on me. It's not what I do."

"What do you do?"

My opening. Thanks, Pepe. "I stop people."

"Huh? Like what?"

"I stop people from leaping off the Golden Gate Bridge. I stop people from jumping onto the tracks in front of BART trains. I stop people from overdosing on Ghirardelli chocolate. Tonight I'm stopping a guy from killing himself."

"Jesu Christi. Where? Who?"

"Here, you."

"What?"

"Pepe, sit quietly and I'll tell you. I am authorized to bring you in for jumping bail." Here Pepe sat straight up and looked around. "If you resist, I am authorized to use force." I had my hand inside my jacket.

The bright lights from the television camera panned to us. Pepe shifted off the stool and started yelling that I had a gun and was going to kill him. Some bikers and other half-drunks came over. Grenville and his football pals joined them as if to lend support. Pepe was screeching...he wasn't going no-fucking-where with me. I held up my paperwork and said it was all official. Anybody who wanted to get in the way would be arrested, too.

"Do you really think you're going to just walk out of here with Pepe all by yourself, bounty hunter?" That from behind me. "Let's fuck this guy over." That from the same voice.

The camera light shifted back and forth. Miss Berry was in Emmy Heaven. Loads of loud shouting. Pepe tried to ease his way back only to get stymied by a big black guy who was hard to move. All-pro linemen had tried it and had failed. I left my gun holstered knowing I could just as easily fire off a random shot and hit somebody innocent.

"Fuck this," I heard the voice again. "I'm going to put an end to this prick." At which time the other linebacker turned and put a fist in the voice that floored him.

Boom! Ping Bodie and his sawed-off peacemaker altered the ceiling. Miss Berry looked at her soundman who gave her a thumbs up. Grenville and the linebacker and some of their friends formed a circle around Pepe who was still screaming. Grenville leaned into Pepe's ear and whispered something that turned off the screaming. About ten regulars from the Congregation of Brotherly Love in the Name of Jesus Christ in the Castro maneuvered into the melee separating the dickheads from the good guys. The bar quieted. The bartender looked at Ping Bodie and pointed at the ceiling and said, "You're going to pay for that."

"No, I'm not," Bodie replied. Then Boom! Another blast into the ceiling. "Not going to pay for that either."

"I'll find all your asses and do you good, you assholes," the bartender shouted.

By now the fate of one Pablo Pedro Perez was of no concern to the rabble in The Top of the Bottom. I put cuffs on Pepe and walked him to the door where a dozen or more cooperating guys had made room for our departure. It was real quiet, so it was easy to hear the bartender call out to Miss Berry, "When's our bar going to be on TV?"

She's a professional, so she didn't laugh. She answered him, "Soon, real soon."

Outside, Grenville said he had to go back in the bar for a minute but that we'd meet at the church where he had some champagne on ice. And some ginger ale. He invited Miss Berry who said, "No way. We're going to have this on television in about an hour. Tune in."

Two linebackers came with me and Pepe to the Bayview Police Station where I turned him and the paperwork in. I got an official receipt that I'd use to claim a generous fee from Severino Carlusconi, my favorite bail bondsman.

Later at Grenville's church we all watched the news on KSFG, sipped some beverages, and got a big kick out of the evening.

"I owe you one, bro," I said to him.

"No you don't. This one is on the house." What a good brother. "The one you owe is the one with the shotgun. Do you even know who he is?"

"Yes. You can meet him on Saturday. He'll be around. Say, what did you go back into the bar to do tonight?"

"I had a visit with the bartender. Learned he owns the place. I reminded him that threatening you and the rest of us was a bad idea. He told me to perform a sex act on myself. I asked him if he'd like to have his saloon turned into a gay bar. You should have heard his reaction to that. Then I told him if he didn't convince me – right then and there – that he was going to forget his threats, I'd bring a hundred gays into his bar every night to occupy every stool, every chair, every table, every square foot on the floor and both pool tables. Then there would be dancing and necking and I couldn't guarantee there would not be more. And the only spending would be on the jukebox at about fifty cents an hour. And if he tried to exercise his right to refuse service to anyone like the sign above his bar says, my large ex-linebacker friends would counsel him on how they would help him exercise those rights. Then I asked him if he agreed with me that after a few nights of this The Top of the Bottom would be known for now and beyond as one of San Francisco's popular gay bars. I added that we could put the word out that the change in theme at his bar was his idea. I'm sure he was about to have an aneurism. Then he told me he got the message."

"You are a fiendish man for someone of the cloth, Grenville," one of his congregants standing nearby said.

Grenville turned to him and said, "Thank you."

I worked the whole room, shaking hands, thanking the guys, telling them how much I appreciated their help. Most of them asked when they'd get to do the same thing again.

40

Grenville put me up for the night in his spare room where I shaved and showered and changed my clothes in the morning before going home to a traffic jam on my street. What was this all about? Five television vans were double-parked outside my building. I had to park a block away, which for San Francisco is a good break. A guy was holding sound equipment behind one of the vans. I asked him what was going on.

"Some private dick almost got himself killed in a shoot-out last night. His office is in that building there. He won't come out. Been banging on the door all morning."

"That'd be that Beault character, right?" I said.

"Yeah, you know him?"

"Sure, I work on the same floor – Bevalaqua Taxes."

"Oh, yeah, I saw that one. You know where Beault is?"

"He moved out of the building the end of last week. Moved down to Sunnyvale. Said there's a lot more money in the Silicon Valley."

"Hey, thanks."

"Don't mention it." I repeated my scam to the other TV crews and the street cleared out. That was easy. "You are a mean man for someone of the law," I accused myself. Being a media star, I could get away with bad behavior. Uh-huh.

I sneaked into the lobby and quickly took the stairs two at a time halfway up to my floor then one at a time when I ran out of breath. No cameras. That stairs thing toggled my switch. I went to change into my gym clothes, passing my phone where the message light was blinking. Not now. I'll do that later after a workout, which I'll need for tomorrow's big show. The Saturday Showdown. I peeked out my door, peered down the stairs, and checked out the street. No paparazzi. At the gym, I acted real humble when staff members said they saw me on television. Me, Mr. Modest. I worked out, washed up, went home and sneaked back in.

Time to listen to the messages. The phone rang.

"So, Mr. Beault, you're a TV star now." The shooter.

"Glad you called. You want the Madagascar Pigeon, am I right?"

"Yes, I do. You ready to hand it over?"

"Tomorrow at Kezar Stadium at one o'clock on the dot. Bring a persuasive amount of American cash, enough to beat your competitors."

"This is unacceptable. I want it now."

"What, you'll shoot up my car again? The police might see that as attempted murder."

"I can aim straight, Beault, so it won't be what you call attempted."

"Something has happened to the statue, meaning I can't give it to you now even if that was my plan. It will not be available until one tomorrow, where I said," I lied. "Be there with money."

I hung up and clicked off my recording gadget with a smile.

I pushed the button to replay my messages. There were fourteen. Six were from television news rooms; five were from people who wouldn't think of hiring any other private eye to solve their problems; one was from an architectural society reproaching me for condoning malicious destruction of property at The Top of the Bottom, a facility, the caller said, that was under consideration for an historic preservation classification; one was from Crystal; and one was from Blough.

I called Blough. After I convinced him that what I did the night before was entirely legal – if a bit melodramatic – I filled him in on what was happening on Saturday at Kezar Stadium. I described my theory, summarized my evidence, and said he was in position to take a load of miscreants into custody if he and a squad of his men wanted to be at the scene. No uniforms, I recommended. I held my breath. "You better not be fucking with me, Beault," was his way of saying he would be there.

It must have been after school hours because Crystal called.

"Ooh, it's you. I seen you on TV. You're a hunk."

"No, you saw me on TV."

220

"That's what I said."

"No you didn't, you said seen."

"So what's the big deal?"

"The big deal is whether you are going to spend your life speaking English or revealing yourself to be an idiot."

"Hey, all I wanted was to talk to you after I, uh, saw you on TV."

"Great, and I want to talk to you."

"Oooh."

"Here's the real deal. Now listen carefully. You never call me again. You throw away my phone number. You listening? Good. If you do ever call me again, I will call your dad. I will tell him just how big a slut you have been with all these calls, and then I will tell him things that may not even be true, but which will, how did you put it before, make him turn purple."

"But..."

"No buts, just go to school and try to learn something, like how to grow up. You got this?"

Through her crying, I got it that she got it. I hung up scratching my head that someday soon this airhead was going to have a driver's license and be eligible to vote. This made me want to upchuck, which made me remember that I hadn't eaten anything all day. I sneaked out my door, sneaked down the stairs, and peeked outside. No TV vans. Whew. I walked to Favonius to have a sandwich and a coffee. And a chocolate fudge sundae topped with whipped cream and a cherry, and if you don't think that wasn't swell, you have much to tumble to. Get this, I walked into the café and Mr. Hui waves and says, "Ah, Mr. Beaurt, me saw you on TV." He got the pronoun wrong but the verb right. He can be forgiven because English is his second language. What do I know, it may be his third or fourth.

41

When I woke on Saturday morning, I saw that the city wore its fog like a can of gray paint spilled over a flower garden. Moist and creeping through every opening in the landscape. Today I loved the fog. It would be just the patina for the staging of justice delivered and menace removed. Get those sons-a-bitches off my ass and the Madagascar Pigeon dead and buried if it wasn't already. Fifty lousy bucks I've pocketed for my troubles over that thing, and I've spent way more than that on gasoline alone just going around to ask questions and get shot at.

I called Grenville who told me a bunch of his churchgoers were walking over to the park while others were driving so there would be cars available in case.

"What are cars going to be needed for – in case?"

"Are you kidding me? What if there's a car chase? Wouldn't want to miss that. This is the best city in the world for a car chase. Remember *Bullitt*? And L.A. gets all the headlines for chases down there. Shoot, Bas, L.A.? No hills. It's all freeway flat down there. No comparison."

"Grenville, you do see, don't you, that this is serious stuff? You are getting way too big a kick out it."

"Can't let you have all the fun, bro."

"Got that right. You're walking?"

"It's less than two miles, we can make it," he chided me. "We'll be there between nine-thirty and ten. Start the game around ten-thirty, eleven."

"Whatever floats your boat."

I scrambled three eggs, microwaved some turkey bacon and popped two sourdough slices into the toaster. This ought to hold me until the post-game barbeque. To be in tune with the outdoor setting of park and football, I pulled on an old sweatpants and a U. of Oregon dark green XXL sweatshirt I bought recently at that Goodwill over on Lombard because it would be warm against the damp fog. I had gone to the Goodwill looking for that jacket of mine Emily donated. I tied on an old pair of running shoes and topped everything off with a New York Yankees baseball cap just to piss people off. I left my guns at home. If I needed to lavish supplemental firepower today with all those armed cops scheduled to be on hand, then my clever little plan was going to be one large cock-up. I drove to the park. The shamus is on the job.

Kezar Stadium, the early home of the San Francisco 49ers pro football team, is tucked into the southeast corner of Golden Gate Park near where Lincoln Way has turned into Frederick Street just west of Stanyan Street, spitting distance from the city's notorious Haight-Ashbury district, which gave rise to the Hippie movement in the 1960s, the successor generation to the Beat Generation of the 1950s. You've heard tell of the flower children. Now their kids and grandkids are there. It's groovy.

Grenville and his churchmen play football on a grass expanse just outside Kezar Stadium unless the field is overrun with kids playing soccer. They don't play on a full hundred yards, they mark off a smaller field with ice buckets and jackets and gym bags. A few of the guys were there doing just that when I arrived.

I didn't see any cops I knew except Dick Headley who I chatted with briefly because he called me over. "Join me at my car, will you?" he said to me. Dick Headley talking to Jaguar Beault...almost a first. He proved to be a very surprising guy. When I got back to the playing area, a few of his officers might easily have been among the park's denizens milling here and there in disguise. If so, they were doing a good job of it. I didn't see any of my suspects either, but likewise they could be hiding in hopes of getting a jump on winning the Madagascar Pigeon. I looked toward Stanyan to see if Grenville and his troop of walkers were arriving and saw a KSFG-TV van parked quietly on Frederick. Nice not to have to worry about parking tickets in one of those vans. Miss Berry and her co-workers call them live-feed trucks.

Shortly, Grenville did arrive holding a carryall I didn't recognize and with about twenty fellows, which put his roster for football at two dozen or more. These guys are serious. All of them, dressed for a day of football, looked like they'd been athletes at one time or another and had not gone to seed. Not just those big linebackers either. You've noticed I have not named them. That's not my prerogative. It's there's.

While the ballplayers were tossing footballs back and forth and stretching, getting ready for the game, Grenville walked over.

"Whatchya got in the bag?" I asked.

"Just my lunch, my helmet, my jock, my cup, a football," he said, "oh, and the family jewels, of course," he laughed. The Protherington family clown.

Over his shoulder I saw Nadine Berry coming our way with two cameramen and a soundman. Full court press, huh?

"Hello, Brother Protherington," she said. "I could use more sun for shooting today instead of the fog. Think you can clear it up, Minister?"

"I do not bargain with God over the weather, my dear."

"Jaguar Beault," she said as if we hadn't met, "you're that new TV star." She seemed to get the biggest kick out of that.

"That was not my doing, that was yours."

"Don't blame me, I was just doing my job."

"So was I," I said.

"Well, whom should we blame?" she asked.

"Rush Limbaugh?"

"Sure, why not, I blame him for everything else."

Just then one of those colorful bike riders pulled up along side of us all decked out in skin-tight riding gear covered all over in product logos and wearing a helmet.

"Good morning, Beault, and the exotic Miss Berry."

"Detective Blough. I hope this is your disguise," I said.

"Well, yes and no. Fact is I ride. I was supposed to do a hundred-miler today, but some private dick jackass conned me into a day of work. Sorry for the rough language, Miss Berry."

"I forgive you, Joe. How's Dominique?"

"Fine, just fine, she'll be pleased you asked."

Then Blough turned to Grenville, stuck out his hand and shook it. "Grenville. How's tricks?"

"Couldn't be better, Joe. Bas here has us all keyed up for a three-ring circus later. I guess you're too busy to play today?"

"That's right. Bas here has me all keyed up, too, and about fifteen of my best boys and girls. I better go. See you around."

Off he rode, bosom buddies with my brother and my lesbian Venus. "Somebody wish to enlighten the slow-witted part of this group as to what just happened?" I stammered.

Miss Berry first. "I've had plenty of chances to work with the lieutenant on crime stories. He's a hardass, but I like him. He's always up front with reporters when he can be. Dominique is his wife. She's a doll. I know their daughter, too."

Grenville next. "Joe's daughter, Francine, is in my congregation. She graduates high school this year. She's kinda finding herself right now."

"And Jaguar Beault, the keen observer, the private detective who deduces answers and uncovers clues to lead to solutions, stared into the space left by Joe." That was me talking.

"Oh, come on, Bas," Grenville laughed at me.

"By the way," Miss Berry said, "the lieutenant likes you. He doesn't like private detectives as a rule, but he sees some good in you. He likes pulling your chain."

"He does it enough, I'll tell you."

Miss Berry called her crew together and had Grenville describe how the game would be played out and how they could best film it. Then they walked around the playing area surveying shots and backgrounds and shadows. Not much in the way of shadows since there was no sun to throw them.

Just before the game got under way – with only a few arguments about who was to play on whose side – I saw Ping Bodie shuffle his way toward some benches and sit down where he had a view of the game. He wasn't wearing his duster, so I presumed he had left his scattergun somewhere else. He knew there would be a police presence.

First possession was settled by the flip of a coin and the game started with the kickoff, really just a punt. They played seven-on-seven with everybody eligible except the center. Substitutions were frequent so that everyone got a chance to get all sweaty. Yesterday the players were friends. Tomorrow they will be friends. But today they were opponents and the game was played to win. It wasn't tackle, it was flag football. Before a flag was grabbed, it was real serious. These guys have done this before. And to think I had considered playing today. What a schmuck I am.

"Have you thought about playing today?" I jumped. Geez.

"Miriam! Didn't see you come up."

"Hi, Bas, are you going to play in the game today?"

"Are you out of your beautiful mind? Watch these people. They are committed. I wouldn't last one down."

"I'm disappointed. I'd like to see you...oh, look, there's Grenville. Grenville! Grenville!" she shouted.

The guys with the ball were huddling at that moment and everyone turned. "Grenville! Grenville!" even louder from Miriam. Once would have been plenty. My brother waved back and headed our way. Miriam didn't wait. She hurried over and threw him a big hug. You don't see Grenville Protherington red-faced very often. This was one of those times. He squeezed out of the hug and put his arm through hers and walked back to where I was standing. One of the ballplayers called over, "Grenville! Grenville! Can we resume play now?" Grenville flipped him off.

"Bas, look, it's Grenville."

"Yes, I can see that. Are you going to introduce us?"

"Oh, Basil, I'm just so happy to see him."

"I guessed. And I suppose if you are going to swoon over somebody, it doesn't count unless it's in public."

A shout and a groan rose from the game. A player was on his back with a few others standing over him.

"What?"

"I got a cramp, a charley horse, in my calf. It hurts like hell."

"Rub some dirt on it and get back in the game or crawl off the field," a player on the other team said to him. Sympathy was not on the roster for today's game.

Miss Berry strolled toward us. Miriam chirped, "That's Nadine Berry from TV. What's she..."

Grenville answered, "She's doing a human interest feature on the game."

"God, she's spectacular looking. Grenville, you're not..."

"She happens to be in my church, Mir, and she thought the game and some interviews would make for a fun show. Want to meet her?"

Miriam is in love with Grenville who is gay. Miriam is now jealous of Nadine Berry, who is lesbian, because Nadine Berry goes to Grenville's church and can see him whenever she likes. Miss Berry has no romantic interest in anyone in the Protherington family. The chances of Nadine Berry stealing Grenville Protherington away from Miriam are less than zero. Now when you have determined how to bring Miriam around to the facts of the matter, write the book. It'll set women studies ahead by millennia.

The game came face-to-face with a water break time out. Five minutes. Miss Berry hurried over to do a few interviews. Grenville saw Lieutenant Blough cycle nearby and went to talk to him.

"I hate her," Miriam told me.

"Hate who?"

"Nadine Berry."

"Why, for heaven's sake?"

"Well, first off, she's prettier than me."

"Forgive me, Miriam, and you know how much I care for you and how beautiful I think you are, but Nadine Berry is prettier than any woman you can name."

"Basil, you sound infatuated."

"With her? What good would it do? I told you, she's lesbian. And I'm not."

"Well, I don't like the way she acts around Grenville."

"Oh, you don't, huh? Think she's going to convert him and change herself?"

"Well..."

"Miriam, you have two doctorates and you are one of our great brilliant citizens, but you are a dumb cluck when it comes to my brother."

We could smell the charcoal burning for the barbeque planned for after the game. Then later we got the aroma of sizzling lunch. I shouldn't have eaten so much breakfast. The game ended. Miss Berry went on with her interviews of the players who migrated to the barbeque pits. Miriam trailed Grenville like a puppy. I fixed up a hamburger and a hot dog, grabbed a couple of bags of chips, and pulled a bottle of water out of one of the ice chests. I know one of the guys pretty well and asked him to do me a favor.

"Sure, what?"

"See that man sitting over there? Take this food to him, please."

"Can do. What is he, homeless?"

"No, far from it. He has a role to play today."

When everyone finished eating, Grenville told Miriam he had something to do and stepped away. He went into the middle of all of us and said, "Good game today, fellas, nobody was embarrassed, no broken bones, no fights..." "Yet," someone shouted and everyone laughed. "... And we didn't need to call 9-1-1." Grenville lowered his voice and said, "The real fun starts in a few minutes. Look around. See people you don't recognize? Yeah, they are some of San Francisco's finest. They've got a job to do. Let them handle it. We're just here to play football, right? Right. We'll help where we can. Just be careful. Now, everybody lower your heads – that means you, too, Basil, (more laughing) – Jesus, look down today on us with your mercy and your kindness. Amen."

"Amen," chorused through the crowd.

"How could you two come from the same parents?"

I jumped and not for the first time today. "Ke-rap," I said, turning. Emily smiled up at me and I instinctively covered my solar plexus.

"Relax, Basil, I'm not in a fighting mood."

"I don't buy that. I've seen you lie." Then I noticed a mid-heighted, well-groomed man biding his time behind Emily.

"Oh," she said, "meet my friend, Archimedes Pym."

I choked on the name. "Pym? I told you not one minute before one o'clock."

"Don't be a putz, Archie's with me." Archie?

"What difference does that make?" I asked.

"Mr. Beault," Pym said, "I'm not here with any hopes of getting the statue. The museum has very limited resources and cannot sacrifice expenditures from other collection centers by spending what the entire museum board felt was an amount beyond our means for the Madagascar Pigeon. I didn't bring any money with me. Emily and I only wanted to see what happens."

"Does this make you feel like a prick, Basil?" The correct answer is yes.

I said, "Criminy, Emily, somebody should bowdlerize your mouth, the way you talk."

"And ESAD to you, too, oh, here's Grenville. Hello, Grenville," she vamped.

Miriam, standing next to Grenville, turned to ice.

"Hi, Emily, you're looking lovely."

Miriam, ice all over, glowered at Emily who paid no attention to her.

"Oooh, I could just kiss you," Emily swooned – in public like you're supposed to.

I couldn't resist, so I said, "That's not all you'd like to do to him." Immediately after which I stepped out of range of any possible attack at my mid-section.

Miriam did not find my joke funny at all. I could tell.

While Emily was making a spectacle of herself over my brother, I said to Pym, "I like her, you understand, but where has that mouth of hers come from? I mean. Not the kind of language you would expect to hear from a lady. Or from a college professor."

"I have to admit," Pym said, "that I am surprised. You seem to bring it out of her, Mr. Beault."

Me. And I was the one who was not surprised. "I'm not surprised," I told Pym, "I guess I just push her buttons over some things best left in the past."

"Besides," Pym said, "it's different at school if she talks that way. Emily has tenure."

Grenville said, "About five more minutes, Bas." I scanned the park and noticed something different. The fog was burned away leaving patchy white clouds in a blue sky. Miss Berry passed by and said, "Your brother's prayer is being answered," as she pointed to the sky. "I knew he would try."

"Maybe, but I put my money on my mom and dad up there."

She gave me a smile that would melt all the snow at the North Pole faster than climate change.

"God, can she be any more beautiful?" I thought.

"Basil, thank you, that is really sweet of you."

"That was out loud?"

She told me yes as she headed to one of her cameramen. Way to go, Mr. Slick. That was real smooth.

I saw Ping Bodie walking toward us with the tall bartender. A couple of minutes to one. There was Phyllis Gunn or Lavernia Lavender. I wondered which until I saw Hugo Blankenship a short way behind her. Lavernia today. Mrs. Smith, along with Pearl and Yvonne both looking very glum, trudging in from Stanyan Street. The Pole and his two abnormals were easy to see. There was John Smith with a scowl on his face. All present except the shooter who nobody knows.

Grenville said something and the innocent observers in the audience for my drawing room revelations spread apart as my statue-obsessed foes filtered in. Mr. Smith yelled out, "What is all this, Beault, who are these people and why are they here?"

"Oh, Mr. Smith, you missed the football game. It was exciting."

The Gunn-Lavender woman said, "I am appalled," as she looked at the big crowd. I did not retort by contradicting her and saying you are not appalled, you are an empty apple barrel. The area quieted.

"I see we are all here except for one person," I said. "I don't know what he looks like. I call him the shooter."

"He's here, Beault," Bodie said, pointing to a slender, gray-headed man who stood near the back. One of the linebackers slipped over behind him. So did two cops.

Mrs. Smith screamed out, "You! Why are you here? He can't be here. He must leave."

"That's enough, Mrs. Smith," I told her. "Give me a while and everything will be clear." Anyway, that is what I hoped. "Most of you know this ordeal – for me anyway – started when Miss Gunn directed a package to my office. It arrived in the hands of Captain Kluszewski who gave it to me before he dropped dead, owing to that excess of bullet holes in him." Groans told me they were pissed at me, but not surprised that I had, indeed, held the Madagascar Pigeon from the beginning. Tough shit, folks. "Yes, I lied a few times about that. I did have the Madagascar Pigeon."

"You dirty..." said The Pole and stopped when a large hand squeezed one of his kidneys. That was thanks to Grenville's handiwork and how he arranged to have each of the suspects covered by two or three of his part-time football players backing up the police.

I pointed at the suspects. "Each of you tried to pry the statue from me by means of force or threat or by buying me. Two of you died trying, Mr. Lorenz and Mr. Westwood. Three murders. And by my count, nine or ten suspects. I got pistol-whipped, taken for auto trips I did not approve, and I got shot at. All for a measly fifty bucks. I held on to the thing to have leverage in what was more than just a race for a dumb statue. It was a multiple murder case. Detective Lieutenant Blough of the San Francisco Homicide Department is all over this case. Sorry, lieutenant, I needed the statue to protect myself. Oh, and here is the funny thing, the Madagascar Pigeon has disappeared."

"What? How?" a few voices called out.

"Gone missing. I don't know how. It was in my...well, I blamed all of you." I drank from a water bottle. "The bird is gone. To me, that didn't matter anymore. There was murder in the fog. I didn't want to be the next victim. That's when I delved into some of you and learned some fascinating things."

One of the TV cameras was stationary up on a picnic table behind the barbeque pits. The other camera was up on the shoulder of a cameraman slowly orbiting the crowd with the soundman and Miss Berry. The TV crew went unnoticed. The focus of the crowd was on me and my spiel.

"By way of background," I continued, "the Madagascar Pigeon is reputed by legend to contain a king's ransom in precious stones. Professor Pym here – an expert in the field – debunks that. How did you put it, 'Those mythmakers were such comedians'? Your efforts, my friends, I am sorry to report, have been for nothing. The prize, which is gone anyway, is worthless, except maybe as a museum curiosity. Nevertheless, you all chased your dreams, and one of you so keen to own it, you murdered three people. Three we know of. All that is left is your greed."

I drank some more water. "I will tell you what happened as best I can reconstruct things. Mrs. Blankenship here, Lavernia Lavender – or Miss Phyllis Gunn when she prefers – was indeed in East Asia where she took possession of the Madagascar Pigeon. Hugo, her husband, or whatever the heck that relationship is all about, had learned that this so-called treasure was in China. Hugo does business with some shady characters in that country. He thought that Lavernia was the one making the trip. Lavernia, Phyllis, who knew, huh?" I laughed.

"After some money probably changed hands in Shanghai, Lavernia, as Phyllis, went about arranging to come home not knowing others were following her with designs of their own on the pigeon and the treasure it was supposed to hold. In time she saw these others and suspected she was in peril. That was when she arranged for the delivery of the statue to San Francisco. To me clandestinely by Captain Kluszewski. Like that? Clandestinely? Anyway, my name shows near the top of the yellow pages listing for private eyes. Someone here advised her to use my address. Lucky me."

I drank again. "Like I said, some of you people sailed on the same boat to San Francisco where the mystery really began. The killer got nervous and hired someone, who knows who, to intercept Kluszewski when the boat docked and grab the statue before it reached me. The killer wasn't very trusting or confident, it seems, or maybe just too greedy, because when it looked like Kluszewski was giving the slip to the hired retriever, the killer shot the captain four times. The loud shooting would have drawn a crowd, so I'm guessing the killer was either distracted or frightened away and left empty-handed because the statue and Kluszewski were gone. How the captain got to my door is an amazing display of dedication to a promise and to an obstinate perseverance. He didn't get a chance to spend the twenty-five hundred bucks Phyllis paid him."

More water. I ventured on. "Now the floodgates open and all you deadbeats come out in search of a toy you think I had. Passport activity for Miss Lavender as well as for The Pole and his partners, Ms. Wu and, er, that guy, showed their passage between the U.S. and China. A birth certificate shows that Miss Lavender is Mrs. Smith's daughter. Mrs. Smith is actually Leticia Crabbe. And this person here, who likes to shoot at my car, is Lavernia's father, Lionel Lavender. Mrs. Smith's new husband is not John Smith as he likes to call himself, but Budlong Haviland Crabbe."

I looked around the crowd. Their attention was riveted on me.

I continued. "The former Mrs. Lavender, or rather Mrs. Crabbe now, Leticia, Mrs. Smith...yes, I know it is confusing...she thought her daughter, either as Phyllis Gunn or Lavernia Lavender, would collect the statue from me. When that didn't happen, Leticia got worried, and when some others got too close to the statue, they – Mr. Lorenz and Mr. Westwood – were shot." I paused and then added, "By Leticia. With a gun. In San Francisco." I sounded like a scene from *Clue*.

"You've ruined everything," Mrs. Smith cried out as she pulled that very gun and fired off a quick shot that got me right above my solar plexus. I went down. I heard bedlam. I saw stars. I thought I had been shot. The preponderance of evidence said that I had been. A policewoman dressed in a sweat suit standing behind Mrs. Smith wrenched the pistol out of her hand. "Oh, daddy," she sobbed as she collapsed to the ground. Bodie went over to her. So did the bartender.

I got surrounded. Grenville, Blough, a couple of his officers, a few of Grenville's buddies. Somebody leaned in to see how dead I was. My chest hurt so bad that I envied Emily's punches that I had previously endured. I heard Blough yell, "Get everyone patted down. I don't want to see another gun come out." His cops were already doing that.

"Somebody call 9-1-1," somebody yelled. Sergeant Headley answered, "The call's in."

Grenville was on his knees holding my hand and asking, "Bas, Bas, you okay?" Fear all over his face. I gurgled.

"He's alive!" Grenville shouted.

I started to move. I wanted to see if I was bleeding. "Don't move!" Grenville shouted again.

"Why?" I asked.

"You've been shot."

"I know," I half-gurgled.

"Then don't move."

"Why?"

"My dumbass brother," I heard Grenville describe me.

"Is he...can he...will he...oh, Grenville, is he okay?" I heard Miss Berry ask.

Grenville reached in under my U of Oregon sweatshirt. "He's wearing a bulletproof vest," he cried out. "He knew this might happen. God, thank you, for the smartest brother on Earth." Then he looked into my face and added, "You stupid jerk." He was crying.

"Let's give him some room," Blough advised. Grenville and one of his husky buddies helped me to my feet. I could stand. I got walked over to one of the picnic tables and sat down. Grenville fussed over me. I drank some water. I got help pulling off my sweatshirt and undoing the kevlar vest. The slug that got me fell out and I pocketed it. A badge of honor I could have done without. The big red spot on my chest was going to be one Hades of a black and blue bruise for a few weeks. But it didn't hurt as much as I thought it should. I thought it was going to be worse because I hadn't ever been shot before and had only heroic ideas about the whole thing. Like Grenville said, "You stupid jerk."

In a few minutes I felt almost whole again, except for the pain. I drank some more water.

"Well, I didn't kill anybody, so I'm going to leave," Blankenship announced.

"As well as I am," The Pole said.

"Oh, please stay," I said, "I'm almost finished, and I'm sure the lieutenant and his squad of officers will have questions for you." Obviously, there was no way these turkeys were getting away from the police presence. Not even counting all the Grenville congregants surrounding them. I tried to stand up but decided to stay seated. Hey, I just got shot.

"As for you, Mr. Blankenship," I said, "you made some very threatening comments to me. I think the penal code will have you book-ended pretty good. The police will also want to look into your dubious import-export activities."

"You can't prove any of this. It's just your word against mine."

"Why, yes, that may be true, Hugo. Only thing, I do have your words." Grenville opened his carryall and brought out a handful of flash drives and handed them to me. "Let's see where yours is, oh, yeah, this one. Your words, your voice."

"And you, Mr. Pole, and your two associates. Taking me on an auto trip against my will. That's kidnapping, I think. That's federal, isn't it, lieutenant?"

Blough, said, "Yes. Maybe we'll do them at the fed level *and* the state. A twofer." I pulled another flash drive. "This one has chapter and verse about that episode. You'll want to run some tests on their guns as well. They seem to have a hankering for them."

"As for our Mr. Lavender, he's already admitted to shooting at me and my car. Bad for the city's image, Mr. Lavender. Spoils the police department's day. They call it attempted murder. San Franciscans really get annoyed at that."

"Mr. Smith, now Mr. Crabbe, you were especially naughty. Trying to hire me to whack your wife. Twice. Let me see which one of these flash drives has you asking me to off her."

Blough's fifteen men and women in the inner part of the gathering now wearing badges hung around their necks identifying them as police officers handcuffed the suspects and advised them of their rights.

We all heard a siren approaching and two of Grenville's friends ran over to Frederick Street and hailed the ambulance, pointing to where I was. The EMTs rushed a gurney over. I didn't need it, thankfully. They worked me over and advised me to go to the hospital. I declined. They gave me some advice about easing the pain. I accepted. They looked around. "What the heck is going on here? You making a movie?" one of them asked. We had to convince them that it was just an innocent day in the park for a little pickup football and a picnic.

"Yeah? When did the rules change and require you to wear bullet-proof vests?" the other one said. No one answered the question.

Blough said, "Thanks for you assistance, gentlemen." The two EMTs shrugged, packed up their stuff and returned to their ambulance.

I drank some more water, took a deep breath to ease the hurt on my chest, and looked at Grenville. He patted his carryall.

"Before these dedicated officers haul your sorry asses over to the police station, it's right around the corner, the Richmond Station, pretty convenient, don't you agree? Before they do that, I want you all to see something."

Grenville reached into the carryall and brought out the Madagascar Pigeon. He set it on a picnic table next to the mustard, ketchup and relish bottles for all to gaze at. Miss Berry's roving cameraman moved in and filmed it for at least a half minute moving his camera this way and that. All the bird fanciers looked at it, glared over at me, and glanced around forlornly to see if they had an avenue of escape. Not hardly. Mrs. Smith, sitting on the ground, turned her head and stared at the statue through her tears, Bodie and the bartender sitting with her.

The Madagascar Pigeon is, as you might expect, a real ugly piece. I mean, how handsome do you think a pigeon is? Regardless, it was drawing a whole lot of attention. Crappy thing like that had caused a lot of stomach ache and worse for a lot of people. And a bullet meant for me.

Miss Lavender inched forward and said, "That is mine. I own it. Give it to me."

"Um, that's not the case, Lavernia," Grenville said to her. "It is actually stolen property from an institute in China." Phyllis/Lavernia was whimpering through this revelation. "It was taken from an antiquities museum. The Chinese authorities have graciously donated it to me – for a modest fee." I looked at him wondering what that was all about.

"Besides, Phyllis," he said softly to her, "you will be going somewhere where this statue would be out of place." She kept whimpering. The cameraman turned to film Miss Gunn, but Miss Berry waved him away.

Grenville continued. "A friend of mine," he looked at a fellow nearby, "made some probes and learned this information from government contacts he has in China. It surprised the Chinese that the statue was attracting any attention at all. It meant nothing more to them than as a curiosity because they have two others." That remark made the would-be statue owners perk up. "Anyway," Grenville said, "it belongs in a museum. It's just a mute statue."

Blough looked at Grenville and me. "That's it?" he asked. We both nodded at him. There was no more to say about the case. Blough told his officers to take the suspects to the station and he'd be there shortly.

Ping Bodie came over. "I'm sorry for everything, Beault. My daughter, what can I say, she was obsessed with this thing, with the fortune she thought was associated with it. We did not see the depth of her problem. My God, she shot you. I am so sorry. And the others. If only..." He choked. "You know what she wanted? She wanted to help Lavernia. Obviously, Lavernia is troubled. She'll need to be hospitalized for the rest of her life. Leticia wanted the riches to pay for that. Her and that Crabbe have no money to speak of. It's all smoke and mirrors with them. And Lavender, he's just a worthless piece of...well, he would have just as quickly taken the statue for himself as help out his own daughter. He's never been around to help. But what Leticia did...turning this into three killings and almost one more – you. I don't know what to say, we're shocked by it. It's just unforgivable. I feel so guilty. I am so sorry."

The bartender said, "I'm sorry, too, Beault, I'm Ty Lavender, Lavernia's brother. What Ping says is true about my father. He's just always been absent. He took advantage of mom when she was young. Now, her life is over. If only we had recognized mom's obsession for what it was. We've been blind. And my sister is, well, you have seen for yourself. She's afflicted. It's been a sad, heartbreaking life for her. She needs, oh God, she needs to be in an institution. I don't know if we'll live this down. Miriam says you might be able to forgive us a little."

"I've been telling Ping and Ty how understanding you can be," Miriam pitched in. "You will be, won't you?"

Miriam? Ping? Ty? What in blazes? Oh, I get it. Ty is a tall, dark, handsome dude who just may be an acceptable stand-in for my gay brother.

"You will, Basil, won't you?" Miriam pressed me.

"Yes, sure, of course. In fact, both of them have been very helpful to me along the way. I owe them."

"God bless you, Basil," she told me as she leaned down and gave me a sisterly kiss on the cheek. She was careful not to hug me. She just saw me get shot. "Please take care of yourself. Get well soon." After Frank and Ty and I shook hands, the three of them walked away.

All of the football players pitched in to clean up the barbeque doings, toss all the trash, grab the ice chests, and give a final look-see to be sure they hadn't left anything behind in the park. Then they filed by to see how I was coming along with my run-in with a bullet. I told them I was on the mend.

Pearl and Yvonne had waited patiently. "You are a pretty amazing detective, Mr. Jaguar Beault," Pearl said. "I have to tell you we are crushed. Only recently – too late – did we start to suspect something all wrong was going on with Tish."

Yvonne broke in. "I wish we hadn't been so shielded to everything. If we could have seen the pressure she put on herself...and then what she did to you today...and the other murders."

"We talked to Ping who told us to talk to you," Pearl added. "Then you told us to be here today, but it was too late to step in and save Tish. We should have seen what was coming." She wiped tears away. "We didn't. We did not see this coming. I hope you don't hold anything against us. You deserve to. Will you, will you hold this against us?"

"No."

"Thank you, Mr. Beault. You've been a prince. We sure hope you are okay. Does it hurt?"

"Yes."

Blough stepped over to us when the two women walked away. "I have to go help with the bookings. Grenville gave me the flash drives," the lieutenant said. "You use those secret agent gadgets to record, uh, stuff?" he said to me.

"Yeah, there're terrific."

"I know. I have to bribe a judge to use mine," he chuckled.

"A speed bump on the way to the truth I don't have to worry over, lieutenant. You know," I told him, "you could call them anonymous tips."

He wrinkled his face and thought for a moment. "Right." Then he looked me in the eye and said, "I feel like an ass. Letting that woman pull a gun. I apologize, Jaguar Beault." I was stunned.

Grenville was standing next to Miss Berry. Blough turned and said to him, "I was just saying to your brother that all along I thought he was a prodigious dumb shit, but I have to take it back now. He's just a normal dumb shit." He grinned at each of us, walked off a few steps to get his bicycle, stopped, turned, came back to the table, picked up the Madagascar Pigeon and asked, "Just what is this thing?"

I smiled and said, "It is the stuff nightmares are made of."

He nodded, set the statue down, then said, "Good job, Basil, I hope you get over the shooting real quick." He walked on pushing his bicycle ahead of him.

Miss Berry called after him, "Can I quote you on that, Joe?"

"No!" he yelled over his shoulder.

"You two are going to be on TV again tonight, maybe all weekend," Miss Berry said. "Me and the guys are going back to the station to cut this into a couple of great stories. Xerxes will love it. Did I tell you he gave me a big raise? He said I'd earned it. I almost believed him. After today it may be true. Basil, I owe you more than I can ever repay. I just about died when I saw you get shot." She stepped in close and softly rubbed across the red blotch on my chest. "This makes for great TV. Did I mention that?" She peered into my eyes. "Again, Mr. Detective, just kidding. Please let's get together, okay? I want you to meet Alana."

"Okay, yes, sure, Alana."

"How about tomorrow?" she asked. "Do you think you will feel good enough?"

"Tomorrow? Yes."

Off she went.

"You like her, don't you?" Grenville said.

"What's there to like? She's plain, not good looking at all, she's got a dull job with no future, she's dumb as a pasta salad..."

"She thinks you're cute."

"Cute, yeah. She thinks Basil Protherington is cute, and she says Grenville Protherington is a God. One of us gets knight in shining armor and I get cute."

"You fucking idiot, she likes you." It was hard not to detect Emily who appeared from nowhere. "You should date her. Hell, you should marry her."

"That's not about to happen, Em, Nadine is gay."

"Poppycock. She is not. Who told you that?"

"She did. Grenville did. If Nadine Berry doesn't know that Nadine Berry is gay, who does? And Grenville doesn't lie, at least not to me."

"They are full of shit then. Archie and I work with hundreds of kids every year. We know what we're talking about. Tell him, Archie"

"She's not gay, Mr. Beault. She clearly is infatuated with you."

I looked at Grenville who had a smirk all across his face. "She's not gay, okay?" he said.

"But..." Now me with the buts.

"She had a real bad experience with a guy a couple of years ago – hey, this does not go past the four of us," Grenville said. "That guy is in jail for a long time. To ward off any more crap from guys, she passes herself off as a lesbian. She didn't adopt Alana with her gay partner. It's her own baby she's raising."

"Built-in family for you, Basil," Emily offered.

"The baby's father died in a car crash just before she had the run-in with the guy in the slammer now. Nadine's known enough heartache. She plans to tell you all about it. Explain to you why she has pretended to be gay. About her husband. About the a-hole, well, she'll tell you. Do me a favor and don't let on that I've said anything to you. She wouldn't mind, but I know she wants to clear the air with you. She likes you a lot."

"Don't worry, I'll keep your secret."

"Okay, only don't use your poker face."

"What? Why? What's that supposed to mean? My poker face isn't so bad."

"Oh, right. Don't you remember in college? Did you ever win a big pot? No. Every time you got something better than a pair of deuces, we'd all fold our hands."

I tried to act like he was wrong. Then I reflected. "Oh drub," I told him.

Things went quiet for a moment before Pym asked Grenville, "What are your plans for the statue now that you own it?"

"I'm giving it to you for your museum. That is, of course, unless Bas wants it."

I gave him a look that he'd seen me use in the past when I thought he was being a jerk.

"No, he doesn't want it. I can tell. Here, take it."

"I don't know what to say," Pym told Grenville. "This is a real coup for the museum."

"I know what to say," Emily shouted as she threw her arms around Grenville's neck. "You are the most wonderful person in the whole wide world." She kissed him hard and then stepped back. Grenville blushed. "Next to my Archie, that is." Archie blushed.

"Thank you very much, you've been very kind to us," Emily said, then added, "even you, Jaguar Beault." She moved in and we hugged and kissed carefully before she walked away with Professor Pym – they were holding hands – and the Madagascar Pigeon. Emily stopped and shouted back, "Send us an invitation to the wedding."

Grenville sat down next to me. "Tell me something. Where'd you get this vest? And don't tell me detective college."

"Guess who you think it was."

"Joe?"

"Close. Maybe so, but it actually came from Sergeant Headley. Curious guy. Probably both of them had the idea."

"It was a great idea."

"You don't have to convince me of that."

"I bet you are glad to be finished with that statue," he said.

"That's a bet you will win every time. Weeks of agony and a puny fifty bucks profit."

"Yeah, puny."

Grenville has a way of laughing inside that percolates before it comes out in such self-satisfaction that you want to punch him in the mouth. Something, of course, I quit trying a long time ago. I looked at him for a moment. "How much?" I asked him.

"Right now I'd say it's north of five million. Could go higher with a final tally. One of my congregants is a jeweler. He really knows his precious stones. He called them primo stuff. Things that maybe no one has seen in centuries."

"How many are there?"

"Sixty-seven. Rubies, emeralds, diamonds, sapphires, trash like that. There were sixty-eight, but I gave him one for his troubles. He's going to deal them for us. It'll be one heck of an auction. Like I said, he calls them primo stuff. A real bonanza. You're rich, Bas."

"No, we're rich. Who got it open? Uh...don't tell me." My brother smiled. "What are you running over there in the Castro?" I asked him, "you're like a universe all your own with every sort of expert."

He just kept smiling. "We're not unskilled, bro, we're just queer." He uses that word when he is teasing himself.

"Wait a minute," I recovered. "How much did you say?"

"More than five million, according to my guy. Likely to be even higher than that. He knows his stuff."

"That's...holy cow, Gren, that's a fortune. I don't believe it. How can that be? Is it true? You're not joking, are you?"

Gren shrugged. "Jackpot time. You win some, you lose some. Today... you won one."

I gawked at him, he smiled at me, I laughed, he laughed, I winced from the gunshot. He said don't laugh too hard. I laughed some more, he laughed some more. The Brothers Protherington. We could have been playing fort like seven year olds for all anyone might think if they were watching us.

"Is this for real?" I asked him. He assured me that it was. "Honest?" I asked him. I wanted to be assured again. He did. I was reassured. I was also in a daze. A bullet to the chest and five mil.

We talked it over and agreed that a portion of the money from the jewels would be divided among the innocent bystanders in the mystery. That would mean Bodie and his grandson, Ty, some for Pym and

Emily to help fund the museum, a big donation to the Police Protective League, nice bonuses to the guys in the church who were so helpful, a new roof for the church, and a trust account for Phyllis Gunn/Lavernia Lavender to care for her hospitalization.

"The rest is for you, Bas," Grenville volunteered, "you've earned it. You and Nadine will need to pay for your kids' education. And maybe you can buy a nice little bungalow and move out of that exotic home and office you occupy."

"You are getting a bunch, too," I said to him. Then I added, "How did you get the statue out of my locker?"

"Oh, come on, that was so obvious. Emily's measurements. You have been sold on those for as long as you've known her." That was true. "Come on over to my place," he said, "I'll drive your car. I'll take the chance that it can make it all the way. Hey, that's another thing. Now you can buy a new car, too. But tonight we'll have a nice safe, bullet-free evening. All the guys are going to want to watch what Nadine puts together on today's football game. A little armchair quarterbacking."

"Okay. Bullet-free sounds good. Hey, Gren, Nadine invited me over to her place."

"Yes, I heard her. She wants you to see her daughter. Are you going?"

"I don't know. I have a pretty full schedule tomorrow. I was planning on folding my laundry and putting air in my tires. But I think I can fit in a visit for a minute or two. Yeah, I think I will go see her. Yeah." We looked at each other and laughed.

"Five million?" I said again.

"More probably," Grenville answered.

I thought about that, and still I could not feel it soak in. I stood up.

"Help me to the car."

I leaned on him across the park. On the way, I said, "Nadine's not gay."

"Nadine's not gay," Grenville said.

The End

244

www.ingramcontent.com/pod-product-compliance
Lightning Source LLC
Chambersburg PA
CBHW072221170626
46813CB00003B/1040

* 9 7 8 0 9 6 1 1 2 4 2 1 2 *